Robert Edric was born in 1956. His novels include *Winter Garden* (James Tait Black Prize winner 1986), *A New Ice Age* (runner-up for the Guardian Fiction Prize 1986), *The Book of the Heathen* (winner of the WH Smith Literary Award 2000), *Peacetime* (longlisted for the Booker Prize 2002), *Gathering the Water* (longlisted for the Booker Prize 2006) and *In Zodiac Light* (shortlisted for the Dublin IMPAC Prize 2010). He lives in Yorkshire.

Acclaim for *Field Service*:

'There has been a slew of novels commemorating the First World War's anniversaries. *Field Service* will be judged one of the best'
John Sutherland, *The Times*

'A masterly analyst of human behaviour . . . Carefully nuanced and engaging . . . Puts the work of most other historical novelists in the shade'
Nick Rennison, *Sunday Times*

'Poignant and moving . . . sensitive, honest yet understated'
Yorkshire Post

'I found this deeply moving; a fine tribute to the early work of the War Graves Commission, which I'll never take for granted again'
Saga

By Robert Edric

WINTER GARDEN
A NEW ICE AGE
A LUNAR ECLIPSE
IN THE DAYS OF THE AMERICAN MUSEUM
THE BROKEN LANDS
HALLOWED GROUND
THE EARTH MADE OF GLASS
ELYSIUM
IN DESOLATE HEAVEN
THE SWORD CABINET
THE BOOK OF THE HEATHEN
PEACETIME
GATHERING THE WATER
THE KINGDOM OF ASHES
IN ZODIAC LIGHT
SALVAGE
THE LONDON SATYR
THE DEVIL'S BEAT
THE MONSTER'S LAMENT
SANCTUARY
FIELD SERVICE

CRADLE SONG
SIREN SONG
SWAN SONG

FIELD SERVICE

Robert Edric

BLACK SWAN

TRANSWORLD PUBLISHERS
61–63 Uxbridge Road, London W5 5SA
www.penguin.co.uk

Transworld is part of the Penguin Random House group of companies
whose addresses can be found at global.penguinrandomhouse.com

Penguin
Random House
UK

First published in Great Britain in 2015 by Doubleday
an imprint of Transworld Publishers
Black Swan edition published 2016

A CIP catalogue record for this book
is available from the British Library.

ISBN
9781784160340

Typeset in Granjon by Kestrel Data, Exeter, Devon.
Printed and bound by Clays Ltd, Bungay, Suffolk.

Penguin Random House is committed to a sustainable
future for our business, our readers and our planet. This book is made from
Forest Stewardship Council® certified paper.

MIX
Paper from
responsible sources
FSC
www.fsc.org   FSC® C018179

1 3 5 7 9 10 8 6 4 2

For

William Ivor Jones, artilleryman
1886–1959

and

Doris Copley, auxiliary nurse
1898–1986

and for their children,
Bill, Bruce and Margaret

The harvest is past, the summer is ended, and we are not saved.

Jeremiah 8:12

Morlancourt, Département du Somme
Summer 1920

Part One

1

Each morning, the small train from either Amiens or Péronne arrived at Morlancourt station and the men waiting for it there were formed into work parties to unload its cargo of building material, supplies and coffins. Until recently, the coffins and corpses had arrived separately, but now, as the days lengthened and finally warmed into full summer, and as the Graves Retrieval and Registration units became fully engaged, it was more usual for the bodies – especially those whose identities had been confirmed – to have already been sealed into their caskets.

Each box was labelled with an embossed metal tag, and often with the same brief details chalked on its lid. Only three months earlier the coffins had arrived polished and with all their fittings attached, but recently they had been little more than simple boxes, showing no true workmanship and none of the effort that had gone into the construction of the earlier caskets. Often – though less and less frequently almost two years after the war's end – these mass-produced caskets were accompanied by other smaller cases marked simply 'Remains', whose lids, in addition to their usual crop of chalked insignia, contained a puzzling pattern of acronyms and question marks.

James Reid stood in the station master's doorway and watched the train arrive. It came at precisely seven o'clock each morning, and he seldom failed to remark upon this precision – the final short blast of steam from the engine timed to coincide with the tolling of the Morlancourt church bell – to Benoît, the station master, knowing that it was something upon which the man prided himself. Reid also knew that if the train left Amiens station early, having come through the night from Pozières or Contalmaison, or occasionally Péronne or Saint-Quentin – a considerably less predictable journey considering the nature of the land in that direction – then Benoît would contact the signalman at the Canal Halt and hold the engine and its cargo there to delay it. And on those rare mornings when the train was running unavoidably late elsewhere, Benoît would open the junction at Quatre Bois or Froissy to get it to Morlancourt for that precise, appointed time.

Passengers elsewhere might complain at the short delays thus created, but few who knew of the train and its sacrosanct cargo and purpose ever did.

As it pulled in this morning, the engine rattling, every linkage of its wheels visible, and slowing with every turn, Reid took out his pocket watch, rubbed its case against his sleeve and flicked open its lid. It was another of the small rituals he shared with Benoît. Reid would joke to the station master that he was checking the train's punctuality, and Benoît, in turn, would reply that this was unnecessary, and that what Reid was really doing each morning was setting the time of his unreliable English watch against the unfailing punctuality of the arriving French train.

As the locomotive finally drew to a halt, with a simultaneous release of steam and smoke from its short funnel, Reid stood erect, drew back his shoulders slightly and saluted the driver. Standing beside him, Benoît repeated the gesture a few seconds later, as though he were an unsynchronized shadow of the other man. The drivers of the train returned the gesture from where they stood on the footplate, their hands and faces black from their work, their eyes and teeth vividly white. Often, these men laughed and shook their heads at the unnecessary formality of the gesture, and their laughter released some of the morning's other small tensions.

A guard would emerge from the rear carriage – invariably Ernaux or André, his son – and a folder filled with dockets and papers would be handed over to Reid, for which he duti-fully signed, and this was then countersigned by the guard.

Upon completing these formalities, Ernaux would wander away from the train, often with Benoît alongside him to discuss some other railway business, leaving Reid to begin his task of supervising the unloading of whatever the small train had delivered to him.

Three months earlier, Reid had written to Wheeler at the Commission Office in Amiens enquiring how much longer he might expect these daily cargoes of the dead, but Wheeler's reply had told him nothing. At the very least, Reid had hoped the deliveries might have been reduced to two or three a week as the larger Signal Cemetery and the surrounding smaller burial grounds, for which he was also responsible, continued to expand and be filled. Perhaps, Reid had suggested, the bodies, coffins and remains might be briefly stored elsewhere until a full load was acquired and then delivered to him. But Wheeler's curt response had made it clear to Reid that his fellow officers in Graves Registration considered this daily arrival of the train, however sparse its load, to be the most expedient method of fulfilling their task. There was nothing Reid might say in reply to this, and so he had kept silent on the matter, and the small trains had continued to come to him at this exact place and upon this exact hour.

Having lodged his satchel beneath the bench beside Benoît's door, Reid walked along the platform to where the men who had come to unload that day's cargo awaited his instructions. There would usually be twenty or thirty of them, sometimes as few as ten, sometimes as many as fifty, all increasingly reluctant participants in the work as the weeks and months passed and they awaited their return home.

When he was occasionally called upon to make short, encouraging speeches to this restless workforce, Reid invariably asked them to consider the importance of what they were doing there, remarking on the fact that, in other circumstances, *they* would expect others to perform the same unhappy duty for them. They would all be home soon enough, and so he asked them to look upon these final duties – these acts of obligation, acts of kindness – as a necessary and vital part of their severance and departure. Some understood what he was trying to say to them; others did not. The men who had been there the longest, and those whose departures lay furthest in the future, understood him best of all. Others, he knew, especially those who had recently been sent to the uncomfortable makeshift barracks at Bray to await their imminent demobilization, resented every word he said to them.

He looked at them now, scattered around the engine yard and the grassy mounds at the rear of the station. It had once been his hope that these men might feel a greater obligation to their work, and that they might even come to gather on the platform in a kind of unofficial guard of honour as the dead arrived. A few came, occasionally, in a desultory, inquisitive manner, but most did not. Most stayed out in the sun, smoking, playing cards or kicking a football until Reid shouted for them to gather together and then instructed them on their few simple tasks.

He was about to do this now when Benoît called his name, and he turned to see the station master coming back to him. Walking in unison beside him – the pair of them looking like the old soldiers they were – was Ernaux.

'What is it?' Reid asked Benoît, waiting until the man had regained his breath. He looked at the ribbons – some his own, some his dead son's – the station master insisted on wearing across the pocket of his uniform.

Benoît cleared his throat and then drew out a cloth to wipe his mouth. Ernaux waited beside him and watched his friend closely.

'There are two passengers,' Benoît said eventually.

'Oh?'

'From Amiens,' Ernaux said.

'Sent here?'

Ernaux handed Reid an envelope and then took a step backwards. It was all he could do to keep his hand at his side and not bring it rigidly to his temple – something he much appreciated doing, and which Reid occasionally indulged.

'Where are they?' Reid asked the guard.

'Waiting,' Ernaux said.

'You sound anxious,' Reid said. 'Have they sent us a general?'

Benoît smiled.

'A general?' Ernaux said. And then he, too, relaxed and laughed. 'A general we would know how to deal with. Besides, all the generals are long since gone. All that remain . . .' He left the remark unfinished.

Are men like me and these others, Reid thought, but he said nothing.

'I only meant—'

'He knows what you meant,' Benoît said, but kindly.

Ernaux bowed his head and Reid put a hand on his shoulder. 'We'll *all* be gone soon enough,' he said. 'One way or another.'

Ernaux glanced at the engine. 'Not while—' he said, and again he stopped abruptly.

Reid finally opened the envelope he held. It was a travel authorization with a note attached, written by Wheeler, requesting Reid to give every assistance to its bearers. He folded the sheet and slid it back into the envelope.

'Are they here?' he asked Ernaux. 'On the train, I mean.'

Ernaux nodded.

Seeing his friend's discomfort, Benoît said, 'They're women. Two women. From England.'

'I see,' Reid said. They had come before – 'Pilgrims', they were called – and they would undoubtedly come again, and in ever greater numbers. The Commission had tried to prevent them from coming, especially at this stage in its vast and constantly expanding plan of works, but had so far been unsuccessful in its efforts.

Reid was distracted from his thoughts by Benoît, who held up his watch to him, suggesting that the task of unloading the train should now begin.

At eight, the small locomotive would be expected to begin its return to Amiens and beyond. The journey to Amiens was only ten miles, but it frequently took over an hour along the damaged track. Beyond Amiens, the timing of all journeys, especially those to the north and east, was considerably less predictable, and on the few occasions when Reid had talked to Benoît of the wider network, the station master had spoken of the distant countryside as though it were now a land completely unknown to him.

Reid started to give his orders to the gathering men, and as he spoke he saw the door of the rear carriage swing open and two women climb awkwardly down on to the platform. Both wore hats and long coats, and both carried cases, which they dropped to the ground and then dragged into the shade of the nearby wall.

2

An hour later, Reid returned alone to stand at the far end of the platform and watch the small train depart. Usually, he was joined by Benoît, but on this occasion the man was absent, having been called into his office. Reid knew that whatever detained him was unavoidable; otherwise he would have been alongside him now to observe the last of their small rituals.

There was no sign of the two women or their cases. Reid had sent word to them explaining that he was unable to attend to them during this one vital hour, and that he would search them out later, when the train had gone, its cargo unloaded and his work at the nearby cemetery underway.

There were a dozen or so rebuilt lodging houses and cafés in the small town, and so finding the two newcomers would not be difficult. All he knew from Wheeler's note was that they had the man's permission to be there. But Reid had little time now to consider what they might expect of him as his day's work began.

The train waited, dripping scalding water, and the driver and Ernaux looked down at Reid where he stood and watched them go. Fifty yards further up the line the signal was still lowered, preventing the engine from leaving the station. There was considerably less urgency attached to this part of the day's timings compared to the train's arrival. The traffic beyond Amiens and Saint-Quentin increased almost daily, especially now that the good weather had arrived and the work of either repairing or dismantling the lines could proceed at a faster pace.

There might soon come a time, it occurred to Reid – and certainly when the cemetery and all those others closer to the river were finally completed and filled – when the branch line to Morlancourt would serve no true purpose and so be closed. And if this happened, he knew how swiftly the station and all its halts and boxes would be abandoned and then fall into disrepair. Benoît and his assistants would be forced either to move elsewhere or – and this was considerably more likely – would lose their jobs completely.

'Are you delayed?' he called up to Ernaux, who took the pipe from his mouth and shrugged.

'Talk of a new bridge across the Sailly road,' he said. 'They're moving the materials. Yesterday, the line beyond Dornacourt was closed for six hours to allow for "priority traffic".' He gave the phrase its telling note.

'English?' Reid asked him.

'That's what we heard.'

Reid tried to imagine where on the reconfigured network of tracks the new bridge was going to be built, and then how it might affect his own work.

The driver said something to Ernaux, who listened intently and then shook his head. He tapped his pipe against the open side of the cab.

'He says we're being delayed because the bastards at Sailly

are deliberately holding up the signals while the track-layers negotiate for better wages,' Ernaux said.

'It's a possibility,' Reid said diplomatically. He guessed that somewhere, perhaps as far away as Arras or Lille, another line was in more urgent use than their own, and that countless others would also be standing and waiting as they now stood and waited – some frustrated by their unknown delay, but most, he guessed, uncaring and uncomplaining and content simply to wait in the warmth.

A further ten minutes passed like this until a note down the solitary signal wire indicated that somewhere a lever had been thrown and that the tracks and their traffic were moving again.

'At last,' Ernaux called down to him. 'We shall no doubt see you tomorrow.'

'No doubt,' Reid called back, relieved to return to his work.

'Unless we return to Amiens to discover that the good earth has finally given up the last of its poor treasures and that our Herculean task here is finished.' It was something Ernaux often said, and Reid always regretted hearing it, largely because the guard expected him to say something equally melodramatic in reply. Once, shortly after his arrival in Morlancourt, Reid had made a remark about the good earth waiting to *receive* the train's cargo, but even as he'd said it he wished he'd remained silent. Afterwards, he had endured Ernaux's comments largely in silence or with a simple nod.

The signal finally rattled on its hinge, and beside Ernaux the driver spun his wheel and pulled out his levers. The engine started to move, screeching as it gained traction and then drew slowly away from the platform.

Reid raised his hand to the two men. 'Until tomorrow,' he called to them.

'Until then,' Ernaux called back.

The engine moved backwards along the track, its empty carriages rattling over the rails.

Reid stood and watched as it began its turn through the gentle curve of the old brickworks cutting and was finally lost to sight.

Leaving the platform, he went first to retrieve his satchel and then to seek out Benoît.

The small office was empty. A kettle sat steaming on the stove, and Reid pushed this to one side. He called for Benoît, but received no answer.

Leaving the building, he returned to where he had watched the gathering men, and saw that though some were still sitting around on the grass, the majority of them had already gone into the larger of the two goods sheds, where the cargo and their day's work awaited them.

Nothing would begin until Reid arrived and gave his instructions, and until his dockets and the coffins and their contents had been tallied. After that, he would direct the men in their work, and within the hour the shed would be cleared. The men who had been working there for some time would explain everything in further detail to the newcomers among them.

Entering the dim and cavernous space, Reid sensed immediately that something was wrong. The men, rather than wandering among the coffins and boxes and calling to each other of the regiments and units they recognized, were all still gathered together at one end of the building.

Several of them were shouting at each other. Jackets and

caps lay on the ground and over the cases where they had been thrown.

Reid called for Drake, his sergeant, and was relieved to hear the man's immediate reply. Everyone turned to look in Reid's direction, and most fell silent at seeing him. He went to them, again calling for Drake.

Drake pushed roughly through the small crowd and presented himself to Reid. Neither man saluted.

'What's wrong?' Reid said.

'The usual,' Drake said. He fastened the buttons on his tunic as he spoke. 'Nothing another few minutes wouldn't have seen sorted out.'

'And by "the usual" you mean . . . ?'

'I mean some smart alec who insists he should be back at home and sipping tea from a cup and saucer rather than still being stuck out here humping corpses and digging graves all day.'

Reid considered his response to this common complaint. Drake might have recently signed on for another seven years, but most of the men now allocated to the Commission were peacetime enlisters, none of whom had seen Active Service. And it was always these men – the men who, as Reid saw it, had the least connection and commitment to the work at hand – who complained the loudest.

'No one is here who has not been rightfully sent here,' he said, shouting, and hearing the distorted echo of his words in the roof high above him. Narrow shafts of sunlight fell to the bare ground through the holes where lost tiles had not been replaced.

Beside Reid, Drake turned to face the surrounding men. 'Hear that?' he shouted. 'And that's an actual officer speak-

24

ing. You might not want to listen to *me*, but you'll do your-selves no favours by ignoring *him*.' He turned to Reid and smiled.

Rather than prolong this encounter, Reid lowered his voice and said, 'Is it anything – anyone – in particular?'

'Bloody newcomers,' Drake said. 'The usual toy soldiers getting their hands dirty for the first time.'

There was some laughter at this. The men in the shed ranged in age from recently delivered nineteen-year-olds to those like the thirty-year-old Drake who had been out there for the past six years. Reid had long since ceased trying to understand how some of these men had found their way to him via the Commission while others were sent out and then called back home without ever leaving their coastal barracks. He wondered if another of his speeches was required, but decided against this. Drake, as usual, was the key to the situation, and he knew from experience that any matter of discipline or discord was best left to the blunt instrument of the sergeant.

'Would anybody like to add anything?' Drake shouted after a long silence. 'Anybody else want to come crying and telling tales to Captain Reid here?'

No one answered him. He was their sergeant. No one ever answered him.

'Good. Because he's a busy man. You want him to shed tears over you when he's got all these other poor mothers' poor bloody sons to take care of?' He waved his arms at the building around them. Every word he shouted came back in that same distorted echo. The mounded coffins and cases lay like a barricade across the open doorway.

'Is that all?' Reid asked him.

'For now,' Drake said. 'If you've got the Registration stuff then we can get started.'

'Of course,' Reid said, and pulled the papers from his case.

Around him, the men slowly dispersed and started their day's work.

3

Reid encountered the two women later that same day. It was early evening, and he was walking along the track between his lodgings and the small wood at Depot Meadow when they appeared ahead of him, rising from the broken line of the embankment and coming directly towards him.

The younger of the two saw him first and stopped walking, reaching out to hold the arm of her companion. It was clear to Reid that his sudden appearance had alarmed her for some reason, and he paused and raised his hand to them, hoping that they might recognize him from earlier.

Having received a wave of acknowledgement from the older woman, Reid continued to where they now stood and awaited him.

'I'm Captain Reid – James,' he said.

The younger woman nodded.

'We were hoping to see you,' the older one said. She held out her hand to him.

Reid guessed her to be in her mid-thirties, perhaps five years older than himself.

'I'm Caroline Mortimer.' She waited for her companion to speak, but the woman said nothing. 'And this is Mary Ellsworth.' She motioned for Mary to hold out her own hand to Reid, which she eventually did, drawing it back after the briefest touch.

'Captain Jessop said we should seek you out,' Caroline said. She repeated '*Seek*' and smiled. 'I imagine you're a very busy man.'

Roger Jessop was Wheeler's senior aide.

Reid was about to answer her when Mary Ellsworth leaned close and whispered to her companion. After this, the younger woman detached herself and continued walking alone along the path towards Morlancourt.

Neither Reid nor Caroline Mortimer spoke as she went, and only when Mary was beyond their hearing did Caroline say, 'Her grief, her distress, remains a great burden to her. Even after all this time.'

It seemed a convoluted thing to say, but Reid made his simple guesses and understood what she was telling him.

Caroline then took out a packet of cigarettes and offered one to Reid, which he accepted.

'She's here searching for the grave of someone she lost,' Reid said.

'Her fiancé. She's on an excursion ticket. I only met her yesterday, in Amiens. It was Captain Jessop who suggested we travel here together. I've been in communication with him and Colonel Wheeler for some time concerning my own arrival here.'

'I see,' Reid said. Neither Wheeler nor Jessop had mentioned this to him. 'I can show her the Registration lists,' he said. 'Let her try to locate where her fiancé might be buried or destined.' He had done the same for others over the past months. 'Has his body been recovered and properly identified?'

'Missing,' Caroline said. 'Three years, apparently.'

'I see.' He looked along the path to the distant figure. 'Then she's likely to be disappointed.'

Seven out of ten of all the corpses currently being recovered and buried remained unidentified. It was a common average at all the cemeteries in the district. If the man had come from a field hospital or clearing station, then his identity would be known. Otherwise, everything would depend on the work of the Graves Registration units working locally.

'I know that,' Caroline said. 'Colonel Wheeler could hardly wait to see the back of the pair of us. She arrived in Amiens with a party of three dozen others, most of whom were going on to the cemeteries at Bray and Suzanne. Only Mary insisted on coming here. She'd heard from one of her fiancé's friends that he'd been killed close to Ville sur Ancre and that he would most likely be buried there or here.'

'If he was found,' Reid said absently.

There was a small communal cemetery at Ville, and two others already starting to take shape closer to Morlancourt itself. It was just as likely that Mary Ellsworth's fiancé – *if* his corpse had been both recovered and identified – would be buried in one of those places.

'It's seldom so straightforward,' Reid said. The smoke from their cigarettes formed a small cloud beside them, hardly moving in the still evening air.

'I understand that,' Caroline said. 'But she needs to do something, to see *something* of where he was lost to her.'

'Of course.' It was why most of the women and families came, and the best many of them could hope to achieve. For some it was everything; for others it at least satisfied the most urgent and painful of their needs.

Neither of them spoke for a moment, and then Reid said, 'And you?'

'What unwelcome burden am *I* about to become to you, you mean? I can see Captain Jessop has told you very little.'

'Nothing at all,' Reid said.

'I see. I was a nursing sister. VAD. I'm here because of the nurses.' She paused. 'Colonel Wheeler assured me you knew I was coming.'

'He makes a great many assurances.'

A month earlier, at one of his regular meetings with Wheeler and other Commission members, the subject had been raised of the burial of twenty nurses, killed at various field hospitals and currently being gathered together so that they might be buried and then commemorated together. The larger of the Morlancourt cemeteries had been mentioned as a likely resting place for the women, but as far as Reid was aware nothing definite had yet been decided. A great many decisions were left unmade at these meetings, and Reid often came away from them feeling he knew considerably less about what was happening in the plots under his supervision than when he'd arrived.

Caroline smiled at the remark. 'Sorry. Please don't worry, I won't get in your way. I knew most of the women personally – women, girls – and I was contacted by the Commission eighteen months ago in the hope that I might be able to help with all the gathering-in and identifications. I have almost complete records for a great number of dressing stations. I was here for over four years, on and off, and our records are better than most. I daresay Colonel Wheeler imagined it would be one less job for him – you – to have to do.'

'I daresay,' Reid said. 'There was mention of twenty women.'

'Twenty-six are currently confirmed,' Caroline said. 'I'm still searching for another seven.'

'There are discrepancies everywhere you look,' Reid said.

Caroline laughed. 'I'm sure there are. Discrepancies.' She reached out and held his arm for a moment. 'I'm sorry,' she said. 'I didn't mean to sound so callous.'

Reid motioned to the fallen trunk of a long-dead tree and they diverted from the narrow path to sit on it.

'If I might be allowed to check my own records against the bodies the Commission has already designated for burial,' Caroline said.

'Of course.' So far none of the nurses had arrived at Morlancourt, and as yet no part of the cemetery there had been designated to accommodate them. It was something he would raise with either Wheeler or Jessop the next time he was in Amiens.

'I do, of course, realize that the odds are heavily in my favour,' Caroline said. 'I doubt if our "missing" or "un-identified" will pose any real problems for you.'

'No, I suppose not.'

He told her the proportions of each category still being delivered to him from the Commission's depots. The numbers surprised her.

'As many as that?' she said. 'I'd always imagined—'

'I think we all did,' Reid said. 'The fact is, the bodies that come to us intact and identified *and* with all their relevant paperwork attached are a relative rarity. In the beginning, perhaps, but these days we struggle more and more to make any valid connection. In addition to which, the mix of reinterments and new recoveries varies every week.'

'I see.' She watched him closely as he said all this.

'The Graves Registration people have teams of men still tracking and tracing and looking for every verification that might help identify someone, but all too often . . .'

'That "someone" doesn't actually exist?'

'"Human remains". Perhaps part of a uniform, hopefully some attached and undamaged insignia. The uncorroborated evidence of a man's comrades, perhaps, but that, too, is an increasing rarity.'

'And so your priority now is simply to gather in and then to decently bury whatever might remain,' she said.

'We know the *names* of all the missing. They'll be commemorated somewhere, somehow, eventually.'

'Just not necessarily in the grave Mary wants to kneel beside and grieve over.' Caroline put a hand to her mouth. 'That sounded uncaring of me.'

Reid shook his head. 'In the years to come there will be thousands like her turning up here and at all the places like it, and most of them will be searching for something they'll never find. I imagine the real trick for them will be to shape and then to temper their expectations.'

Every grave would at least contain *someone*; there would be no so-called 'duds'.

In the distance, a train passed along the line towards the vanished hamlet of Merissy, slowing where the station had once stood, and both of them turned to watch its progress. The driver sounded his whistle at the lost stop and a thin plume of smoke rose briefly above the tracks.

Caroline brushed small flies from her face. 'How long have you been here?' she asked him.

'In Morlancourt? Four months.'

'And before that?'

'I arrived in March 1916.'

'The same month I lost my husband,' she said.

'Oh. I—'

'Happily, *his* body was quickly recovered and he was recently reinterred in the Courcelette cemetery beyond Pozières. I was there before going on to Amiens. I daresay your own plot here is in a similar state.'

'I know Courcelette,' Reid said. 'The man in charge – Jameson – is doing a good job there.'

'I was told by the Commission that there might be a nurses' cemetery there, too, but that seems unlikely considering the relatively small numbers involved. Captain Jessop told me that in the beginning there had been a notion to bury the nurses and other medical staff throughout the cemeteries, but that there were now far too many of these – burial grounds, that is – for this to remain a practical option. I suppose I should be grateful that so *few* of us were killed.'

'Do you know the circumstances of the women destined to come here?' Reid asked her. It seemed a clumsy question and he regretted it as soon as he'd spoken.

'How they were killed, you mean? I know what the Registration documents tell me – just as you know what yours tell you, I suppose. I know the dates and places and causes of death and suchlike, and I'm long familiar with all those wonderful phrases that have recently been concocted to do their calm and reassuring work. I was reading just yesterday that a committee has been set up to decide on a name for what's just happened.'

'The war, you mean?'

'The war itself. All its engagements. They seem insistent on something much grander.'

'No doubt,' Reid said, and the pair of them smiled.

'Are you married?' Caroline asked him. 'Engaged?'

Reid shook his head. He could hear splashing from the river in the distance and the shouting of men, carrying like the whistle of the train on the still air. The men, he imagined, might even be his own labourers.

'We were watching them work earlier,' Caroline said. 'It all seemed very confused.'

'I can imagine. I prefer to look on it as organized chaos.'

'In the knowledge that out of that chaos will soon come peace and calm and order?'

'It seems a lot to hope for.'

Caroline Mortimer took a deep breath and said, 'When my husband was killed, I received several letters from his friends telling me how swift and straightforward everything had been, how little he had suffered. I was even reassured that his body had been unmarked.'

'I see.'

'I daresay you wrote similar letters yourself.'

'Some,' Reid said.

'Many?'

'Enough to want never to have to do it again. Enough to want all of this to be over and done with, and for it to truly mean something to all those who need it in order to get on with their lives.'

'People like Mary Ellsworth, you mean?'

All of us, Reid thought. *You included*. 'Yes, people like Mary Ellsworth.'

Caroline lit another cigarette. 'I daresay the same few

stories will be told over and over,' she said. 'About how men died.'

'A lot will depend on what people want to hear.'

'The grieving survivors.'

Reid bowed his head. 'You'll have a grave. You'll know your husband is buried there.' He knew it was a harsh thing to say to her, and so he looked at her and waited for her nod of agreement and forgiveness.

'I'm thirty-eight,' she said. 'Mary Ellsworth is barely twenty. I'm twice her age, old enough to be her mother. My husband and I were married for nineteen years.'

'Children?'

She shook her head. 'Mary, on the other hand—'

'She already has a child?'

'She lost the child she was carrying when she learned of her fiancé's death.'

'She told you that herself?'

'I seemed to know everything there was to know about her and why she was here within minutes of meeting her.'

'Give me the man's name,' Reid said. 'I'll search the registers for her. I can talk to a few others. A lot of stuff's just arrived at the Commission from the Army Graves people. Does she still have all his details?'

'Every single one of them. All committed to memory. Everything imaginable. Whereas I . . .' She hesitated. 'Whereas I sometimes have days when I cannot even remember what my husband's voice sounded like.'

They sat in silence for a while, listening to the distant men and the humming of the insects which filled the air around them.

Then Reid said, 'You should go to the rise above Sailly.'

He pointed ahead of them to where the horizon rose slightly.

Caroline shielded her eyes and looked.

'It's perhaps a hundred feet high. A mountain in this part of the world.' He, too, peered into the distant haze. In the west, the sun was low in the sky, adding its glare to the land. 'If you walk up it and then look back towards Albert, you can just about make out the beginning of that order you were talking about.'

'The order emerging out of chaos. No – the order you are *bringing* out of chaos.'

'Another of those too-grand notions,' he said. 'Another illusion.'

'Perhaps,' she said. 'But it's what so many now crave.'

'I suppose so,' he said, knowing she was right.

Behind them, the church bell at Bray pealed the hour, and they both sat without speaking until this finished and as the simple dying note then faded to silence.

4

The next morning, following his usual duties on the platform, Reid was beckoned by Benoît into his small office. The station master closed the door behind him and indicated the only two chairs the cramped and overcrowded room contained.

Reid, again understanding the need for these courtesies and observances – especially upon the stage of Benoît's own small part in the drama of the changing world around them – sat down and laid everything he carried at his feet. Benoît then offered him coffee, which he accepted with forced enthusiasm. The drink was invariably thick and dark and bitter, and it was all Reid could do to sip it without screwing up his face. Benoît took great pride in his coffee, and to have refused him this particular pleasure would have been close to an insult.

Eventually, his preparations finished, Benoît put down his own cup and saucer and leaned towards Reid, both hands on his knees.

'I have heard alarming things,' he said.

'Oh? Concerning?'

'From Ernaux.' Ernaux – this link with that restless wider world – was a constant source of alarming news.

'I was with him a few moments ago,' Reid said. 'He said nothing to me.' Reid spoke French well enough to understand most of what Benoît said to him, but he occasionally struggled with the man's growled accent, with his colloquialisms, and with the lost words and abbreviated language he commonly used. It had long been clear to him that Benoît, despite Reid's occasionally faltering replies, believed he, Reid, understood perfectly everything he was told.

'He works regularly at the Doullens depot,' Benoît said. 'And sometimes further afield. At Abbeville and Beauvais.'

'Has something happened there?' Reid was keen to start work, knowing that the men now gathered beyond the station yard would do little until receiving his instructions.

'Ernaux says that in the Saint-Quentin yards there are many unidentified French corpses and remains that are assigned identities that cannot truthfully be said to be their own.'

'I see,' Reid said. He wondered at the nature of Benoît's concern and considered what to say to him.

'Ernaux says that bodies at Saint-Quentin have become little more than an inconvenience for our own administrators.'

'I'm sure everything is—'

'He believes it is a great conspiracy.'

'Conspiracy?'

'Of silence. Of convenience. Of greater powers holding sway.' Everything Benoît now said was framed in this melodrama.

Reid remembered his conversation with Caroline Mortimer and wondered what similar cold and evasive reassurances he might offer the man.

'I daresay a great many things are done these days for reasons we may not yet understand,' he said.

'According to Ernaux, the workers at the Abbeville yards throw the sacks of remains from the carriages to the ground as though they were sacks of potatoes. There is no proper accord, no respect.'

'I know,' Reid said. He doubted if the story were true, but could not suggest this. 'So perhaps we are more fortunate than most, here in Morlancourt, in being able to afford *our* dead the respect and dignity they deserve.' Despite sounding like another of his tired speeches, it was a good answer and he could see that Benoît appreciated it and the compliment it contained.

'Of course,' Benoît said.

In an attempt to steer them on to another path, Reid said, 'I was sent an order last week warning me against interring German remains by mistake. Forty graves at the French national cemetery outside Serre were dug up because someone – presumably another of your own officials – believed German remains had been buried there in error.'

'I suppose there are some mistakes none of us can afford to make,' Benoît said, shaking his head.

'Precisely,' Reid said. He knew that Benoît and Ernaux had worked together throughout the war and that the bond between them was strong. Whatever Reid said, he would be careful neither to contradict nor insult the guard.

'The station master at Froissy told Ernaux they had a train pass through there yesterday carrying nothing but bones.'

'Bones?'

'For one of our great ossuaries. You English lay out your pretty cemeteries like cloths at a picnic, while we French pile up our skulls and bones in a few vast charnel houses for the grieving relatives to visit.' He shook his head again at the unhappy thought.

This divergence in practice was frequently discussed among the senior members of the Commission, and Reid had been instructed never to comment publicly on the subject. A great many reciprocal but fragile arrangements and confused understandings still existed between the two countries' Commissions and their architects.

The French had their own cemeteries, of course – locally, there was the military ground alongside the line at Bray, at Cerisy, and the recently commissioned burial plot on the road north of Etinehem – but it was invariably the ossuaries which attracted the most attention and caused the greatest disquiet among the French themselves. Reid already knew how Benoît felt about these plans.

'I imagine they'll make memorable monuments,' Reid said. But Benoît was not convinced of this, and so said nothing in reply.

Reid knew the old man was remembering his own lost son, badly injured at Verdun, who had then died less than a month later in the hospital at Mantes la Jolie on the Seine. Benoît and his wife had retrieved the boy's body and brought it back to Morlancourt for burial at their own expense. Benoît had told Reid all this in the smallest detail the first time the two men had exchanged their histories.

'I suppose you and I understand these things better than most,' Benoît said eventually.

'I suppose we do.'

'Ernaux and I, we are just old men doing what all old men must do – grumbling about a world that has changed beyond all recognition, and which has finally slipped beyond our control and understanding. And soon the work here – your work – will be completed and the line closed and the world will change again.'

Reid said nothing in reply to this, merely nodded, relieved that Benoît's lament required nothing more of him. He was distracted briefly by a line of men moving past the office window, running from where that morning's cargo had just been unloaded back out into the sunlight beyond the platform's end.

'They are anxious to start their work,' Benoît said.

Reid heard Drake shouting at the men to move faster. There was no purpose to this seeming urgency, just another of the sergeant's irresistible impulses finding its target. Most of the men laughed and shouted to each other as they ran, paying little attention to Drake.

'I should go,' Reid said.

'Of course.'

'Thank you for the coffee.'

Benoît smiled at this. 'But you would much prefer a cup of your Earl Grey tea?'

Reid retrieved his papers and rose from his chair. He remembered the monthly packages of tea his mother had sent to him, the sudden sharp aroma as he peeled away the packaging. 'Not at all,' he said.

Eight coffins and the additional remains of seventeen men had been delivered to him. A smaller cargo than during the previous weeks, and perhaps the cause of the men's high spirits now.

'Ernaux also heard from one of the drivers that deliveries to the cemeteries between Villers-Bretonneux and Moreuil are ended and that the few bodies still intended for Moreuil and Morisel will now be redirected either here or to Cerisy,' Benoît said.

'I daresay it was bound to happen.' Reid knew from recent reports which burial grounds were to be restricted in their construction, and which were destined for seemingly endless expansion. Some places, he knew, had only ever been intended as small, almost intimate collections of graves – the graves of individual regiments, say, or of men who had fought and died together at a particularly notable engagement – whereas other burial grounds had been altered and enlarged in accordance with need.

He wished he had been better informed by the Commission of their eventual plans for Morlancourt, but all his recent queries on the matter had been met with either uncertainty or diversion. He read nothing untoward into these responses; they merely confirmed in his own mind that many of his superiors knew as little as he did about how and when their great shared enterprise would be completed.

What he did know for certain, however, was that the cemetery at Moreuil was about to be expanded rather than declared finished, and that the land at Morisel had recently been acquired for a German burial ground. He revealed nothing of this to Benoît, unwilling to contradict anything Ernaux might already have told him.

He waited in the doorway as the last of the men ran past him, some of them offering casual salutes as they continued along the platform.

Then Drake came to him and reported that everything was loaded and ready to be taken to the cemetery. He called to Benoît over Reid's shoulder. Even after six years in

France, Drake spoke only a dozen or so words of French, and, however brief or amicable the exchange, he invariably pronounced each one of these as though it tasted sour on his tongue.

5

Once a fortnight, Reid was summoned by Wheeler to attend a Commission meeting either in Amiens or, more recently, as its ruins were finally cleared, in Albert. The latter was closer and easier to reach from Morlancourt, but wherever these meetings were held, Reid regretted the time they wasted and the delays they caused him. By his own reckoning, a morning or afternoon once a month would have achieved just as much.

He went to the gatherings primarily to report on all that he and the other cemetery-builders had already achieved, and to offer vague predictions and qualified recommendations for the weeks and months ahead.

The day's business was usually followed by an extended meal – Godbert's and Chez Joséphine in Amiens were the current favourites – at which Reid's attendance was also obligatory, and at which Wheeler and others among the Commission's grandees held forth with self-congratulatory speeches concerning all that was currently happening.

The sole benefit of these outings was that Reid was able to see Alexander Lucas, his counterpart and liaison officer in the local Investigation and Retrieval branch of the Graves Registration department. It was Lucas's task to discover lost or forgotten graves – usually by collating information supplied to him by the returning local inhabitants and from letters sent to the Commission by men who had long since returned home and who had only lately responded to the War Office's appeals. Alexander Lucas was then responsible for the retrieval and identification of the newly located corpses prior to their reburial, usually now at Morlancourt and the surrounding plots.

Reid and Lucas were the same age, but Lucas was already seven years married and with a five-year-old daughter. The two men had not served together, but had later discovered that they had both been in the hospital at Boulogne at the same time, and had afterwards taken part in actions at Chaulnes and Maricourt. It was at Maricourt that Reid had received his leg injury, following which he had been sent home on two months' leave. Alexander Lucas, meanwhile, had been invalided from the Army for four months following the Armistice, returning first to Southampton and then to Napsbury. Following a further month of convalescence in the Peak District, he had finally returned home to Nottingham to his wife and daughter.

Upon his recovery, Reid had applied to be considered for a post in either the Imperial Commission or the Graves Registration Service, both of which were only then calculating their approaches to the work ahead.

For three months following his own return to France, Alexander Lucas had been appointed to oversee the work of the Retrieval units in that part of the Somme valley, and it was during this time that he and Reid had met and become friends.

Reid travelled to Amiens on that morning's returning

train, the sole occupant of a carriage and four goods wagons. In the beginning, he had often travelled in the cab with Ernaux and the driver, but he had seen how his presence made the men uneasy, and so afterwards he had insisted on riding in one of the carriages, telling Ernaux he had paperwork to complete before the day's meeting began.

Pulling into Amiens now after the short journey, Reid was pleased to see Alexander Lucas waiting for him on the recently rebuilt platform. It had become Lucas's habit to wait for his friend like this so that the two of them might spend some time together prior to these unwelcome diversions from their real work.

Reid stepped out and Lucas came to him. Ernaux shouted to them from the cab and Reid called back his thanks.

Because the train would not return to Morlancourt until the following morning, Reid would have to ask at the several Army depots and transport yards in the town if any vehicle was going in the direction of Morlancourt later in the day. He was rarely unsuccessful in this, and most of the drivers were happy to make the short detour from the Bray or Sailly roads, where a good enough surface existed. Recently, however, he and Lucas had spent their evenings together in one of the town's small hotels, the two of them not parting until the following morning – Lucas to wherever he was currently working and Reid often returning to Morlancourt on the train delivering his own supplies.

Both men had less than a year left to serve. Reid had recently considered extending this, but Lucas talked only of getting to the end of his time and of returning home for good. It was his intention, he told Reid, to resume his work as an architect and eventually to set up his own practice.

Waiting until the engine had pulled away from the platform, the two men went to sit beneath the station awning.

'What's that?' Reid asked, indicating the sheet of paper Lucas held, which he had been reading upon Reid's arrival.

'I applied for a mobile bath unit from the dozen sitting unused behind the Royal Warwicks' ordnance store and Wheeler has denied me.'

'On what grounds?'

'On the grounds that it is summer and that there is plenty of clean water elsewhere for my diggers to use. Where? Not where we're digging, there isn't. Everywhere might be starting to *look* dry and solid, but the water's still there a foot or two down.'

Immediately following the end of hostilities, the corpses and remains were collected together daily in great numbers – hundreds on some days – and the majority of these had come from long-known and properly marked sites, however makeshift. But the fact that so many hitherto unsuspected bodies were still being discovered and retrieved almost two years later had come as a surprise to many in the Commission, and it was why the plans for the laying-out at Morlancourt and elsewhere were now constantly being revised.

'Where are you working?' Reid asked.

'A farmer reported a grave of at least thirty men over at Lihons. Yorks and Lancs. A further twenty somewhere along the Roye road, buried and then lost some time during the March retreat. Oh, and – ' Lucas searched his pockets and pulled out a second folded sheet of paper – 'we received a report only yesterday of between ten and thirty "unknowns" in your neck of the woods. Place called Prezière. I say "place" . . .'

'I know it,' Reid said. 'What's left of it. I think the Lanca-shire Fusiliers fought there.'

'That's who we've got written down. A well-digger came across a mass of rotting flesh and equipment. When we've finished at Roye I'm coming over for a look.'

'I'll find you somewhere to stay,' Reid told him. Prezière, he knew, was little more than a brick-strewn field, long since overgrown, and with the vestiges of a crossroads somewhere amid the rubble.

'I don't suppose you've heard anything?' Lucas asked him.

'About the bodies?' Reid shook his head.

'A man called Clarry,' Lucas said, again reading from the sheet. 'Rebuilding his farm at a place called Malesterre.'

The names meant nothing to Reid, but he felt certain that Benoît and the other inhabitants at Morlancourt would know where the place had once been. 'I'll make enquiries for you,' he said.

'The bodies at Lihons had everything we needed,' Lucas said. 'Someone had sealed all their details in bottles. Thirty men, and we had them all retrieved, laid out, bagged and identified in a single day.'

'I remember them,' Reid said. 'They're docketed for the Lihons national cemetery, but we're starting to think the French will want the place solely for their own. It's marked out for behind their old front line.'

'Does it matter *where* they go?' Lucas said, continuing to read from the sheet.

'I daresay if—'

'The poor beggars along the Roye road came from every regiment under the sun. Retreating armies. There

48

were Africans among them, infantry and labour brigades. Wheeler is pushing for separate cemeteries.'

'It's what the Canadians, Australians and New Zealanders want, too,' Reid said, remembering another of Wheeler's recent edicts. 'The Africans will probably go to Delville.'

Neither man spoke for a moment, both conscious of the short time remaining to them.

Eventually, Alexander Lucas said, 'Wheeler told me I should instruct my digging teams to carry pails with them so they could find water to clean themselves. Plenty of rivers and canals, he said. What on God's earth does he think they're actually washing off their hands after a day in a two-year-old mass grave?'

'Does he never visit you?'

Lucas smiled. 'He sends one of his minions – lapdog Jessop, usually, poor man. I daresay your end of things is much more to Wheeler's liking. I even—' Lucas stopped speaking and looked down at the sheet he held, which was now shaking slightly, betraying the sudden tremor of his hand. He watched this for a moment until it became still again.

'Are you all right?' Reid asked him.

'It comes and goes,' Lucas said dismissively, and Reid knew by his tone not to persist.

'You said my end of things?'

Lucas laughed. 'All your tidying-up. There's already talk of commemorative ceremonies, Wheeler presiding.'

'What sort of ceremonies?' Reid said, knowing that these had been planned, but convinced that the first of them was still a considerable way in the future.

'When the cemeteries are complete, I suppose,' Lucas said.

'I don't know – something. He'll probably want you to retire to a respectable distance from the cemetery walls and gate-houses and then start building hotels for him.'

'Hotels?' It was a ridiculous suggestion, however it was meant.

'For the tourists.'

'Two women turned up at Morlancourt,' Reid said.

'Only two? Consider yourself lucky. The hotels here and in Saint-Quentin are already thriving on the trade.'

After a further few minutes, the pair of them left the station and walked out into the streets beyond.

Everywhere they went there was the clamour of re-building and of tradesmen and shopkeepers operating their businesses. Fenced depots filled many of the cleared sites, and soldiers and their equipment were still evident everywhere. The air was filled with the smell of petrol and woodsmoke.

Lucas indicated a table and two chairs set out on the brick pavement ahead of them and they sat down again. A waiter appeared and took their order for coffee and cognac. Despite it being only mid-morning, Lucas insisted on the spirit, saying that the wine at the meal later would be carefully rationed.

'The word is that Wheeler will be making one or two of his pronouncements,' Lucas said, draining his glass and gesturing to the waiter for it to be refilled. Reid held his hand over his own. 'Jessop let slip that he's in the running for some promotion or other.'

'In connection with his work on the Commission?'

'What else? Grand Panjandrum Wheeler. Who knows, we two – you and I, we lowly diggers and scrapers – might find ourselves drawn aloft in his golden wake towards that same shining glory.'

'But only once we've washed the mud off our hands and faces,' Reid said.

'And the rest.' Lucas raised his second glass. 'To reflected glory,' he said.

'Glory in all its forms,' Reid said, squinting in the sunlight, which set ablaze the liquid in his own raised glass.

6

Work on preparing the cemetery at Morlancourt had started prior to Reid's arrival, but the first bodies had not been delivered until he had been in charge there for almost two months. He had arrived at the place alone and unprepared. His workers and all their equipment had followed piecemeal and unannounced, and only with the completion of the repairs to the railway embankment at Chaulnes was any true and organized progress made.

To begin with, Reid had been given a map of the actual ground to be prepared, along with a traced overlay of the eventual shape and configuration of the cemetery. It had been immediately apparent to him that whoever had created the plan to be imposed on the ground had never actually visited the place itself. The cemetery design demanded near-level sections, or land only gently undulating. But the fields and open spaces at Morlancourt contained a small river, and ridges and slopes upon which no truly straight lines could be imposed without considerable groundwork beforehand. In addition, there was a low scarp along its western edge, where the soil was lost and the underlying chalk revealed at the surface.

Only upon his first full exploration of the site did Reid

discover that there were several slender paths and a broader rutted track running over the land which were still in regular use by the local farmers and their labourers. These same men created even further delays by insisting on harvesting the sparse remaining winter crops already growing on the site.

Most of the land had by then already been requisitioned by government order prior to being leased to the British. Some of it, Reid later discovered – almost a third of the total site – had been donated voluntarily by the landowners themselves, often because they could no longer find the men to work it.

As Reid had anticipated, local disputes over ownership and long-held rights took up a great deal of his time during those early weeks, and were the cause of his first true conflicts with the Commission members in Amiens.

Men still worked at lowering and grading the steepest of the slopes and then covering the exposed rock with soil excavated from elsewhere at the site. The stream along the cemetery's eastern edge was cleared of sediment and channelled via a succession of buried culverts in that part of the emerging cemetery. But this in turn had led to neighbouring farmers demanding to have their own water supplies returned to what they had once been. One man insisted that the diversion and channelling of the stream had caused flooding in his dairy yard.

Often these complaints were founded on genuine grievances; at other times the locals made their demands for compensation simply because times were still hard, because they held others responsible for their losses, and because nothing, even now, was as guaranteed or as certain as it had once been for them.

Reid prided himself on having become adept at deciding

which of these demands and complaints he might legitimately pass on to the Commission and which he might more readily contest and dismiss himself. It was Wheeler's unrecorded opinion that the demands should *all* be dismissed and that everything should remain in abeyance to the greater good.

The major obstacle at Morlancourt, it quickly became clear to Reid, was the remains of the wood along the road to Sailly which, though clearly marked on the original map of the area, was absent from the Commission's own plan of how the finished site would eventually appear. Almost a hundred graves were marked in their ten perfect rows where the shattered stumps and mounded roots now stood. Reid had insisted on both Wheeler and Jessop visiting the site with him, and afterwards sending him the heavy equipment and additional men required to excavate the stumps. Without mechanical diggers, the removal of a solitary tree took a dozen men a whole day to achieve, and Reid had calculated that there were the remains of almost two hundred still to be cleared.

Now, almost four months later, the majority of these still stood along the Sailly road. The bulldozers and diggers had come, but only for a short time, and had proved largely ineffectual in the confined space, frequently breaking down and needing to be returned to Saint-Quentin for repair. Their replacements had come erratically, and then only after long delays.

There had been comparatively little damage to the land surrounding Morlancourt until the final months of the war, and because the ground had not been repeatedly churned and reconfigured over the preceding years, much of the overlying earth was compacted and dry, and the strata beneath it still lay in solid layers.

Only where the land to the south approached the Somme with its flood plain, marshes and porous channels did water remain a problem for other burial grounds, and Reid knew well enough from his meetings with the engineers what changes and delays were now being caused there by repeated flooding and seepage. The Canadians at Cerissy, for instance, had been forced to reconsider the whole of their first chosen site because of the unstoppable rise of the groundwater there.

The slow progress in removing the trees at Morlancourt remained a constant source of friction between Reid and Wheeler. Recently, however, there had been talk of leaving what remained of the small woodland intact and of acquiring a further small field above the lane to Etinhem to accommodate the graves. The delays in completing these changes remained Reid's greatest frustration, and in the meantime Wheeler insisted on the continued removal of the peripheral trees in case the plan proved unsuccessful.

Where the woodland remained undamaged, it was an attractive feature of the site – especially on the crown of the slight rise above the Sailly road. With its mix of oaks and beeches at its centre, it reminded Reid of the Gloucestershire village where he had lived and played as a boy, and where he had later walked with his father before the man's early death.

Elsewhere on the designated land, the levelling of its lower contours and the filling in of hollows proceeded more quickly and easily, and Reid was soon able to see how the finished pattern of graves would eventually come to look over large areas. He recognized the great virtue in the simplicity and uniformity of the Commission's plan. And as Wheeler frequently reminded him, the visiting relatives would see only what they had come to see and nothing of what had been there before their arrival.

As spring had turned to summer, and as the work had finally started in earnest, it had become a habit of Reid's to wander over the whole of the site upon the completion of each day's work – both to see exactly what had been accomplished by his workers and to gauge his overall rate of progress. Most of what he saw on these solitary walks pleased and impressed him. The recently dug and refilled graves were as yet bare and stark across the dark earth, but already there was an emerging notion of that greater order.

Only beyond the eastern edge of the cemetery had the war left its lasting mark on the ground at Morlancourt: a line of four large, perfectly spaced craters along the course of a track connecting the station with the lock gates beyond Vaux. Perhaps the track had once been targeted as a link between the two places – though neither had been of any true significance other than as easily traversable ground for retreating troops – but it was more probable that the shells had fallen randomly. In all likelihood, the craters, long over-grown and already filling with rubble from nearby ruins, had been there since the war's earlier incursion. Reid frequently found himself reading the ground like this – something still done more by instinct than by any necessary calculation.

Each crater possessed a low rim of surrounding earth, and all that would be required of the farm labourers who might eventually be sent to reclaim the lost ground would be for this loose soil to be shovelled back into the hole from which it had been blasted.

Upon completing these evening excursions, and often

finding himself walking as the sky all around him darkened with the setting of the sun, Reid would return to his lodgings and look out along the few streets of Morlancourt and wonder how often its inhabitants – many of them only recently returned to their homes and livelihoods – looked along those same streets and gave thanks for what, amid so much destruction elsewhere, had survived of the place. He wondered, too, how many of those people cursed him for what he was now there to undertake.

On one occasion, Reid had returned to his lodgings later than usual, and as he'd walked home he'd been surprised by the sudden appearance of a dozen draught horses galloping up to him on the other side of a hedge through the thickening darkness. The animals had come snorting and neighing to the hedge, and the rising drumming of their hooves had sounded to Reid exactly like the noise of a distant, rolling barrage. He guessed the horses had only recently been released from their own day's labours and were running off their hours of constraint. The first of the creatures had shied away upon seeing him there, and the rest had then turned and galloped back across the open field.

7

Caroline Mortimer came out of the Morlancourt church-yard and stood in front of Reid where he sat beside a stone trough. 'I went to the vantage point you recommended,' she said. She positioned herself between Reid and the sun, enveloping him in her shadow.

He had been half-asleep when she'd spoken to him.

He shielded his eyes to look up at her.

Behind her, others from the congregation made their way out of the church and through its small burial ground. The church roof had recently been repaired using sheets of corrugated iron. All of the shattered windows had been boarded over and the door replaced, but the simple squat structure remained sound enough to be used. There was already a fund being built up to strengthen the tower and to replace the solitary damaged bell, which now pealed with a dull, flat note.

In the churchyard, many of the slabs and memorials had been removed and lay stacked against the wall. Benoît had explained to Reid how these would soon be put back over the burials they commemorated. The path that encircled the low mound upon which the church stood came down to wrought-iron gates and the trough beside which Reid sat.

An old, undamaged yew stood taller than the building itself and cast a circle of impenetrable shade over the ground beneath it.

'Were you inside?' Caroline asked.

'I'm afraid not. But I still enjoy sitting and listening to the hymns.' He moved to one side, allowing her to sit beside him. He nodded to the people he recognized. Benoît appeared with his wife and, as usual, told Reid what he had missed by not attending the service. Benoît's wife pushed her husband to one side and told Reid to take no notice of him.

Reid searched among the other locals for those few of his own workers who attended the services. A dozen or so soldiers came out and congregated by the stacked stones, smoking and trying to attract the local girls with what little French they had learned. He knew that others among his team of diggers would come to the service held in the early evening. Most of the remaining men would still be in their beds; and some, he knew, would be sleeping further afield in Albert or Saint-Quentin, where they had spent the previous evening. He turned a blind eye to these 'Sunday leaves' and insisted to Drake that he did the same. Drake agreed, but only reluctantly, and the concession remained a constant marker in the ever-changing balance of expediency and regulation between the two men.

'We sang in French,' Caroline said. '"All Creatures That On Earth Do Dwell" and "Worthy Is The Lamb For Sinners Slain".'

Reid didn't recognize the latter and so she sang a verse of it for him.

'I'm none the wiser,' he said when she'd finished. He saw

what pleasure she derived from singing and he complimented her on her voice.

'I was in the choir at home,' she said. 'In Lincoln.'

'The cathedral?'

She laughed at the suggestion. 'My parish church. Shortly before I last left home, a subscription was started for a memorial to be set into one of its walls.' She looked away from him as she spoke.

'Benoît tells me there's talk of something similar here,' he said. 'Once the new bell's cast. He's probably leading that committee, too.' He looked along the lane to where Benoît and his wife were walking home.

'Were many killed from here?' she asked him.

'I don't know. Benoît lost his only son. I daresay the names and numbers are well enough known by now to keep the masons busy for some time to come.' It only then occurred to him that her husband's name would in all likelihood be included in her own local memorial.

'I suppose so,' she said. 'Today the visiting curé told us all that we should never stop giving thanks for the fact that this place was largely spared. He told everyone it was their own personal miracle. He said that the Lord had wrapped His hands around the place and kept it safe from harm.'

'I see,' Reid said. He imagined Benoît listening to the words.

'A woman got up and walked out at hearing him,' Caroline said. 'Everyone waited for her husband to go after her and fetch her back, but he never left his pew. I could hear him crying from where I was sitting at the rear.' She rose briefly to exchange greetings with a solitary woman who passed beside them. It surprised Reid to hear her speak French so fluently, and he remarked on this when she sat back beside him.

'I was here for four years, remember,' she said. 'Many of our orderlies were French.' She leaned forward and searched along the street. Most of the sparse congregation had dispersed by now, but a few still lingered in the sun. 'I was hoping to see Mary.'

'Your companion? Wasn't she at the service with you?'

'She told me she preferred her own God.'

'Is it not the same one, then?'

'She called them Papists.' She laughed at the remark. 'Besides, she's been unwell ever since she arrived.'

'Oh?'

'She says she can find no *purpose* in life.'

It was clear to Reid that Caroline did not want to discuss the younger woman at any greater length.

'I should have come to find you,' he said. 'To show you the plans for the nurses' graves. It's just that, as yet, there's very little to see. Only their names and numbers on a plan which bears no resemblance whatsoever to the place itself. We're still waiting to hear for certain where our Cross of Sacrifice and Stone of Remembrance are to be positioned.' He had finally received the rudimentary plan for the nurses' graves from Wheeler, having told him of Caroline Mortimer's arrival.

'Someone told me recently that the French are considering using concrete crosses,' she said.

'Concrete on a metal frame. For their concentration cemeteries, yes.'

'But concrete – it seems . . .'

'It seems French, that's all.'

She smiled at this. 'Sergeant Drake told me that the graves

in the British burial grounds were being laid out to resemble units on parade, facing east towards the enemy. And that whatever else the final planting-up includes, roses will be planted so that at some part of every day the shadow of one of those roses will fall on to every British grave.'

Now Reid smiled. 'Those of us in charge on the ground are convinced that the Commission has an office somewhere marked "Fanciful Notions".'

'Still . . .'

'Yes, still . . .'

'Drake was kind enough to show me over the ground,' she said. 'I lied and told him you'd said it was all right for me to see where the nurses would eventually be laid to rest. I went to him after walking to the centre of the place.'

'Was it any help? I mean, did it make anything clearer to you?'

She considered this. 'The place was much larger than I'd imagined. I suppose that's to be . . . well . . .'

'We've found a good spot for the women,' Reid said.

'Drake showed me. I asked him when the bodies were coming, but he didn't know.'

Reid closed his eyes in thought. 'Wheeler thought some-time in the next month. I'll let you know as soon as I hear anything more definite. It's a plot beside the stream, close to one of the paths. Wheeler also said there was talk of a separate memorial for them.'

'Oh? Is that likely? I don't think—'

'Like almost everything else, nothing's been decided for certain yet. If I hear anything more . . . To be honest, at present Wheeler's more concerned about the imminent arrival from Neuville of an executed man.'

'Is he against it? Personally?'

'He gives that impression. The Commission overall has been in favour of their inclusion from the very start.'

'I imagine most of the poor souls . . .' She tailed off.

'Besides,' Reid said, 'Parliament has spoken. And I daresay all our elders and betters are growing weary of the constant outcries and assaults they must for ever fend off.' He stopped abruptly and then signalled his apology to her for this gentle outburst.

Neither of them spoke for a moment, and then Caroline touched his sleeve briefly and said, 'Did you know someone?'

Reid nodded absently. 'I knew *of* a man. A boy. Ninth Devons. He's buried at the Dartmoor cemetery. He'd already absconded six times before he was caught and charged and tried. Twice while on Active Service. He was given every opportunity. It seemed to me at the time that everyone involved simply ran out of patience with him. He was barely old enough to be here. They should have done the decent thing and sent him somewhere out of harm's way.'

They were interrupted by the appearance of Mary Ellsworth, who came quickly, running almost, round the corner of the lane leading to the rear of the church. She seemed surprised to find them so suddenly in front of her.

Reid rose to greet her and offered her his seat, but she stopped a few yards from them and came no closer. She seemed wary of the pair of them. Or perhaps wary of Caroline Mortimer only because she was in Reid's company.

Caroline, too, rose from the bench. She went to Mary and held both her hands. She told her to join them.

'I didn't know where you were,' Mary said accusingly.

'I told you yesterday. I was at the service.'

'I meant afterwards. I was waiting for you to return.'

'I met Captain Reid. We were talking.'

Mary Ellsworth looked back and forth between them as though doubting what Caroline had just told her.

'Is something wrong?' Caroline asked her. 'Has something happened?'

Mary pulled herself free and took several paces away from her. 'I wanted to see you, to talk, that's all,' she said.

Reid sat back down, hoping to put her at her ease.

'Are you coming?' Mary said to Caroline.

'Soon,' Caroline said. 'I wanted some air.'

Clearly angry that the older woman had not done as she'd asked, Mary Ellsworth turned and walked briskly away from them.

'Perhaps you should go to her,' Reid suggested as Caroline watched her leave.

'I'm not her guardian,' Caroline said, though not unkindly. 'I've been away, in Amiens. I only returned last night. She wanted to come with me, but I told her I had work to do and that she ought to stay here.'

'Work in connection with your nurses?'

She shook her head. 'The bodies of six women were found in a grave at Acheville, beyond Arras. The Registration officer in Amiens sent word to me. It turned out they were nuns and novices from a convent in Liège. Their own graveyard was lost to them during the war and these six had been buried in the plot at Acheville. They'd all been exhumed and identified by the time I arrived. I could have returned immediately, but the few remaining sisters invited me to stay the night and I accepted. Mary can be very demanding.'

'I can imagine. Has she found out anything more about her fiancé?'

'Nothing positive. The resident superintendent at Vignacourt—'

'Vesey – Peter Vesey,' Reid said. 'I know him.'

'He apparently had four graves assigned to men with the same surname, but none of their details matched up with Mary's fiancé. Same regiment, but different companies and dates.'

'It's more common than you'd imagine,' Reid said.

'So, once again, her hopes were raised and then dashed.'

'Did she go to Vignacourt?'

Caroline shook her head. 'When I told her I wouldn't be able to accompany her, she insisted on coming to Acheville with me. I told her to go alone, that the journey would be straightforward. To be honest, I didn't want her with me at Acheville. If the women there had turned out to be nurses, then I would have had things to do. You know how it is. It's why she's angry with me now. I don't blame her. I doubt if she truly knows herself what she wants or expects from any of this.'

'She'd be better off back at home,' Reid said.

'Wherever she was, I doubt things would be any different. Besides . . .'

'Besides, you appreciated your time alone at Acheville?'

'I did. I promised I'd return before I left for England. The place is half-destroyed, but the nuns are carrying on with their lives there as though nothing has happened. It has always been a nursing convent. I went to prayers with them. I knelt on the bare earth and listened to them whispering and murmuring all around me for an hour. They are growing vegetables again, and breeding ducks and rabbits. They collect frogs from nearby ponds. The oldest of the six dead was ninety, the youngest only fourteen. The sisters dug their new graves and reburied them. Several of them worked in the hospital in Arras. I had French nuns with me at the casualty clearing station at Abbeville, and later at Roisel. They were afraid of nothing, those women.'

'Unlike—'

'Yes, unlike Mary, who now, it seems, is afraid of almost everything she encounters.'

It wasn't what Reid had been about to say, but he let the remark pass.

After this, she held out her hand to him and said she ought to go after Mary. Less than ten minutes had passed since her abrupt departure.

'Of course,' Reid said, rising again. He'd hoped they might have spent longer together, but again he said nothing.

'Will you come and visit me?' she said.

'Of course.'

She took a step away from him, then turned and saluted, and he had already half raised his arm when she laughed and lowered her own.

He watched her go, seeing her pass in and out of the light and shadow of the lost buildings as she moved along the street, pausing occasionally to exchange greetings with the few villagers still gathered there.

8

Two days later, Reid was waiting on the platform when Alexander Lucas and a dozen or so others climbed down from the train carrying that day's deliveries. Lucas saw him and came to him through the congregating men.

'En route to Prezière,' he said. 'Jessop's arranging for transport from here. I spoke to him earlier. According to him, the lorries should already be waiting.' He looked beyond the station to where Reid's men were again gathering on the verge.

'Nothing so far,' Reid said.

'Which is precisely what I expected.' There was neither anger nor disappointment in Lucas's voice.

They were then approached by Drake, who complained that Lucas's men were getting in the way of the train being unloaded.

'And the station master in Amiens complained that we were in the way of your coffins being loaded,' Lucas said.

Drake smiled and shook his head.

Reid told him to set their own men to work.

'I have half a ton of equipment. Picks and spades, mostly,' Lucas said. 'I'll tell my crew to stay out of the way until your stuff's off.'

'The driver will insist on sticking to the schedule,' Reid warned him.

'And then spend three hours back in Amiens doing nothing?'

'Probably.'

'Most of what we need will be on the lorries,' Lucas said. He shouted instructions for the dozen or so others who had come with him.

'Is that all of you?' Reid asked him, surprised to see so few men.

Lucas left him briefly and went to the rear of the train, where he now told his own labourers to help the men unloading the coffins. There was friendly competition between the two groups.

When Lucas returned, he took Reid's arm and guided him into the empty waiting room. Sparrows flew from side to side across the low ceiling. The room was dimly lit, cool in the morning shade, and filled with the dust which rose from its bare boards.

Lucas sat opposite Reid on one of the simple benches and the two men lit cigarettes. It was clear to Reid that Lucas had brought him away from the others for a reason.

'Have there been new discoveries?' Reid said. 'At Prezière?'

Lucas opened the case he carried and took out a rolled map and several folders fastened with string. He unrolled the map and showed it to Reid.

'This is you,' he said, tapping a finger at the centre of the sheet. 'And here's Prezière. At least, here's where it once was.'

'How many bodies do you expect to recover?'

'Our latest estimate – accounts vary – is between thirty and forty.'

'So many? I didn't think there'd been any major engagement there.' Reid studied the map more closely, trying to remember where and when the lines had come and gone in those last confused months. 'At Hargicourt, perhaps, when everything was overrun. But Prezière? Do you have any witnesses?'

'Apparently, we're going to retrieve between thirty and forty corpses that were laid out with all their insignia intact *inside* a barn, which afterwards collapsed on top of them and hid them from sight for two years.' His scepticism was clear.

'A makeshift morgue, then?' Reid said.

'Possibly. Our most reliable witness – the farmer who owns the barn, which had been a fodder store on the edge of his land – said that he only returned there in May of this year to find the building with its roof and upper walls caved in. There was no other significant damage around the place and so he left it alone and got on with what needed doing elsewhere on his property. We know the Ninth and Fifth Manchesters and the Second Lancashire Fusiliers retreated over the land sometime during that last Easter, and that the Germans followed them and often overtook them as far west as Albert.'

'So do you believe the bodies were gathered up afterwards and laid there by the Germans?'

'Unlikely. They were making five or six miles' progress each day by then and stopping for nothing. There was a sizeable depot at Combles and they were keen to get to it before it was destroyed. We've learned most of this from our own records and other eye witness accounts.'

'What, then?'

Lucas sat in silence for a moment before answering.

'Wheeler believes we're retrieving the bodies of men who were taken prisoner and who found themselves rounded up into the building.'

'And who were then killed there—'

'By "means unknown", yes.' Lucas rolled up his map.

Only then did it fully occur to Reid what Lucas was suggesting to him. 'Surely, you don't believe . . .' he began to say.

'According to the farmer – the man's supposedly waiting for us there now – the few corpses he was able to make out beneath the rubble appeared to have been badly burned, scorched black.'

'Scorched?'

'That was the word he used. It's not usually what happens to bodies, however the men were killed.'

'Perhaps the building caught fire and that was why it collapsed in on the men,' Reid said.

'The farmer says the collapsed joists and other timbers and tiles show no signs whatsoever of the same fire.'

Neither man spoke for a moment. It seemed to Reid that all further speculation about how the men had died two years earlier was pointless.

'Will the bodies be sent here, do you think?' he said eventually.

Lucas nodded. 'They were originally docketed for Hargicourt, but Wheeler believes it's best all round if they now come here, and as soon and directly as possible.'

'I doubt—'

'He wants me to retrieve them, identify them – which shouldn't be too difficult – and then make the arrangements to deliver them directly to you, rather than to one of the sorting depots. He's already got Jessop working on the paperwork. Once I've started work at Prezière, and we all get a clearer picture of what did or didn't happen there, then Wheeler will set everything in motion at his end. He insists it's all for the best, and to be honest, I tend to agree with him.'

'Even if what you uncover points to . . . ?'

'Yes.'

'I see,' Reid said. It was the first time bodies would have come to Morlancourt like this. 'Does Wheeler want *me* to do anything?'

'"Let expediency be our watchword." All Wheeler wants is for you and me to make everything run as smoothly as possible for him. I doubt it's anything more or less than we do already.'

'Even if you do find evidence of the deliberate killing of prisoners?'

Lucas smiled at this. 'I said exactly the same to him. He looked as though he was going to explode.'

'He surely can't want everything to be ignored or dismissed without at least—'

'Can't he? Besides, like I said – he may have a point. What good would stirring everything up and causing the men's families all that doubt and anguish serve? Who among them wouldn't far rather just know that their loved one had finally been found and then buried here? You can see his point, surely? Besides, he as good as told me that if *I* couldn't deal with all of this quickly and quietly, there were plenty of others he could call on to do the work for him. He also hinted that a great deal of what *he* wanted had been sanctioned by others higher up.'

'In the Commission? The War Office?'

Lucas shrugged.

They sat in silence for several minutes, listening to the noise of the men outside unloading the train's cargo.

'Wheeler will need to provide me with all the necessary paperwork,' Reid said eventually.

'Jessop's got everything in hand. We have the names of all the men in the Manchesters and Lancashires who answered the last roll-call before the Germans came running across the fields at Prezière. At least now twenty to thirty wives and mothers will have their uncertainty ended and their minds put to rest.'

'But only because you'll keep the truth from them and tell them what they want to hear,' Reid said, immediately wishing he'd stayed silent.

'Of course I'll tell them what they want to hear,' Lucas shouted at him. 'Just as I'll tell Wheeler what *he* wants to hear. And just as *you*'ll tell them all where to come and lay their flowers, where to come to kneel and to cry and to remember their heroic son or husband or brother killed in a painless instant while gallantly fighting for his friends and king and country.'

Reid was accustomed to hearing these unguarded remarks from Lucas, but seldom had he heard the man express himself so vehemently or within the hearing of others.

They were distracted briefly by the rising noise of approaching lorries.

'Your transport,' Reid said. He watched as Lucas clasped his hands together and then released them. 'How long will it take you?' he asked him.

'Wheeler's given us a week. As I say, identification should

72

be straightforward, and that's what usually takes up most of our time.'

'Even if the bodies are badly burned?'

Lucas bowed his head and held his face in his cupped palms. 'Sorry about that,' he said.

Reid waved away the apology.

'Wheeler's opening gambit was to give us three days.'

'Could it be done in that time?'

'Probably. I told him we needed ten and we settled on a week.'

'Because he knew what he was asking of you and was in no position to argue?'

'Something like that. However long it takes, he wants the first of my paperwork with you by the end of the week. The sooner we start, the sooner we finish. He wants the first of the bodies delivered to you on your smoky little train by this time next week.'

'I'll allocate the plots as soon as I get the names,' Reid said.

'I'm sure he'd appreciate that. He even suggested to me that the three of us should get together for dinner one night. A pat on the back for all our hard work under such trying circumstances. He's probably already preparing a little speech.'

They were interrupted by a knock on the open door, and Drake appeared. A man in a full, clean uniform stood beside him.

'Ah,' Lucas said.

The man came forward and Reid saw the clerical collar beneath his tunic.

'The padre was looking for Lieutenant Lucas,' Drake said.

'Chaplain Guthrie,' Lucas called to the man. 'Come and meet your parish gravediggers.'

The man looked unhappy at the remark. 'Captain Reid,' he said to Reid, holding out his hand and pointedly ignoring Alexander Lucas. 'I believe your charges await you.' He motioned outside.

'My charges?'

'He means your bodies,' Lucas said.

'Of course,' Reid said. He rose and shook the chaplain's hand.

'I was about to tell you,' Lucas said, unable to hide the amusement in his voice. 'The Commission has recently felt the need for – what? – shall we call it a greater degree of spiritual rigour and religious guidance in all its affairs and efforts.'

The chaplain looked over Reid's shoulder to where Lucas still sat behind him. 'As much as I appreciate your candour and your somewhat unnecessary introduction, Lieutenant Lucas, I am here, as we all surely are, to serve the greater good and to—'

'Ah, that again,' Lucas said.

Guthrie turned back to Reid. 'Jonathan Montague Symes Guthrie,' he said. 'Chaplain to the Royal West Surreys, and latterly – as Lieutenant Lucas has already somewhat clumsily suggested – adviser on spiritual matters to the Imperial Commission.'

'Are you here to assist at Prezière?' Reid said.

'And much more,' Guthrie said, smiling.

'*Much* more,' Lucas said softly, and Reid heard the warning in the words.

Meaning what? That the man had been directed by Wheeler

to watch over and report on what now happened at Morlancourt?

Lucas rose from where he sat and began to gather up his possessions.

Outside, a horn sounded, followed by shouting from the gathered men.

'Captain Lucas's lorries are here,' Drake said. 'And a motor car.'

'My sturdy chariot,' Lucas said, going out on to the platform. 'Now all I need are my bow of burnished gold and my arrows of desire.'

Guthrie shook his head at the words. 'He displays his heathen's credentials and appetites like other men wear their medals and ribbons,' he said.

'I know,' Reid said, doing his best not to smile.

Guthrie followed Alexander Lucas out towards the lorries.

Reid went to the doorway. At the edge of the station yard, Lucas was already standing in the passenger seat of the car and looking down at everything around him. He called out instructions and his men immediately started loading their own scattered equipment.

9

Reid spent the remainder of the day in the cemetery. Work continued on channelling the small stream and keeping its water away from the recently excavated graves. He had argued against deepening the culvert, but Wheeler had insisted on this. It seemed to Reid that all it had achieved was to increase the flow of water in its new course. He made a note in his log to request a visit from one of the Commission's supervising engineers the next time he met with Wheeler. Meanwhile, he calculated which of the short lines of graves on the cemetery's higher land might now be excavated without delay in readiness for the bodies Alexander Lucas would soon deliver to him.

At mid-morning he blew his whistle to signal a break. The men immediately stopped what they were doing and congregated on the few patches of long grass. They ate and drank and smoked. Most sat in small groups, and a few of the younger ones kicked a ball back and forth. Reid wanted to tell them to rest after their labours, to save their strength for what was left of the day ahead, but he had long since learned to say nothing. He would allow them half an hour in that heat, and except for the few men who now approached him with questions or who came to him for fresh instructions, he remained apart from them.

He sat against a tree at the edge of the small copse overlooking the slope and brought his log of works up to date. Some of the men, he saw, still carried the pieces of oil cloth they had used to sit on during Active Service. The material, in addition to keeping their backsides dry, was widely considered a preventative against piles. Reid himself had once organized the distribution of such pieces from the factory in Bapaume, when the mayor and his aldermen there had made a ceremony of handing over the damaged rolls. The factory itself had lost its roof and most of its walls and had soon afterwards been abandoned and fallen into ruin.

He was close to finishing the log when someone called to him and he shielded his eyes to look around him. The voice had come from behind him, somewhere in the trees, and the sound of someone coming through the undergrowth caused Reid to rise and turn. The voice called again, and this time Reid recognized Jonathan Guthrie. He called back, and a moment later the chaplain appeared amid the thin trunks. There was someone following him, and Reid watched as Caroline Mortimer was finally revealed. She came along the same narrow path a few paces behind the man.

'We heard your whistle,' Guthrie said, emerging into the open. 'I must say, I doubt I shall ever hear the same thing again without the sound sending a chill up my spine.'

'No,' Reid said. At the beginning of the work on the cemetery, he had rung a small bell, but the sound of this had not carried, and the newly arrived workers had complained about every minute lost to them.

'We met on the far side of the hill,' Guthrie said. 'Caroline was explaining her own duties here.'

'Duties?' Reid said.

'To her fallen nurses,' Guthrie said.

'Of course.' It surprised Reid to hear the man, only so recently arrived, call her by her Christian name.

'I was showing Reverend Guthrie the view towards the river,' Caroline said. 'When the land beyond the canal is restored and planted again, it should provide a beautiful setting for your cemetery.'

'I suppose so,' Reid said.

It was something he had not considered. It had always surprised him to see how swiftly the farmers had reclaimed and then planted their land as the fighting had come and gone around them. Even when the local population had been forcibly evacuated *en masse*, they had invariably returned at the first opportunity to resume their work, despite all the warnings to wait until the land was made safe again.

'They do a pretty good job,' Guthrie said. 'At Aubigny they filled in the most enormous craters and were ploughing over the old trenches and picket lines within days of our departure. I daresay we shall be wondering where everything went before we know it.' He looked around him at the scattered men. 'Should they not be working?' he said.

Reid heard the note of disapproval in his voice. 'On a break,' he told him.

Guthrie pulled back his cuff and looked at his watch. 'I see,' he said.

Caroline Mortimer came away from the chaplain to stand beside Reid. 'I hear you're being delayed by flooding,' she said. 'The villagers know everything.'

'I'm sure they do,' Reid said. He pointed to the stream. 'Whoever drew up the plans probably imagined it to be a lot

78

smaller and considerably more intermittent than it actually is.'

'It's water,' Guthrie said, but nothing more.

The three of them then sat together at the edge of the trees.

'And you?' Reid asked Guthrie. 'Do you have a specific duty here?' It was something he had been considering since meeting the man earlier in the day.

'As I believe I told you, I was chaplain to the Royal West Surreys. Over the past year I have officiated at a great many of their burials. Brigadier Ronaldson was assiduous at locating as many of our lost and missing men as humanly possible. He's back at home now. I promised him I would continue to do what I could. I'm here for another three months, on attachment to the Commission. You might say I am finishing the job for him.'

This answer left Reid none the wiser, and he tried to remember if any of the Surrey dead had already been assigned to Morlancourt.

'You will no doubt be aware, of course, that a number of recently retrieved Surreys are to come to you here,' Guthrie said.

'Of course.'

'Then, naturally, I shall perform my duties here on their behalf.'

Reid could only say, 'Of course,' again.

Guthrie took off his cap and wiped his forehead with a clean white handkerchief. Everything he said continued to sound both detached and rehearsed. 'I was hoping you might show me on your plans where the graves will eventually lie.'

To hide his ignorance, Reid explained that he would

need to consult the maps in his room back in Morlancourt. He guessed that some of the men awaiting delivery would remain unidentified. 'Perhaps you might be able to help with identification where necessary,' he suggested.

'Of course,' Guthrie said, but with little conviction. 'Though I daresay the opportunity for that, like a great deal else, is already long past. I knew a good many of those men personally. I wrote to their families.' He glanced at Caroline Mortimer sitting close beside him. 'I told Colonel Wheeler – Edmund – that he must avail himself of my services at all times. The war itself may be long over, and all that . . . I spent a week in the Flesquières salient when the pits there were uncovered. A hundred and seventy bodies were removed, and all of them – imagine that, Captain Reid – all of them, every single one, were fully and properly identified. I daresay there were many other instances when not a solitary corpse was afforded that same privilege.'

'Many,' Reid said, uncertain how they had come so swiftly on to this other path. He wanted to signal to the man to watch what he said in front of Caroline.

Catching something of Reid's concern, Caroline herself said, 'I am equally fortunate in knowing the identities of every one of my nurses. I, too, wrote to their families – their parents, usually – and I gained considerable balm from both writing those letters and receiving their many replies.' She closed her eyes as she said this, perhaps remembering the women.

'At Havrincourt,' Guthrie went on, almost as though she had not spoken, 'I held a service close to our support artillery. The shells flew over our heads as we knelt and prayed. Nine-fives, long-distance jobs.'

It seemed an odd remark to make, and Reid was reminded of an incident when three of his own men had been killed by a solitary shell that had fallen on the railhead at Brouchy, which had landed a dud but had then exploded the following day as the men were loading timber for new trench work.

'I mention this because it is my intention to hold a service here,' Guthrie said loudly, distracting Reid from his thoughts.

'Sorry?'

'A service. I shall hold one here, at the cemetery. Soon. Sometime in the coming weeks.'

'While the work is going on?' Reid said. 'Surely not?'

Plans had already been made by the Commission for inaugural ceremonies when all the nearby burial grounds were completed and handed over to their eventual keepers.

'You'll need to talk to Wheeler,' Reid said, angry at what Guthrie had just proposed, but convinced that Wheeler would prevent whatever the man was planning while the ground itself remained in a state of such obvious turmoil and disarray.

'I've already done so,' Guthrie said. 'Edmund told me I must do whatever I see fit to honour the Surreys – everyone, in fact.'

'I doubt if—' Reid began to say.

'In fact, I was rather hoping you might see your way to rearranging your schedules somewhat – I doubt they are set in stone – so that all the necessary graves are dug and filled at the same time. Edmund certainly seemed to believe this to be well within your capabilities. He told me to tell you that you might contact him directly if you have any concerns regarding what I've just asked of you.'

Reid saw how completely he had been outmanoeuvred.

He quickly calculated the changes required to his schedules, and what extra work this might entail, especially in light of Alexander Lucas's earlier revelation. He was convinced that Wheeler – *Edmund* – had only agreed to Guthrie's proposal because it had been put to the Commission in a manner that had made it difficult for anyone to refuse him. It would be almost impossible, Reid knew, especially given the labour and transportation required, to reinter all the Surreys either soon or at a single ceremony, even if this *had* already been sanctioned by some distant figure at the Commission.

'We usually manage ten to fifteen burials a day,' he said. 'To correspond with the bodies delivered to us each morning.'

Guthrie considered this, clearly aware of Reid's objections to what he had just proposed. 'I shall be seeing Edmund later this evening,' he said. 'Perhaps he and I might consider things then at greater length.'

'And say what?' Reid said. 'Like I say, the pace and routine of the work here is dictated to us by the number of bodies – mostly reinterments and new retrievals these days – sent to us from the Graves depots. Most days we fulfil our quotas, and other days we fall behind. Even here, some men are interred and then later removed for burial elsewhere. It's more common than you'd think. I imagine even Colonel Wheeler—'

'Please, I meant no criticism of you or your achievement here,' Guthrie said. He looked at Caroline and smiled as he said this, as though expecting her to share his surprise at Reid's objections. He then held Reid's arm for a moment and

Reid felt himself flinch at the man's touch. 'And I certainly never meant to cause you any offence, Captain Reid.'

Everything Guthrie said and suggested kept Reid at a disadvantage.

'No, of course not,' Reid said, regretting even this small concession. He looked away from Guthrie, watching a group of diggers who lay along the low banks of the stream and scooped water from it in their cupped palms. He regretted more than ever Caroline Mortimer's presence beside them.

'Perhaps I might be able to do something similar for my nurses,' she said hesitantly. 'A small ceremony, I mean. Something separate from whatever Colonel Wheeler intends at a later date.'

'I hardly think—' Guthrie began to say, but stopped abruptly when she turned to him and held his gaze.

'I don't see why not,' Reid said.

The graves for the women were already dug and waiting. Every man who had worked on them had known who they were intended for, and greater care than usual had been put into their preparation on that account. Several of the diggers had even approached Reid to say that they would appreciate some further element of ceremony to the day's routine when the women finally came to them. Given the usual constraints, Reid had promised them he would do his best. Perhaps what Caroline was now suggesting – after all, she was unlikely to be refused by Wheeler – would be the perfect solution.

Guthrie looked again at his watch and, seeing this, Reid took out his whistle and blew on it. Caroline had already covered her ears with her hands, but the sound surprised Guthrie and he gave a start, afterwards laughing at himself.

All across the cemetery, men rose from where they had been lying and sitting and walked singly and in small groups back to their work.

"'See them toil in the fields of the Lord',' Guthrie said, then he too rose and without a word to either Reid or Caroline, walked quickly down the slope towards the road.

10

Reid saw nothing of Alexander Lucas for the whole of the following day. As agreed, he had arranged a room for Lucas in his own small *pension* and had anticipated spending the evening with him upon his return from Prezière. But by ten that night, Lucas had not appeared, and neither had his men and their lorries.

When Lucas did finally come, at six the following morning, he was alone and driving himself. He sat in the street beneath Reid's window and sounded his horn.

Reid went to his window and Lucas beckoned for him to go down to him.

Reid arrived at the car and started to tell him about the room he had arranged.

'I'll bring some of my stuff later,' Lucas said, interrupting him, yawning, and showing little interest in what Reid was telling him. 'It's a Hudson,' he said, meaning the car. 'Last time, they gave me a Daimler. Beautiful machine. I own a Sunbeam at home.' He yawned again and stopped speaking.

It was clear to Reid that the man was exhausted. 'Did you get your bodies?' he asked him.

'We made a start,' Lucas said.

'You were there all day and night?'

'Some of us.'

Lucas started the engine and drove them out of the village, stopping a few minutes later alongside the near-empty Ancre canal.

'What is it?' Reid asked eventually as the two men walked along the embankment.

Lucas arched his back and swung his arms. 'Wheeler sent a despatch rider to await our arrival,' he said. He sat down on the slope, his feet only a yard above the surface of the green and stagnant water.

Reid sat beside him. Insects swarmed over the surface of the drained channel and rushes grew along most of its length. Its faintly sulphurous smell filled the warming air.

'Because of what he already knew you'd find there?' Reid said.

'It's possible. The rider was there to tell me to make the site secure, keep everyone out, and to make sure that every body we retrieved was properly identified – as far as possible – and then fully logged. To be honest, having seen the place and the bodies, my concerns remain elsewhere.'

'Meaning what?' Reid said, already guessing.

Alexander Lucas rubbed his face with both his hands. 'The bodies were more severely burned than the farmer's account had suggested.'

Reid watched ripples along the surface of the canal where sluggish fish rose to take the flies.

'Was the farmer there?' he said.

'He was working in the fields during the day, but he left in the evening before I could talk to him. I camped in the ruined barn.'

'With the bodies?'

86

Lucas smiled. 'With the bodies. We counted thirty-six of them. None of them are covered as such, just lined up on the ground under the rubble of the collapsed building.'

'And the burning?'

'Like I said – worse than I'd anticipated, but in most cases still only superficial. The corpses were certainly all intact. It looks to me as though somebody poured petrol or paraffin over them and set them alight.'

'Were you able to make your identifications?'

'They'd been there almost two years. Nothing was instantly identifiable, but most of them were in some kind of uniform and with kit attached. There are some indications of looting – not many watches or cigarette cases or small arms, for instance. But there they are in their neat and tidy rows all the same. Believe me, I wish all our retrievals were as easily accomplished.'

'Does their being laid out like that suggest that whoever did it was – I don't know – showing them some measure of respect?'

'It's a possibility. I've seen it before, though usually with far fewer bodies.'

'Then perhaps they were simply gathered up and laid out by men who assumed they'd be collected by our own teams afterwards,' Reid suggested.

Lucas shrugged. 'Besides, as Wheeler keeps reminding me, all that matters now is that we've actually found and recovered them.' He yawned and stretched.

'And not the circumstances of their deaths?'

'I think we all know where that particular line was long since drawn.'

Reid didn't fully understand the remark, but said nothing.

A dragonfly appeared in front of him, iridescent blue and emerald green, hovering motionless and then flicking itself away from him.

After a silence, he said, 'Will it delay you?'

'I'm not sure,' Lucas said. 'I daresay Wheeler will only breathe easy when everyone's been boxed up and handed over to you. "The earth must bear its secrets," and all that. Besides, who among us is still truly looking for answers or for explanations?'

'Perhaps,' Reid said.

After a further silence, Lucas said, 'Jessop let slip that the old man lost his nephew out here – July 'sixteen – and that he was making discreet enquiries about having the boy's body repatriated so that his sister could bury him in the family plot. The family plot – that sounds like a good solid ending to the story, don't you think?'

'I doubt if the Commission—'

'Wheeler *is* the Commission,' Lucas said angrily.

But Reid knew that Wheeler, because of his position, would be more bound than most to abide by the rules concerning repatriation. Besides, it had long since been decided that all recovered bodies would be buried as close as possible to where they had fallen, and wherever possible in the company of their dead companions. In the early days, as all these rules and practices were still being decided, wealthier families had petitioned the War Office and had then made their own private arrangements to retrieve their dead. Almost from the start, the Commission had been keen to prevent this. Wheeler, Reid knew, would have no say whatsoever in what happened to the body of his nephew.

'It might be wise for you to become answerable to someone other than Wheeler,' he said to Lucas, knowing how evasive he sounded. He knew, too, how unlikely Lucas was to act on this advice.

'I know,' Lucas conceded. 'But I gave the man my word that I'd do all I could. He's as powerless as the rest of us in the matter, I know that.'

'I could alter some of my schedules and let Wheeler know that we are ready and waiting here,' Reid said. 'I could make the burials a priority.'

Lucas nodded at this. 'I imagine he just wants everything done by the book. I – we – need to go through the usual motions for him, that's all.'

'Can you trust your men to say nothing?' Reid said.

'Most of them don't care one way or another. All *they* want to do now is to wash their hands and get back home. They might all be serving men, but not many of them *act* like soldiers. I lose two or three every week when the Monday Orders arrive in Calais.'

'Same here,' Reid said.

They were distracted briefly by the appearance on the far bank of several men carrying wicker baskets, who rose to the skyline and then followed the canal in the direction of the lock at Ancre. Reid recognized several of them from Morlancourt and he called to them. They were eel fishermen lifting the traps they had set the previous evening. Two of the men held up the sacks they carried. The sacks swung and twisted with the writhing of their living contents.

'They sell them,' Reid told Lucas, adding that his own landlady had already served eels to him.

'When they finally prised open the lock gates in Albert,' Lucas said, 'the water fell only slowly and they pulled out hundreds of the things – thousands – three and four feet long, some of them, and thicker than a man's arm.'

'I suppose—'

'They'd been feeding on disintegrating corpses for months. It was the submerged bodies that had jammed the gates. The locals said bubbles had been rising all that time. We were called in to take away the remains – French, mostly. Believe me, we were only too glad to hand them over.'

'The creatures here are barely a foot long,' Reid said, causing Lucas to laugh.

The fishermen and their baskets were now in the far distance and out of earshot, their outlines melting into the haze already rising off the land. In places, thin wisps of steam rose from the surface of the canal.

'So what do you make of friend Guthrie?' Lucas said.

'He came out to the cemetery,' Reid said. 'Apparently, he's planning some kind of ceremony for the West Surreys about to be buried there.'

'Oh, he does like to raise his blessed palms in benediction over everyone and everything he encounters,' Lucas said, again doing nothing to disguise his dislike of the man.

'He's overbearing, that's all,' Reid said.

'Holier than thou, you mean?'

'Which he is,' Reid said. 'Holier than us.'

'He buried them at Fricourt, Varens and Hédaville,' Lucas said. 'He used to hold services every morning and then again in the evening for anyone who wanted them.'

It was beyond Reid to ask Lucas what grudge he held against Guthrie. 'He was with Caroline Mortimer,' he said.

'Your nurse?'

'The bodies of her women will be with us soon enough.'

'And did Saint Guthrie promise to see *them* safely delivered up into Heaven, too?'

'He offered to do *something*,' Reid said. 'For which Caroline Mortimer was grateful.'

'I'm sure she was.' Lucas squinted into the rising light. 'Ignore me,' he said. 'It's been a long night. Wheeler said he'd send us an earth-mover from the Pioneers' depot. Not that it'll be much use in a space like that.'

'The man occasionally shows willing,' Reid said.

'Doesn't he just? And then makes sure everyone knows it. He told me he'd wait a little longer before coming out to Prezière himself. Said he didn't want to get in our way.'

'I suppose ultimately—'

'Ultimately, he'll do exactly what he's told to do, just like the rest of us. No one is going to be here for ever. I have men who would set off walking home right now if I told them they could go.'

'Enough have tried it,' Reid said.

'And I daresay a handful succeeded. When I first came out here I had a commanding officer who insisted on giving a map to everyone under his command who wanted one.'

'Of here, France?'

'Of this part of the world. Nothing too specific, of course. The coastline, cities, railways, towns, big rivers, that sort of thing. To be honest, the maps looked ancient, fifty years old at least. The point is – and this was why he handed them out – they also showed the southern half of England, London up to the Midlands, and all the Channel ports from Dover round to Plymouth. Something a serving man could look at and see roughly where he was in relation to his home. Something he could put his finger on and then draw a connecting line.'

91

'Something to reassure him,' Reid said. 'Like the Romans and their lines of sown mustard seed which flowered yellow each spring and allegedly pointed all the way back to Rome.'

'I suppose so,' Lucas said.

After that, neither man spoke for several minutes.

The smell from the water grew stronger in the rising heat. Birdsong filled the open land behind them.

Eventually, Reid looked at his watch. It was almost seven. 'I ought to go,' he said. There were no bodies arriving that morning, but Drake and a dozen men would already be at the station to await the delivery of their other supplies.

The cemetery lay in the opposite direction to the one they had taken out of Morlancourt and Lucas insisted on driving Reid there.

Passing back through the village, they saw the fishermen sitting at tables on the street, already surrounded by the women of the place, who were taking out the writhing eels and inspecting them, seemingly oblivious to the way the creatures coiled themselves around their hands and forearms. Previously, Reid had seen the men chop off the eels' heads as they were sold and then watched as they had continued writhing just as vigorously afterwards.

11

The following morning, shortly before his departure for the station, Reid was washing when there was a knock at his door. He had spent the previous evening with Alexander Lucas, and he imagined this to be him now. They had arranged to meet later in the day, prior to Lucas returning to Amiens to deliver his preliminary report to Wheeler. But upon pulling open his door, he was surprised to see Caroline Mortimer standing there.

'You were expecting someone else,' she said, waiting to be invited into the room as Reid pulled on his shirt and continued drying himself.

He told her about his plans for the day and waited for her to speak.

She looked quickly around the small room and then sat in its only comfortable chair.

Reid rubbed his wet hair vigorously. He looked in the mirror hanging above his basin and saw Caroline Mortimer studying his back.

'You were wounded,' she said.

Reid slapped a hand over the two scars high on his shoulder. 'It was never much,' he said. 'Spent shrapnel, that's all. There and my leg.'

Caroline rose and came to him where he stood. She pulled away his shirt and then kneaded and stretched the skin around the scars.

'They were badly stitched,' she said.

'They were *quickly* stitched,' Reid said.

'What happened? I'm sorry – none of my business.'

'It was at Bécourt,' Reid said. 'The last March. It seems all we ever did for a fortnight was withdraw, look over our shoulders and then withdraw some more. And by "withdraw"—'

'You mean—'

'I mean run, yes. Everywhere you looked during that last spring, there was confusion. Years and years of next-to-no real progress whatsoever, and then *that*. I was sent to assist in the retrieval of some of our forward guns. Small pieces. The artillerymen were making up their crews, gathering together horses and limbers. We were just about done, only one or two firing pins to be removed, when half a dozen shells fell among us. I was wounded and concussed. I was unlucky, that's all. I felt very little – at least not until I came to. I was picked up straight away and taken to the hospital at Albert on one of the gun carriages.'

'A close friend of mine nursed at the place,' Caroline said. She smiled at the sudden, unexpected memory, and Reid felt her fingers press harder into his shoulder.

'Not then, I hope,' he said.

'No – earlier. She was moved back to the base hospital at Le Havre just before Christmas the previous year.'

'Is she . . . ? I mean . . .'

'Safe at home. She went from Le Havre to Roehampton, and from there back to Southampton, where she started out.

94

She was married six months ago and she's expecting her first child in four months' time.' There seemed a comforting, re-assuring order and symmetry to the story.

'I'm pleased for her,' Reid said.

'Me, too.' She saw his relief, the different story he might just as easily have blundered into.

'Someone took out the shrapnel – like I say, already spent, by all accounts – and stitched me up. And an hour or so after I'd recovered consciousness we were all shipped from Albert back to Boulogne, to the civilian hospital there. I was more or less left to my own devices for a full month afterwards.'

'Did you anticipate being sent home?'

'I'm not sure. I doubt it. But I suddenly seemed a lot closer to leaving, simply by being there at Boulogne.'

'When we had the time, we sometimes opened up and cleaned out wounds already dealt with at the field stations,' she said. 'Too many men suffered from infections after-wards.'

'No such luxury,' Reid said. 'I was examined every day, told I was coming along nicely, and then discharged at the end of the month. By then, the rout had more or less come to a standstill. I was told I was eligible to apply for a further month's leave, but there seemed little point.'

'Oh? Surely, a month without—'

'Three of the men who'd been with me at Bécourt were killed outright by the shells. Another ten were injured worse than me. I'd known most of them for at least the past year. Going home seemed . . . unnecessary, somehow.'

'Unnecessary?'

'I'd seen a lot of men go home and then come back. It

made things harder for some of them. Especially the ones with wives and families, children.'

'Of course,' Caroline said. She left him where he stood and went back to the chair, sitting beside his unmade bed and looking out at the street below. There were already people moving along it, the sound of hooves and of lowing cattle as the animals were driven to the fields.

Reid pulled on his shirt and straightened his hair with his fingers.

'And so you went back,' Caroline said eventually.

'To a place called Montigny. A long way behind the new lines. We were billeted in a place that had seen nothing whatsoever of the fighting. The rest of the regiment had come on through the old battlegrounds. We were in a line twenty miles further back than where we'd started from two years earlier. My service card was stamped "Recuperation Duties". I suppose in a way it's how I eventually ended up here.'

'Were you able to stay there until everything was over?'

'Pretty much. We were in and out of the reserve lines for the summer, but it was a quiet sector. The truth was that after that last push and long retreat, everybody I'd known for any time was more or less exhausted. We all seemed to have had our own lucky escapes during those hectic weeks, and we were simply relieved to be able to rest and to catch our breath. I was in Montigny from April until August, and then after that we were moved to support the Queen's Own, west of Amiens. The Australians were there, and a tank corps. When the Armistice came, I was at Caulières, supervising depot work on the Amiens road. I was in another hotel, and the men were billeted in all the surrounding houses. On the day of the Armistice, our senior officers got everyone to assemble on the banks of the old reservoir at Vaux, hundreds of us. We were there at first light and we stayed there until the church in the valley bottom finally struck eleven.'

'I was in Le Touquet,' Caroline said. 'On the day itself we were busy from the night before – thirty serious wounds. Half the men died. We were told to take all the drink off the men coming into the dressing stations.'

'There was plenty to drink at Vaux,' Reid said absently. 'We all waited until the bells started ringing and then everyone celebrated.'

'Everyone?' Caroline said, but more to herself than to Reid.

'No, I suppose not. That evening, I heard that two men had drowned in the reservoir. They drank too much and then went swimming. Hundreds did. The men were discovered missing only the following day. Their bodies were found at the reservoir overflow the day after that. They'd been in a tunnelling company, miners. We were there for another month, until Christmas, and then one by one the companies were disbanded. Most of us, the officers in particular, went from Active Service into the reserve battalions. We were known as "disembodied". I was home by Christmas Eve and then called back here at the end of the following February.'

'Here?'

'Saint-Quentin first. I washed up here three months later to oversee the laying out of the plots between Querrie and Péronne. I only came to Morlancourt earlier this year.'

'I see,' she said.

Reid wondered at the seeming simplicity of the story he had just told, the days and the years it enclosed. Only then did it occur to him to ask her why she had called on him so early in the day.

'I came for Mary,' she said. 'Something of a surprise. Captain Jessop let her know late last night that her fiancé's body has been located and that he is actually being delivered to you here today.'

'Today?' Reid had little idea of the identities of the men being delivered to him each morning until he read the dockets that accompanied their corpses. 'Are you sure?'

'Captain Jessop seemed certain. Colonel Wheeler had asked him to look out for him. It was always likely that he'd be sent here, and sometime soon, but no one knew when. Apparently, his name was on the list sent to Colonel Wheeler yesterday afternoon. Mary's already calling it a miracle. Before she got the news, she was talking about returning home. To be honest with you, I was encouraging her to go.'

'I won't see the list of names until the train gets here,' Reid said. 'Ernaux makes something of a point of handing it over.'

She smiled. 'I can imagine.'

'I've saluted more often on that platform than anywhere else while I've been over here,' Reid said. He finished dressing, buttoning his jacket and then brushing the dried earth from his sleeves and shins. 'What's the man's name?' he asked her.

'Andrew Copley,' she said.

The pair of them fell silent at the sound of footsteps in the narrow corridor outside.

'That might be her now,' Caroline said, and she went to the door and looked out before Reid could stop her. But there was no one there and she went back in to him. 'Don't worry,' she said. 'No one saw me – either then or when I arrived.'

'It doesn't . . . I mean . . .' Reid said, feeling himself redden at the half-formed lie.

'She's been waiting in my room for the past hour,' Caroline said. 'She told me late last night about her news. I told her I'd come to see you to ask your permission for her to be at the station when the train arrives. She wants to be with the coffin for a moment before it's taken out to the cemetery. Can you arrange that for her? I mean, is it allowed?'

Reid considered what she was asking him.

'Would it have been simpler if we'd simply turned up un-announced at the station?'

'What is she expecting?' Reid said. 'More often than not, the coffins arrive with names and numbers chalked on them. We affix their plates here only once their actual plots are confirmed and ready for them.'

'She just wants to see it, that's all.'

'Sometimes we get caskets containing body parts, and occasionally the Registration people at Saint-Quentin chalk that on the caskets. It can all seem a bit brutal.'

'Compared to a proper funeral and burial?'

He nodded. 'Does she know any more?'

'Such as? Oh, I see. Apparently, Jessop was able to tell her that her fiancé's identity had been confirmed and that he'd previously been interred close to where he'd died. The body arrived in Saint-Quentin two days ago. She insisted on me coming to see you.'

'And if I say no, she'll come anyway?'

'I imagine so,' Caroline said.

'Will you be with her?' he said.

'It's what she wants. She turned up at my room already wearing a veil.'

'Is she still there?'

'I imagine so. I told her I'd go straight back to her.'

Reid looked at his watch. 'Go back to her. Give me some time to get the train unloaded. Bring her closer to eight. I'll need to find out what else is being sent. I'll sort something out with Drake.'

'Of course. She's grateful for anything you're able to do. As am I.'

Collecting up his case and satchel, Reid held open the door for her and she left the room ahead of him, descending the stairs to the street, where they stood together for a moment longer before parting.

'One thing,' Reid said after she had taken several steps away from him. 'You must persuade her to stay at the station. Afterwards, I mean, when I leave with the coffins for the cemetery.'

'Of course.'

'It's important,' Reid said. 'It's difficult enough work for the men, without—'

'Without a woman wailing in grief while they're labouring?'

'Yes, exactly,' Reid said, angry at this unthinking remark.

'I'm sorry, I didn't mean to sound so crass,' she said. She reached towards him.

'No, I know,' he said, and before she could answer him – apologize further, perhaps – he turned and left her for the station and the men already gathering there.

12

Later, approaching eight, Reid went to join the two women where they waited in Benoît's office.

Mary Ellsworth rose immediately at his appearance in the doorway.

'A few more minutes,' he told her, careful to keep himself between the woman and the door.

'Monsieur Benoît treated us to his coffee,' Caroline said.

Benoît, who had been sitting with the two women, dismissed this kindness with a wave. 'It is . . . an occasion,' he said.

Caroline looked at Reid and he nodded slightly to let her know that everything was going to their vague plan.

'My sergeant will let us know,' Reid said. He could hear behind him the noise of the men removing the last of that morning's cargo from the train. He saw that while Benoît's and Caroline's small cups were empty, Mary Ellsworth's remained full to the brim. Caroline rose beside the woman and took it from her, emptying it in a single swallow as Benoît rummaged in a drawer.

'Monsieur Benoît was telling us about his son,' Caroline said, indicating the photograph on Benoît's desk.

'Ah, yes – he, too, had a fiancée,' Benoît said.

Reid tried to remember if he already knew this. 'Of course,' he said. He took the photo Benoît handed to him. It was of a boy and a girl, neither of them looking older than fourteen or fifteen.

'It was taken a year before the war started,' Benoît said. 'She now lives in Roubaix. She was married a few months ago. A Belgian, a miner.'

It seemed to Reid that a lifetime of loss, despair and regret were let out in a single breath.

'She's very beautiful,' Caroline said. She took the picture from Reid and showed it to Mary, but the woman remained too distracted to look. She, too, listened to the voices of the men on the platform.

Reid regretted having come away from the work so soon. All the time he had been with the others, he had expected either Mary Ellsworth alone, or Mary and Caroline together, to appear among them, demanding to see the body of Mary's fiancé.

'Seventeen bodies,' he said. 'Only six unidentified.' He wondered why he'd said it, what it might signify to the women.

'Are the unidentified treated any differently?' Caroline asked him, glancing at Mary, just as a teacher might glance at a shy child reluctant to ask its own questions.

'Not at all,' Reid said, understanding her motive, and grateful for the opportunity to fill the small room's awkward silence with something other than more silence. Even by leaving the door open, he sensed that some of its tensions had already been released.

'You bury them amid the known?'

'We do. They lie with their comrades, with the men who would have been familiar to them. The hope is that their families will come and decide for themselves where their own lost son or husband or brother might lie.'

'I imagine many will take great comfort from believing they know where they are,' Caroline said. Everything she said was more for Mary's sake than her own.

'There was originally some idea of using different stones, but the Commission decided that they should all be the same.' Reid looked at Mary as he said this, but it was clear to him from that same distracted gaze that nothing either he or Caroline now said penetrated her concern.

Just as he was considering what he might say next, Drake appeared beside him in the doorway.

'Sir.' Drake saluted sharply, and Reid returned the rare gesture.

'Are we ready?' he said.

'We are, sir. I've told the men to draw the lorries and carts down the road a pace or two so that there's no noise while the ladies . . .'

'That's considerate of you. Thank you.'

'Sir.'

'Yes, thank you for everything,' Caroline said. 'You must all be very busy men without . . . distractions like this.'

'It's nothing, Miss,' Drake said. 'In fact, I think—' He stopped abruptly.

'No, please, go on,' Caroline prompted him. She moved closer to the man.

'I was going to say that, in a funny sort of way, I think the men . . . I think they *appreciate* being able to do something like this.'

It surprised Reid to hear Drake speaking like this, but he said nothing.

'You mean to be able to connect what they're doing here – all their hard and dirty labour – with what it will come to mean to the people who actually *knew* the men they're burying?' Caroline said to him, again more for Mary Ellsworth's sake than her own, and again looking to the woman to add something of her own. But still Mary remained silent.

'That's it exactly,' Drake said. 'Some days, we take twenty unidentified bodies off that train and dig twenty holes, lower them in and then cover them over with no real sense of . . . of . . .' He faltered, suddenly self-conscious in front of Reid at what he was trying to explain. He looked at Mary Ellsworth. 'Being able to do this for the girl, well . . .'

Mary finally turned to look at him, and Drake fell silent and bowed his head.

'We understand you perfectly,' Caroline said to him. 'And I'm certain that your kindness here today will be a great consolation to a great many people for a considerable time to come. Mary?'

'Yes,' Mary Ellsworth said. She drew down the veil that had been folded back over the small hat she wore.

'Good,' Drake said, and then, 'Right.' He saw the photograph Benoît held. 'Your boy?' he said to him.

'And the girl who became his fiancée,' Benoît said, handing the picture to him.

'I see.' Drake looked at the two children and then handed the precious possession back to the old station master. 'It's a grave loss for you,' he said.

'I bear up,' Benoît said absently.

'Of course you do,' Drake said. 'That's what men like you

and me do – we bear up. Mostly because we know there's nothing else for it. We bear up; that's what we do.'

Benoît slid the picture into his pocket. 'You're right,' he said. 'We bear up because others cannot. Perhaps they too will find that same strength in the months and years to come, but for now, so soon afterwards, they do not possess it, and so we – men like you and I, Sergeant Drake – we bear up and we provide that strength for them.'

Reid translated all this for Drake, who nodded in agreement at everything Benoît said.

'That's right,' Drake said. 'That's exactly right. We play the waiting game, you and me, Benoît. We wait and we wait and we wait for everything to finally right itself and then we make sure everyone else is still standing upright.'

Reid translated again.

'We bear the true weight of the world on our shoulders,' Benoît said. He held a hand over his pocket and his heart.

'We do that,' Drake said. 'We bear that sorry weight. And who knows, it might only get lighter by a solitary ounce every passing year, but we still go on bearing it.' He clasped Benoît's shoulders with both hands, and Benoît stiffened and held up his chin at the unexpected gesture.

And once again, it seemed to Reid, he saw precisely what made Drake the good sergeant that he was.

When Drake released Benoît, he turned to Mary Ellsworth and held up his arm for her. Mary quickly slid her hand beneath it and allowed herself to be led outside.

Reid shared a glance with Caroline, who watched Drake and Mary and smiled at them.

Then she came to Reid and waited for him to present his own arm to her, which he did, and which she held. She then beckoned for Benoît to do the same with her other arm.

They left the office and walked out on to the silent platform. Caroline slowed the pace of the two men she held, allowing Drake and Mary to draw ahead of them.

They reached the dim and cavernous space of the goods shed.

Inside, they gathered back together.

Drake released Mary Ellsworth and came to Reid. He indicated where the solitary coffin now stood at the far end of the room on a makeshift trestle.

Moving closer, Reid saw that the full name of Mary's fiancé, his service number, regiment, and dates of birth and death had all been recently stencilled neatly on the coffin lid. All the usual chalked details from the Saint-Quentin depot had been scrubbed away. In addition to this, someone had laid a clean white handkerchief beside the man's name and placed on this a small bunch of wild flowers – mostly daisies, which grew in abundance along the verges between the station and the cemetery.

Mary Ellsworth said, 'Oh,' at seeing all this.

Reid expected her to go quickly to the coffin and perhaps to embrace it, but instead she held back. She turned to Drake. 'I . . . would you . . . ?' She wanted him to go with her.

'My pleasure,' Drake said. She again held his arm and the two of them went forward alone.

'The man is forever a surprise to me,' Reid whispered to Caroline.

'No – you underestimate him, that's all,' she said. 'He hides himself.'

'I suppose so.' Her remark had sounded simultaneously dismissive and kind.

'Or perhaps Mary's fiancé had a sergeant just like him and the boy wrote to her telling her all about the man,' she said. She continued to hold the arms of both Reid and Benoît.

'Perhaps,' Reid said.

Closer to the coffin, Drake and Mary Ellsworth stopped walking, and the woman finally went forward alone. She touched the casket and then walked from one end of it to the other. She laid her hand on the stencilled name for a moment, and then on the clean white cloth and the flowers. Her quiet sobbing echoed slightly in the high, empty space.

Eventually, Reid, Caroline and Benoît walked to the box and waited in a line beside Drake.

From where they stood, Reid could see the other men beyond the station, gathered in silence to watch the small, impromptu ceremony now taking place there.

'Perhaps you might say something, sir,' Drake said to Reid, who was unprepared for this.

'I don't know. Do you think . . . ? I didn't know the man.'

'I'm sure she'd appreciate something,' Caroline said.

Reid detached himself from her and moved closer to Mary Ellsworth and the coffin. He saw where a solitary cart and its two horses waited on the road.

Mary Ellsworth turned at his approach. 'Please,' she said.

'We forget,' Reid said, clearing his throat. 'We forget at our peril, and to our eternal shame, what sacrifice this man' – unable to read the stencilled details from where he stood, he tried hard to remember the name Caroline had told him two hours earlier – 'what *all* these men who now pass through this place made on our behalf. They came and they fought and they died and were injured in ways far too many for us to count. They came here and they did all this because they had a *reason* to do it all. Many because they had a duty to fulfil, and just as many others because they knew that what they were fighting for – what they were fighting to *protect* – was at the very heart of everything they believed in, everything they possessed, everything they held dear. They fought and they died to protect and to keep safe for others everything that was dearest and most precious to them – everything that, without which, their own lives would have become unbearable – unliveable, even – and without all true purpose.' He paused.

Beside him, he saw Caroline nod and then lower her face to the ground. Beyond her, he saw the wetness on Benoît's cheeks and chin.

At the coffin, Drake now stood alongside Mary and held her arm again.

'And what we do here, today – what hundreds of other men do in hundreds of other places just like this one – what we do here in our work is to honour and to serve these men in a way no others can. Many thousands – millions, in fact – will have no real idea of what these men endured, how they fought, and how they suffered and died, but many of us here – many of us entrusted with this work – will know precisely what they endured and how they suffered and how they died.' He paused again, wondering if he'd said enough, or if even more was required of him. He knew that, in all likelihood, he would only repeat himself.

Benoît took out a handkerchief and wiped his face.

'In the years to come, this land will return to how it once was, how it once looked, and a great many of its recent up-heavals and tragedies will be forgotten. But what will *never* be forgotten will be the men – men such as Andrew Copley here,' the name came to him as he spoke – 'who gave their own lives so that the lives of those countless millions of others might now resume their rightful, *peaceful* course.'

Mary Ellsworth half turned to him at hearing her fiancé's name.

Reid listened to the quiet drumming of his words in the space above him.

'Men never die where they live the fiercest,' he went on. 'And they live the fiercest where they are loved the deepest – in the hearts of those who love them who they leave behind.' They were lines from a poem he had learned at school, but whose title and author he could not remember. He stopped talking and lowered his eyes to the ground.

Caroline held his arm again.

Benoît lowered his own eyes and mumbled a prayer.

At the coffin, Mary Ellsworth took a few paces back, and Drake retrieved the handkerchief and the flowers and gave them to her. Then he took something small from his pocket and gave that to her, too. He stood close to her for a moment, as though he were about to clasp her like he had earlier clasped Benoît, and then pull her to him and embrace her. But instead, he simply said something quietly to her and then turned and marched back to the others.

'They were fine words,' he said to Reid, stopping and turning on his heel.

'I didn't really—'

'They were fine words. You said what needed to be said. You did what mattered – what counted – and you did the pair of them proud.'

'Thank you.'

Mary Ellsworth finally came back to them, and Caroline went to her and held her.

'Thank you,' Mary said first to Reid, and then to Drake, who closed his eyes briefly and then turned to the distant coffin and saluted.

Seeing this, Reid did the same, followed a moment later by Benoît.

Mary did nothing to clear the tears running down her face.

Waiting until the two women had walked back out on to the platform, Drake called to the men on the waiting cart to come in and collect the coffin.

'You went to a lot of trouble,' Reid said to him. 'I appreciate that. As, I'm sure, does Mary.'

'It seemed only right,' Drake said. 'I held back one of the carts instead of a lorry because the horses seemed more fitting.'

'Of course.'

'It's only a pity that we can't do something similar for the rest of them,' Drake said.

'Their time will come,' Reid told him. Then he asked Drake what he had given to Mary at the coffin.

'I gave her a cap badge from one of the boxes of insignia they occasionally send us. He was in the Fifteenth Battalion, West Yorkshires.'

'And did you tell her it was actually his, her fiancé's?'

'I did. So may God and all His angels forgive me for that.'

'She'll treasure it,' Reid said.

'Good,' Drake said. 'Because there won't be much else to keep her going, and especially not after she gets back home.'

The blunt remark surprised Reid. 'Oh? You seem—'

'I am,' Drake said. 'My sister lost her bloke. They were going to be married, too. Twenty-First Entrenching Battalion. I never liked the man, myself, too bloody full of himself, but I saw what it did to her. Three years ago, Third Ypres. She was twenty-nine.'

'I see,' Reid said. 'And did she . . . ?'

'Did she what? Did she get over it? Never. You see her now, you'd swear she was nearer fifty than thirty.'

Mary Ellsworth, Caroline, Benoît, and now Drake. Reid saw how tightly all these other small wreaths were woven.

The men loading the coffin called to Drake, and he left Reid and went to them. He climbed on to the cart with them, and Reid watched as the driver turned the horses to face the lane leading to the cemetery. The clatter of their hooves on the hard surface sounded long after they had gone from his sight. Bright sunlight obscured the countryside beyond and left its own black suns at the centre of his vision. Rubbing his eyes, he went to join the others waiting for him on the platform.

Part Two

13

Alexander Lucas was waiting for Reid at Amiens station. They had both earlier attended another of Wheeler's meetings, at the close of which Wheeler had called Reid to him.

Now, approaching Lucas on the empty platform, Reid carried the rolled charts Wheeler had insisted he take with him back to Morlancourt. They were copies of the plans that had been made of the recently confirmed cemeteries at Cerisy and the Lancashire Dump cemetery at Aveluy Wood, and Reid still wondered what use they were likely to be to him at the much smaller Morlancourt.

Lucas took one of the rolled sheets, opened it and studied it. He was as mystified as Reid as to why Wheeler had given him the plans. His best guess was that Morlancourt was now being considered for expansion. It had happened elsewhere, where the number of bodies retrieved had exceeded expectations.

The suggestion alarmed Reid and he was unable to conceal this.

'Or perhaps he now wants something as grand as Cerisy at Morlancourt,' Lucas said, amused by Reid's reaction to his deliberate provocation.

'The bigger cemeteries will hold ten times the number of men,' Reid said. 'The ground at Morlancourt isn't anywhere near suitable for that kind of expansion.'

'If you say so,' Lucas said. He sat with his bare feet on the cold stone of the platform, his boots and socks on the bench beside him.

'I thought at first he wanted to talk about the planting,' Reid said.

'At Morlancourt?'

'In these plans, the gardens and beds are drawn in and the plants all named.' He turned the sheet to show Lucas, who continued to show little real interest.

'He could have told you anything you needed to know in the meeting itself,' Lucas said. 'God knows, it was filled with every other kind of irrelevance.'

Both men were unhappy at having wasted another day at Wheeler's insistence. And now, because of the further delay, they had missed the regular train back to Albert and were waiting on the chance of an engine from distant Abbeville passing through the station on its way to Paris. Lucas had already spoken to the station master, who had promised him that if an engine did come, he would signal for it to stop.

'Holly, box, rowan, lilac, dogwood, privet, syringa, laburnum, laurel and cherry,' Lucas said, reading the names from the plan. 'How very English.'

'That's the point,' Reid said. 'Besides, I imagine they all grow easily enough over here, too.'

'I once turned up in Péronne,' Lucas said, 'to find hundreds of Zouaves there, all of them picking cherries in an orchard. They'd been ordered to assemble in a nearby field and then they'd seen the harvest underway and had decided to get involved. Hundreds of men in full uniform up rickety ladders and shaking fruit from the trees.'

'They're planting the colonial cemeteries with trees and shrubs from the colonies,' Reid said. 'Maples, eucalyptus, acacia, that kind of thing.'

'Here?' Lucas said, and then, 'A year ago we retrieved a party of East Kents – the Buffs – from Guillemont, their pockets and knapsacks bulging with cobnuts. Someone who'd known the men said they harvested the things back at home. I'd never heard of them. They were all killed in a late cut-up at Guillemont in a stand of trees there. Apparently, the runner with the order for them to withdraw never came closer than three miles to them.'

'Where are they now?' Reid asked him.

Lucas shrugged. 'I handed them over to your people and that's the last I saw of them. Perhaps Wheeler just intends you to start preparing for your own planting at Morlancourt.'

'Perhaps.' Reid took the plans back, rolled them up and tied them securely.

A small train passed on the far track, its open wagons filled with French soldiers. The men waved and shouted to the few others waiting in the station as they moved slowly through it. They were all young men – what the French called 'bleuets' – and in all likelihood had seen nothing of the war, only its aftermath.

'Have you heard anything from home of late?' Reid asked Lucas.

Lucas looked away.

'I'm sorry, I didn't mean to pry.'

'You aren't,' Lucas said. 'It's just that things between the

117

two of us – Elizabeth and me – have been . . . what should I say? – unsettled? – for some time now.'

Reid waited. Some men spoke endlessly of home and their families, whereas others hardly mentioned those things. Lucas was one of the latter. Some men believed that by talking endlessly of those other lives, they maintained a strong connection to them; others seemed equally determined to keep the two existences as far apart as possible.

'If Susan hadn't been born . . .' Lucas said finally.

'What, you would have separated? Divorced?'

Lucas rubbed a hand over his face. 'It's possible, yes.'

'Are things . . . ?'

'I was last home four months ago. Ten days. We seemed to do nothing but argue with each other. About everything. Perhaps not argue, exactly, but nothing seemed right; everything seemed to have changed. Everything seemed off-kilter between us. Apart from which – and I don't know which I took the hardest – my daughter seemed hardly to know me. Everything I tried to do with her, everything I said to her, seemed only to make her apprehensive, wary of me.'

'And you think it's all this,' Reid said. 'Your work here?'

'That's certainly what Elizabeth believes, though in truth it was probably more of a convenient excuse for both of us than anything more . . .'

'But it must have *some* bearing, surely?'

'I'm sure you're right. Of course it must. Although I daresay the simple fact of my absence doesn't help matters.'

'No,' Reid said. 'I suppose not. Have the two of you decided anything?'

'Not really. How can we while I'm still over here and she's there? The best we could manage to agree on was to wait

118

until I was back for good and then see what remained to be salvaged.'

'For the sake of your daughter?'

'For Susan, yes. It all seemed a bit ridiculous to me at the time. Hundreds of thousands of families having to make do without husbands and fathers, and there *we* were talking about things as though we were planning – I don't know – an outing somewhere.'

Everything Lucas said made it clear to Reid that he wanted to say as little as possible on the subject. Reid wanted to ask him if he ever spoke to his wife about the work he undertook there, but the question was beyond him.

'They put up a tin chapel at Guillemont,' he said eventually. 'The Royal Kents. I saw it when the Commission was choosing its plots.'

'It was already there when we were retrieving the bodies,' Lucas said. 'They sprang up in lots of places. Wayside pulpits.'

'They painted it white,' Reid said. 'The chapel at Guillemont. Whitewash, I suppose. Someone had hung copies of paintings – Old Masters – on its walls.'

'I remember. We took the first few corpses inside. Until it became obvious that we'd need considerably more space, that is.'

They were interrupted by the station master, who came to Lucas and confirmed that a train from Abbeville would definitely be there in ten minutes. Lucas thanked the man and gave him a cigarette, which he took and slid behind his ear. Lucas then offered him several more, which he also took. He saluted the pair of them before returning to his duties. Both Lucas and Reid returned the gesture.

'I was at Étaples soon after Guillemont,' Lucas said,

watching the man go, picking up the thread of their conversation and keeping it on the same cold course.

'*That* place,' Reid said.

'I saw a boy walk into the sea there. In full uniform and with all his kit, his rifle in his hands. All too much for him.'

'He drowned, you mean?'

Lucas nodded absently. 'I sat and watched him at a distance. I shouted to him, to anyone who could hear me, but he just kept on walking until he went under the waves. They found him washed back up later the same day.'

'There were forever stories of that place,' Reid said. 'Most of the men I put out of the line on Excused Duties were sent there for a week or so. God knows why.'

'Probably because it showed them there were worse places to be than the front itself.'

'It's a possibility.'

Neither man believed this.

'A good number of the men recruited into the Retrieval units came straight from the Excused Duty rosters at Étaples at the time of the Armistice,' Lucas said.

'I was always glad to see the back of them,' Reid said. 'Did you know the circumstances of the boy who drowned?'

'Not really. Only that he was young, and that that place was all he'd ever known of the war. Apparently, he'd arrived from Dover less than a fortnight earlier.' Lucas leaned forward and sat with his elbows on his knees, his head down. He looked at his bare feet. 'My heels are cracked,' he said, and then laughed. 'From standing in water. I've been given some ointment by the MO. He told me I should get fresh air to them as often as possible. I did try explaining to him how difficult that might be.'

A moment later, they heard the clanging of points being switched and turned to watch the Paris-bound engine moving slowly and laboriously towards them, spurting smoke and steam as it came, scraping and grinding, and then letting out a long, exhausted wheeze as it finally stopped alongside them.

The station master reappeared and spoke to the driver. He beckoned to Lucas and Reid and indicated for them to climb up on to the driving platform. The engine pulled no carriages and so they would return to Albert alongside the driver.

'We could stay on the thing all the way to Paris,' Lucas said, leaning out of the cab to look along the tracks ahead of them.

'We could,' Reid said, the words more mouthed than spoken.

Beneath them, the station master blew his whistle and waved a flag, and the engine pulled away from the platform as slowly and laboriously as it had arrived and resumed its broken journey.

14

The following morning, Reid again waited with Lucas, this time at the Morlancourt station for Reid's daily train. Lucas had spent the night in the town and was now on his way to resume the retrieval of the bodies at Prezière.

The train was uncharacteristically late that day, and by twenty past seven had still not arrived. At Reid's urging, Benoît telephoned Saint-Quentin, only to be told that the engine had departed late – he was not told why – and that it was currently somewhere between La Boiselle and the halt at the old Gallaton junction. He conveyed all this to Reid, who in turn told Drake and the waiting men.

Lucas had been sent word the previous evening that Jessop would be arriving in Morlancourt to accompany him to Prezière with the intention of reporting directly to Wheeler on the work there. When Lucas had attempted to raise the subject at the previous day's meeting, Wheeler had refused to include it on the agenda. Lucas had screwed up the note telling him of Jessop's arrival and had thrown it into the gutter where he and Reid were sitting outside a bar.

'Perhaps *everything* sounds better to Wheeler coming from one of his own,' Reid said to him now. He stood at the edge of the platform and looked along the line towards the distant signal box.

Lucas sat with his head down. Reid guessed he was nursing a hangover, and that this coloured the resentment he felt at Wheeler's behaviour.

It was the first time in three months that the train had not arrived on time, and whatever the reason for the delay, Reid knew that the whole of his schedule for the day ahead would be disrupted.

'Sit down,' Lucas said to him angrily. 'You'd have been told if there was anything seriously wrong.'

Reid doubted this, but said nothing.

'Perhaps it's late because Jessop wants a leisurely breakfast,' Lucas said.

It was an apology of sorts.

Further along the platform, Benoît emerged from his office and came to them.

'The train is still beyond Gallaton. I spoke to the signalman there. Ernaux told him that there had been a delay in the loading, something unexpected. If they're beyond the signal, then they'll be here in' – he looked at his watch and pursed his lips in calculation – 'fifteen minutes.'

'Good-oh,' Lucas said, settling himself back against the cool wall, stretching his legs, closing his eyes and folding his arms across his chest.

'Yes, "Good-oh",' Benoît said, amused by Lucas's response.

'And Ernaux said nothing else about the delay?' Reid asked him.

But Benoît just shrugged. It would have been impossible for him to have contacted the train itself at one of its manned halts and to have spoken to the guard directly.

'You heard the man,' Lucas said. 'Fifteen minutes. You can stand down, the bloody show's been delayed.'

Reid smiled at the remark and went to join him in the shade of the station canopy.

Benoît returned to his office, promising to let Reid know if he heard anything more.

'I heard about the boy,' Lucas said. 'Your little funeral service.'

'It was Drake, mostly,' Reid said.

'The man who told me has got two brothers soon to be buried over at the Suzanne Number Three. He said he wanted to imagine the same kind of thing being done for them there. He's a good man. Every leave I give him, he goes straight to the cemetery to see where they'll be. He's the last of the family. He's talking about staying over here when his time's up.'

It sometimes seemed to Reid as though all these stories were like small white clouds floating and slowly evaporating across a vast warm blue sky.

'I wonder what Jessop really wants,' Lucas said, his eyes still closed.

'To be told that you've retrieved the bodies, identified them, and that they can now be safely registered for burial, I should imagine,' Reid said.

'Another happy ending, then.'

Before Reid could respond to this, he was distracted by someone calling his name, and both men looked along the platform to see Jonathan Guthrie coming towards them.

'That's all we need,' Lucas said. He pulled his cap low over his brow and pretended to be asleep.

Guthrie arrived in front of them. 'No train?' he said.

Reid told him of the delay.

Lucas gave a snore and pretended to wake up. 'Oh, it's you, Guthrie. And I was having such a wonderful dream.'

Guthrie looked at him suspiciously for a moment, and when he turned back to Reid, Reid avoided his eyes.

'Oh? A dream about what?'

'I was back at home, with my wife and daughter, in the garden. It was warm, like today, and we were in the shade, just like here, and my wife was laying out food and drink, and my daughter was climbing on me, insisting that I play with her. I doubt I could ever imagine being happier.'

Reid considered how this contrasted with what Lucas had told him the previous day.

'Then it was a good dream, indeed,' Guthrie said, still with a note of suspicion in his voice, as though suspecting Lucas were about to play a joke on him. 'I envy you, Lieutenant Lucas. I truly do. As, I imagine, do many others.'

Lucas, unprepared for the remark, could not answer him, caught in his own small deception. He rubbed a hand over his closed eyes.

'How long now until you return to them?' Guthrie asked him.

'My service commission's up in eight months, next spring.'

Reid again sensed his friend's reluctance to say more on the matter.

'And then what?' Guthrie said. 'I mean, what will you return to, your profession?'

'I was an architect,' Lucas said. 'Recently qualified. I was what's called a late starter.'

'I see.' Guthrie turned to Reid. 'The train – will the delay affect your work?' he said.

'I daresay. Perhaps I'll get Drake to crack the whip a little harder.'

Only Lucas laughed at the remark.

Guthrie stood apart from them. 'I saw Caroline Mortimer yesterday evening,' he said. 'She was with the unfortunate girl. She told me what happened, what you did. The girl herself showed me the cap badge and the flowers she had been given.' Everything he said betrayed his anger at what had happened in his absence, at his exclusion.

'And?' Lucas said to him.

'I merely wish Captain Reid here had seen fit to include *me* in the whole affair, that I had perhaps been given some advance notice of what he was about to undertake – without authority, I might add.'

'There was no time,' Reid said. 'I only learned of the man's arrival an hour before he came.'

'Nevertheless, I might still have been informed. Proceedings might have been delayed. Surely I might have contributed something in my capacity as—'

'Your capacity as what?' Lucas said.

Guthrie stiffened. 'In my capacity, Lieutenant Lucas, as a Man of God. I would have thought that much at least was obvious, even to you.'

'*Even* to me?' Lucas said. 'Of course. And I don't suppose it ever occurred to you for a single instant that whatever you might have added to the proceedings, Man-of-God Guthrie, would have been precisely what no one else there wanted.'

'I don't think—' Reid began to say, before being cut off by Guthrie.

'Why, Lieutenant Lucas? Because once again – and by no

126

one's consent except your own – *you*, and you alone, know what is best for everyone concerned? You, and you alone, know best what everyone else *needs* at times like this?'

'It was all something of a makeshift event,' Reid said as Guthrie drew breath. '*Nothing* was planned. *No one* knew what was needed, or even what the outcome of the thing was likely to be. I had no idea that Drake and the men would do what they did. They did it for the girl, Mary, not because . . . because . . . The truth is, it was done out of *need*, out of simple, straightforward need, and out of common decency and humanity. It was done for her, that's all.' He stopped abruptly, conscious that he had been shouting.

Further along the platform, several men came out of the goods shed to see what was happening.

'Of course,' Guthrie said eventually. 'My apologies. Perhaps you misunderstand me, Captain Reid. I simply—'

'What did she say to you?' Lucas said to Guthrie.

'Sorry?'

'The unfortunate girl – Mary Ellsworth – what did she say to you when you saw her with Caroline Mortimer?'

'I don't . . . I mean, she was clearly overcome by the occasion. She said very little. As you might imagine, the conversation was mostly between Caroline and myself.'

'I'll bet it was,' Lucas said. 'And so all this self-righteous indignation today is on your own account and not hers?'

'This is intolerable,' Guthrie said, looking to Reid for his support.

'No, it isn't,' Lucas said. 'I'll ask you again – what did Mary say to you?'

Guthrie remained silent for a moment. 'She told me she was grateful for everything Captain Reid and his sergeant had done for her. She's little more than a grieving child. Of course she was grateful.'

'Now she's a child,' Lucas said to Reid. 'He'll be telling us next she doesn't know her own mind.'

'I'll say no such thing,' Guthrie said. He turned his back on the two men and walked away from them towards Benoît's office, where he stopped and looked along the tracks.

Reid waited until Lucas looked at him and then he shook his head. 'Stop pushing him,' he said.

And then, before either of them could speak again, Lucas's arm started to shake. With his other hand, he reached up and pulled Reid closer to him so that he was hidden from Guthrie, who continued looking in the other direction. Then he clasped his shaking arm and held it tight at the elbow.

'Talk,' he said to Reid, his voice betraying a slight stammer. 'Just talk.'

And so Reid resumed talking to him, his voice low, telling him of the problems the delayed train was likely to cause him. And then, when he could think of nothing else to say on the subject, he warned Lucas of the problems *he* was creating by his continued hostility towards men like Guthrie, Jessop and Wheeler, and the likely consequences of this. And as he spoke, he saw that Lucas's trembling arm slowly became still and that he was finally able to release it.

'Finished?' Lucas said, smiling.

'Forget I said it,' Reid said. He motioned to Lucas's arm, and in response, Lucas raised and then swung it.

'The MO says it's nothing. Apparently, time is a great healer.'

'It's been—'

'I know,' Lucas said. He took out a cigarette and lit it,

holding it up for Reid to see. 'See?' The rising smoke wavered only slightly in the still air.

Along the platform, Guthrie turned and came back to them.

'The train's coming,' he said. He pointed to the distant thin plume of steam. 'Edmund sent word to me that there would be some Surreys on board.'

'Is that why you're here?' Reid asked him.

'It is.' Guthrie unfastened his pocket and took out a Bible, from which hung a slender scarlet ribbon.

'Do you want to say something before we unload them?'

Guthrie looked around them. 'Perhaps in the shed,' he said.

'Of course.' Reid left him, calling for Drake and the others to assemble on the platform.

The train itself finally appeared and drew level with its marker outside Benoît's office. By Reid's reckoning it was forty minutes overdue.

Benoît reappeared and went immediately to Ernaux. He spoke briefly with the man and then came to Reid.

'No bodies,' he said. 'No bodies and no coffins.'

Reid looked at Guthrie, who was already standing in prayer at the platform's edge. 'Then what?'

'Stones. Two wagons filled with headstones. According to Ernaux, there are a hundred of them. It took a long time to load them. No one expected them.'

'Including me,' Reid said. 'The first weren't scheduled to be here for at least another week.'

Throughout most of the Commission sites, the original wooden crosses and other temporary markers were being replaced by engraved stones, and whenever he saw these elsewhere it never failed to surprise Reid what a great difference they made to the sites they adorned. At Bray Hill almost all of the dilapidated markers had been replaced, whereas at the nearby Brontay Farm cemetery – as at Morlancourt – not a single clean, white engraved stone had yet been set in the ground.

Lucas came to join the two men.

'They've sent us headstones,' Reid said.

Lucas looked along the line of the train. 'No Jessop?'

'No passengers,' Benoît said. 'Ernaux says the weight is too much for the axles.'

Lucas walked along the carriages calling for Jessop.

Seeing that something was wrong, Guthrie came to Reid and Benoît. 'I was told that men of the Surreys would be arriving today,' he said.

Benoît waited for Reid to answer for him, which he did.

At the end of the platform Reid saw Drake and a dozen others approach one of the wagons. Drake climbed on board and then reappeared a moment later, cursing loudly and kicking the side of the open doorway.

15

Later, shortly before work at the cemetery was due to finish for the day, Drake sought out Reid and told him there was something that required his attention. The sergeant was caked from his chest to his feet in pale mud, which had dried in the heat and now flaked from him where he rubbed at it. He stood beside Reid, his hands on his knees, panting to regain his breath.

Reid waited. He knew Drake had been overseeing work on the graves close to the intermittent stream along the cemetery's eastern edge.

Eventually, Drake stood upright and spat heavily.

'More problems with the water?' Reid said.

'Every foot we dig out on those two far lines' – he pointed to the distant holes – 'just fills up again. We're getting no-where fast.'

Reid had already allocated the graves for Alexander Lucas's imminent arrivals, and he wanted the graves to be ready when the bodies from Prezière arrived.

'Digging deeper just encourages the water to come in faster,' Drake said. 'It's even started to appear in some of the roadside graves.' He swung his arm to the shallow holes at the bottom of the slope. 'The sides are crumbling.'

The two men set off walking towards the stream. A group of two dozen diggers had already stopped their work there and were sitting along the line of the banked hedge.

'And then there's him,' Drake said to Reid as they approached, indicating a man who stood with a bicycle at his feet.

'Who is he?'

'A local. He seems to know everything there is to know about the place. Everything's "low" this and "low" that.'

'It means water,' Reid said.

Drake stopped walking. 'I'd never have guessed.'

'Sorry,' Reid said.

'I heard enough of them screaming for it after the cock-up at Bouchoir to know exactly what it means,' Drake said.

They arrived amid the gathered diggers, and the Frenchman came directly to Reid. Reid recognized the man from Morlancourt, but did not know him. He held out his hand to him, and the man took it and shook it vigorously and then started talking and hardly drew breath for five minutes. The diggers along the hedge mostly ignored him, smoking and talking among themselves.

When the man had finished, Reid said to Drake, 'He's telling me that a stream rises and floods here every winter. It's a tributary of the Somme. It floods without fail and covers all this area. Apparently, it's been far worse since the canal and its feeders were damaged. It was never this bad in the summer months before. He says the water's backing up as far as the railway.'

'Meaning we'll never be rid of the problem here?' Drake said simply.

Reid shrugged and let out a long breath.

The Frenchman pulled Reid to one side and pointed to-wards the open country to the north.

'He reckons there's a second intermittent stream which appears and runs from the Ancre to the Somme along our western edge.'

The Frenchman continued his emphatic gesticulating.

'Apparently, we're digging the new graves across the likely flow of *that* stream. According to him, all we're doing here is exposing the buried flow. However hard we try to keep the water out, it'll just rise up again.' Reid tried to calculate where else on the restricted site he might now relocate the flooded graves. Whatever he decided, it would be one more delay, and one more cause of conflict between himself and Wheeler.

When the Frenchman had gone, Drake called for the men to gather closer, and Reid then repeated to them everything the man had just told him. Few of them showed any real interest in his concerns so late in the day.

Some, imagining they were about to be told to work for longer, called out in tired frustration, causing Drake to shout for silence.

Sensing their mood, and wishing that the Frenchman had come to see him much earlier in the day, Reid assured them that their day's work was finished.

'Leave the flooded graves alone. I'll look at my plans and work out where to dig next.' Several of the men cheered at this, prompting another rebuke from Drake. But even as Reid said all this, he knew that any alteration to either his plans or his schedule – both now closely watched by Wheeler – would be difficult to achieve.

'All on the word of a Frenchy?' one of the unhappy men shouted.

'He knows what he's talking about,' Drake said. 'Be-sides . . .'

'Besides, what?' Reid said.

'He showed me his ribbons,' Drake said. 'He was in it from start to finish. There won't be many like him.'

'I see,' Reid said.

'It still doesn't give him the right to come here and start shouting the odds to us,' the same man said. 'Not a Frenchy.'

'This is his country, his home,' Reid said.

The man seemed surprised by the remark. 'So?' he said.

'Which means—' Drake began to say.

'Which means he's already long back at home, while we're still here digging away and still with no real sign of our dis-charge dates,' the man said.

It was a brave interruption, but Drake knew better than to respond to it.

It had been the original intention of the Commission to employ considerably more local workmen on the cemeteries, but at Morlancourt this had never happened, and instead the Army's time-bound regulars and peacetime conscripts had been directed to the work.

The cemetery-making, especially on that part of the old battlefield, had exceeded all expectations, and only once the work had started had the labour shortfall been fully appreciated. Men were frequently moved from site to site as required. Some smaller plots were begun and completed in a continuous effort; others were laid out and then worked on at intervals.

Recently, it had been revealed that where local diggers were employed – usually farmers and their labourers unable to return to their lost farms – those men were paid at a higher rate than the soldiers, and this too had caused unrest. It was why, Reid knew, his own workforce often worked so slowly, and why, like today, they quickly voiced their complaints at any additional burden placed upon them.

'So everything gets altered on *his* say-so?' another man called to Reid.

'No – on *my* say-so,' Reid said.

Few were convinced by the answer.

Before Reid could say any more, the Morlancourt church bell sounded in the distance, signalling the end of the day's work. Across the whole of the site, the labourers started to gather up their tools. Barrels of water stood by the cemetery entrance and men hurriedly washed themselves, dipping their heads into the barrels and scooping the water over their shoulders and chests with their cupped hands. They dried themselves in the day's heat and with their vests and shirts.

The men around Reid walked away from him in twos and threes, and he watched them go.

'Everything is a source of grievance to them,' he said to Drake.

'They're soldiers. What do you expect? Worse – they're soldiers without a war. Besides, most of them are hardly even that – soldiers – and none of them had any of this in mind when they signed up and learned how to salute.'

'No,' Reid said. 'I suppose not. Though I still wonder at their mistrust of the French.'

'It's not *all* the French,' Drake said, smiling. 'Most of them get up to Saint-Quentin at the weekends.'

Reid understood what Drake was telling him and laughed.

'Besides,' Drake went on, 'some of us old hands have good reason – to mistrust the French, I mean.'

'Oh?'

'I was at Noyes,' Drake said. 'The French withdrew from our right flank in the night without saying a word. Left us out in the open. I only got back by the skin of my teeth.'

'And losses?'

'Too many. The French were two miles back in their own reserve lines when we next saw them.'

'I see.'

Drake looked slowly around them at the half-flooded graves. 'Wheeler's going to be none too happy with this little set-back. No bodies today means they'll probably send more than usual tomorrow and the day after that. It's going to put us even further behind, not getting them into the ground regularly.' He lit a pipe and sucked hard on it, filling the air with the sharp aroma of its tobacco.

Reid had not yet told him about the likelihood of the bodies retrieved at Prezière coming directly to them, and soon.

'I'll have another look at our layout,' he said. 'There's still plenty of land over on our western boundary not yet allocated. I daresay we might even make life a little easier for ourselves.'

Drake laughed at the suggestion. 'If you say so.'

The two men walked towards the cemetery entrance and the crowd of men now gathered there.

'What about you?' Reid said to Drake.

'Me?'

'Your extended service.'

Drake laughed again. 'Funny you should ask,' he said. 'I was thinking only the other night where I might be posted next, when this little lot is finally over and done with.'

'Do you have any preference?'

'Preference? In this man's army? Mind you, I'd like somewhere warm, for a change. I was listed for Mesopotamia before I ended up here. I walked down the gangplank at Boulogne with a bag full of tropical kit and dosed up on all sorts of tablets in preparation.'

'Why the change?'

'Who knows? I daresay somebody's plan had taken a turn for the worse and I was another one of those men pushed into an unexpected hole.'

'"Once more unto the breach" sort of thing?'

'Oh, I've seen a lot of breaches in my time. It's a noble-sounding thing, is a breach.'

'But the reality—'

'Is precisely that. It took us six hours to cover those two miles at Noyes.'

They arrived beside the men and Drake went immediately to their centre, where he organized them into groups to await the lorries which would soon arrive to return them to their barracks. Some already stood on the mounded stores there, searching the hazy horizon for the tell-tale signs of exhaust smoke.

16

It was four days since the first of the freshly engraved head-stones had arrived. There had been no further deliveries of these, and so far this first consignment remained stacked beneath a tarpaulin in a corner of the goods shed.

Reid returned to them for the first time on his way back from the cemetery to his room. He already knew from having visited the smaller, half-completed cemeteries at Bray and Etinhem what dignity the finished, upright stones conferred on those places, what spartan order and sense of completion they brought to the hitherto disorganized plots.

He pulled back the tarpaulin and read the names and other details already crisply carved into the smooth, polished surfaces. Portland stone. At Bray, the morning sun caught the chiselled surfaces of the upright slabs and then turned them to different colours throughout the course of the day. At Etinhem, at dawn, the lettering of the stones already planted there seemed gilded by the light of the rising sun. The two hundred French crosses seemed insubstantial by comparison.

At the bottom of the stones their earlier, stencilled details were still visible. These would be hidden and lost when the stones were sunk into their concrete foundations along the heads of the rows. Most of the graves in most of the smaller cemeteries were now laid out in lines of ten, making each row and then each grave easier to find amid the broader plots.

Reid was pulling the tarpaulin back into place when he became aware of someone else in the vast space, someone sitting at the table he himself occasionally used to deliver his instructions to the men. At first he imagined this to be Benoît, but as his eyes became more accustomed to the light, he saw that it was Alexander Lucas sitting there.

Lucas sat with his feet on the table, and as Reid approached him, he saw that the man was exhausted. He had been absent from his room in Morlancourt for the previous two nights.

'I was beginning to think you'd absconded,' Reid said, drawing up a crate and sitting opposite him.

Lucas wiped his face with a cloth, doing little more than create a new pattern in the sweat and dirt with which it was covered.

'Orders from above,' he said.

'Where else?'

'I just got back a few minutes ago. I came in out of the heat.' He took up a canvas bag from the floor and laid it on the table.

Reid started to tell him what had happened during his absence, but then fell silent.

'The bodies are ready to come,' Lucas said. 'Jessop came today. Wheeler wants you to sign them off.' He pushed the bag across the table towards Reid.

'Are the bodies all identified, then?'

'Every single one of them.'

'And Wheeler's happy to do that – to see the men buried without any further inquiry into how they might have been killed?' It occurred to Reid that he was voicing these concerns more for Lucas's sake than for his own.

Lucas held up his palms. 'Soapy Joe Guthrie agrees with Wheeler that it's the only sensible – the only *honourable* – course to take.'

Reid motioned to the bag on the table.

'All the necessary paperwork,' Lucas said. 'You see what a nice neat little package everything has become. Wheeler wants you to prepare and allocate the graves, bury the men, and then sign everything and return it to him.'

Reid pulled the bag towards him. 'It might just be for the best,' he said.

'Of course it might.' Lucas leaned back in his chair and yawned.

Reid opened the bag and looked briefly at its contents.

'The youngest was eighteen, the oldest fifty-two,' Lucas said.

'And were your suspicions concerning—'

'Any suspicions I might *once* have had have all been blown away in Wheeler's chill and cleansing wind,' Lucas said. He paused and looked directly at Reid. 'Just as everyone told me they would be.' He picked up the cloth and wiped his face again, this time pushing it into his mouth and rubbing his teeth. He drank from his canteen, tipped back his head and gargled, afterwards spitting the water at his feet. 'We found sixteen clear head wounds,' he said. 'Over thirty of the corpses had suffered post-mortem burning. I'm only telling you this because none of it is actually mentioned in the files.'

'I see,' Reid said. He pushed the papers back into the bag and closed it.

'Jessop went to great lengths to make it perfectly clear to

me that under no circumstances was I to add any of my own – what was the phrase? Oh, yes – "unwarranted concerns" to the documentation,' Lucas said.

'Things like this must happen all the time elsewhere,' Reid said, immediately wishing he hadn't.

'I'm sure they do,' Lucas said.

'Meaning?'

'Meaning they happen elsewhere, and not under *my* supervision,' Lucas said.

'I'm sorry,' Reid said. 'Perhaps Wheeler himself is being put under pressure.'

Lucas refused to respond to this, merely shaking his head.

In Lucas's eyes, Reid knew, he was as complicit as any of them in Wheeler's scheme to retrieve and then bury the desecrated bodies.

'Jessop said he'd come to you personally when everything was done,' Lucas said.

'To make sure the men—'

'To make sure your signature was everywhere it needed to be. Just as mine already is.'

'Right,' Reid said. He wondered how he might now change the subject.

'Besides,' Lucas went on, 'Wheeler's reasoning is probably right – what are these forty-two compared to all the hundreds of thousands of men who have vanished completely? At least this lot have finally been retrieved and identified and will be laid to rest. What of those hundreds of thousands of other ghosts left to wander endlessly out there, shouting to be found?'

It was an uncharacteristically melodramatic thing for Lucas to say, and Reid hesitated before speaking.

'At least we know the names of all the men,' he said. 'They'll all get their monuments somewhere, eventually.'

'Of course they will,' Lucas said. 'And thus – just as Wheeler decrees it – will *everyone* be safely gathered up and delivered back into the fold.'

'That was always the plan,' Reid said, aware that everything he now said was a further disappointment to Lucas.

They were distracted briefly by an engine moving slowly along the track beyond the doorway. Both men turned to look, but neither of them recognized the driver or guard. There were no carriages attached, and the engine seemed to be about to come to a halt with each slow turn of its wheels. But it continued moving and passed from their view.

The small trains passed through Morlancourt several times each day, and occasionally Benoît said even he had no true idea of where they had come from or where they were going, let alone their purpose. To Reid, because they exhibited no urgency, and because they carried neither cargo nor passengers, they always seemed somehow lost, wandering aimlessly, a kind of dying momentum made manifest in all those tons of grinding and wheezing machinery, and driven and directed by men who were themselves becoming ghosts of their own former vigorous and purposeful selves.

When they could no longer hear the engine, Reid said, 'When will they come, the bodies?'

Lucas shrugged. 'Soon, I imagine. Tomorrow, the day after.' He continued watching the world outside the shed. 'Someone said they were testing the rebuilt line towards Bonnay,' he said absently. 'Perhaps they're settling the beds.'

'Will you be staying here tonight?' Reid asked him.

'In Morlancourt? I hope so.' Lucas hesitated a moment and

then searched his pockets, finally pulling out an envelope. 'This arrived yesterday. My wife's unwell.'

'Oh?' Reid remembered the conversation he'd had with Lucas at Amiens station and wondered what to say.

'Her mother sent it. She's gone to stay with Elizabeth.'

'Is it serious?' Reid said.

'I don't know. There's a suggestion it might be scarlet fever. Apparently, there have been other cases locally. Any excuse and the woman would have moved in. It was posted eight days ago. There's been nothing since.'

'Surely that's a good sign,' Reid said. 'Perhaps she's already recovered.' He was grateful, finally, for the chance to turn in this new direction.

'I've written back asking for more details. I wonder, do we still have censors?'

'I don't know,' Reid said. It was three months since he'd last written to anyone at home.

Lucas rose from where he sat and gathered up his few belongings. Reid picked up the bag of documents, and the two men walked from the cool and dim interior of the building out into the warmth and light of the early-evening sun, which was already falling towards the far horizon, and which cast their shadows across the platform and on to the tracks.

Fifty yards up the line, the small engine sat motionless, exhaling thin plumes of steam and smoke, and dripping water, looking more than ever like the lost and exhausted creature it had become.

17

The next day, Reid was working at the cemetery when one of his workers came to him and indicated the car sitting at the entrance. A solitary man in uniform had already climbed out and now waited by the road.

'Can't he come to me?' Reid said, unwilling to leave his work; he was running behind schedule and expecting the bodies from Prezière at any time.

'He told me to fetch you,' the man said. 'Said it was important that he saw you alone.'

Reid gave instructions to the men he was with and then walked to the entrance.

As he approached, he finally recognized Roger Jessop, and the man's unexpected presence there made him wary.

Upon his arrival at the car, Jessop held out his hand, and this too kept Reid on his guard. Jessop then suggested they walk a few paces away from the nearby men.

'It looks good work,' he said, waving at the cemetery without really looking at it. 'Good progress. Edmund is forever singing your praises. Everything taking shape, and all that.' It was the first time either Jessop or Wheeler had been to Morlancourt in the past two months.

'So have you come to make an assessment for him?' Reid

said. 'Concerning the bodies from Prezière?' He wanted Jessop to get to the point and then to leave.

'Prezière? Oh, Good Lord, no, nothing like that. They'll come in three days' time, by all accounts.' He spoke as though Reid had already been told this, or as though the information were of no consequence to him. Or perhaps the seemingly casual remark was a deliberate attempt to play down everything that would now soon enough be concluded. 'No, no, Edmund's taking good care of that particular . . .' He left the remark unfinished and concentrated on fastening a button which had come undone on his tunic.

'So what is it?' Reid prompted him.

'In fact, I daresay he would have been here himself – Edmund, that is – if he wasn't so damn busy. "Desk-bound", he calls it. Tethered to his pieces of paper and his meetings.' He spoke as though Reid had said nothing. He looked at his watch. 'In fact, at this very moment, he's at another of his interminable conferences. In Doullens with someone from the Chamber of Deputies to go over the Perpetuity of Sepulchre question. Sepulchre? Sepulture? I can never remember. Big gathering, pow-wow. It's still a cause for some concern, apparently.'

To Reid, it had always seemed too grand – too *weighted* – a term for what was essentially an arrangement about the long-term cost and maintenance of all the British cemeteries on foreign soil.

'The Quatre Fils,' Jessop said. 'The meeting. The name of the restaurant. It's a different world. Hardly a brick out of place. The Quatre Fils d'Ayman. A different world entirely.'

Reid had visited the place only once, soon after his arrival. The restaurant was reputedly the grandest in Doullens, and largely used now by the wealthier visitors touring the battle-fields, Americans mostly.

Motioning to the lane he had just driven along, Jessop said, 'I wonder if we might walk.'

'Because of the reason for your visit?' Reid said, finally losing patience with the man.

Jessop cast him a hostile glance. 'If you want to put it like that, yes.' He smiled and nodded to a group of nearby men.

Put it like what? Reid wanted to shout, *Just get on with it.* The man was as adept as Wheeler at orchestrating these un-necessary and unsettling dramas.

Eventually, Jessop walked away from the entrance until he came to the shade of the trees which overhung the narrow space. He stopped and leaned against one of the smooth, pale trunks. Reid joined him and leaned against the bank there.

'You've finally got the man coming from Neuville,' Jessop said, his voice low. 'A few days' time, perhaps. He was flagged up to us by the depot at Péronne.'

'You mean his body?' Reid said, remembering. The old clearing-station cemetery at Neuville was being dismantled and its corpses distributed elsewhere.

Jessop took off his cap and wiped his brow. 'The executed chap,' he said. 'Name of Etherington. 1915. Sad affair. Eleventh Royal Warwicks. Edmund just wanted to let you know in advance. You know . . . in case . . . well, I'm sure you understand. He said you'd appreciate the gesture – forewarned, and all that. You've already taken delivery of some of the same mob, I believe.'

Taken delivery.

'Eighteen,' Reid said.

'Sorry?'

'Royal Warwickshires. We've already buried eighteen of them.'

'Laid to Rest. Good. Then perhaps the poor chap's in the right place, after all. God rest his soul. In accordance with the new directives, Colonel Wheeler wants him put in with the others, everything kept . . . Well, you know better than most, I daresay, how feelings run where these things are concerned.'

Not really, Reid thought, but said nothing.

'There are still plots available in the same row,' he said eventually, looking back over the cemetery and trying to remember exactly where the Warwickshires were buried amid the spreading lines.

'Good, excellent,' Jessop said. 'Fact is, Edmund asked me to be quite specific on the point. He'd much prefer—'

'If the man was buried at the centre of his companions?'

'Spot on,' Jessop said. 'Spot on. Shove him in among the honourable dead, and all that. Keep everything . . . well . . .'

Hidden away? 'It's where he deserves to be,' Reid said.

'Of course it is, of course,' Jessop said. 'Edmund's sentiments precisely. Good man, good man.'

A few months ago, there had been a short-lived labour strike at the Cerisy-Gailly cemetery when four executed men had been sent for burial among their own battalions.

'We'll exhume one of the others and lay him at the end,' Reid said, quickly calculating the time and labour necessary for the work.

'Good show,' Jessop said, clearly relieved that this part of his errand was done. 'Edmund said you were a safe pair of hands, that he could rely on you.'

To do what I am told, Reid thought, but again said nothing either to make Jessop suspicious or to delay his departure. Everything that had passed between them, he knew, would now find its way back to Wheeler.

'I suppose these chaps will be turning up all over the place,' Jessop said. 'In fact, it's a wonder no one—'

'What was the charge against the man?' Reid said.

Surprised at being interrupted like this, Jessop said nothing for a moment. 'Etherington? I'm not entirely certain. Desertion, I should imagine, same as most of them. Though 1915 – cowardice, perhaps. I haven't actually seen the paperwork myself. Edmund's your man for that. Though I daresay it hardly matters, not after all this time.'

'It will matter to those who knew him and who might one day come to see his grave,' Reid said.

'Quite. Of course. You're perfectly right. And that's why we must all endeavour to do our best for the poor chap. In fact, just the other day we were discussing the likely numbers where visitors were concerned. Here, everywhere.'

'Did you come to any conclusions?' Reid said.

'Not really. Hard to predict a thing like that. It's Edmund's belief that most of the families – lower ranks, Kitchener's boys, that is – won't have travelled very far from where they were born. Hard to see how they'd manage to get all this way. I suppose to most of them, all of this will seem like—'

'A foreign country?'

'Quite, quite. Parliament is already talking about setting up funds to assist the most needy. I daresay people might come once, but after that, only the better able and better travelled will continue to visit.'

'Then let's hope Parliament comes to the right decision,' Reid said.

148

'Quite,' Jessop said again, the word like a palm held to Reid's chest. 'Besides, there are also all the Dominion chaps to consider. Imagine the problems *those* particular families will encounter.'

'Do we know where Etherington was from?'

'No idea. Like I said, Edmund's your man for the paperwork. Royal Warwick? Could have been anywhere. I think perhaps the Black Country somewhere. Probably another of those boys only too glad to turn his back on the factory floor, eh?'

'Probably,' Reid said. He looked along the curving line of the lane, through its pattern of alternating bright sunlight and deep shade where the trees still stood. In parts, it was like looking along a tunnel.

'So I can inform Edmund that you're fully apprised and likewise prepared?' Jessop said.

'Of course,' Reid said, sensing that the man was at last ready to leave.

'And all this Prezière business,' Jessop finally said, glancing away as he spoke.

'The graves are ready and waiting.'

'And Lieutenant Lucas . . .'

'Gave me most of the paperwork yesterday,' Reid said.

'Good, good, excellent.'

'So you can inform Colonel Wheeler – Edmund – that both Lieutenant Lucas and I have followed his instructions to the letter.'

'I merely intended to ascertain—'

Reid laughed at the words and Jessop fell silent.

Then Reid turned away and walked back to the cemetery entrance.

Jessop walked quickly to catch up with him, determined, Reid supposed, to have the final word.

'As a fellow officer,' Jessop said to Reid's back, 'I shall not, of course, repeat any of what—'

'Do whatever you please,' Reid said, unwilling to turn and face the man again.

'Good, right,' Jessop said. 'Then perhaps Chaplain Guthrie might get better sense out of you when—'

'Guthrie? What's any of it got to do with him?'

Jessop smiled at the remark and all it revealed. 'Perhaps if you'd allowed me to finish speaking.' He caught his breath. 'Colonel Wheeler thought it only right and fitting that someone – in this instance, Jonathan Guthrie – say a few words at the interment.'

'And Guthrie, naturally, jumped at the chance.'

'I would prefer to say that the chaplain acceded gracefully to Edmund's suggestion. But yes, he will attend and officiate at the burial. Or if not at the actual burial itself – you know how keen the Commission is to keep all these things until the proper time – then at least at the man's delivery to you, at the final part of his journey.'

'His journey?'

'Here, to you, to the cemetery,' Jessop said. He swatted the flies from his face. 'Damn things,' he said.

'You get used to them,' Reid said.

'*You* might.'

The two men arrived back at the cemetery entrance, where a solitary block of stone marked the beginning of its proposed gate.

Jessop put on his cap, straightened it, ran a finger along the curve of its brim and then turned and walked back to his car.

Reid walked more slowly to join him.

'I shall need one of your chaps to crank the engine,' Jessop said. He climbed into the driving seat and sat rigidly with his hands on the steering wheel.

Reid went to the engine and turned its handle.

'Not you, for God's sake,' Jessop shouted to him. 'I meant for one of your diggers to come.'

The engine spluttered and fell silent.

It started at the third attempt and Reid stepped away from the car as the fumes from its exhaust drifted towards him.

Jessop waited a full minute before letting out the brake and slowly steering the car forward. He called to Reid, but Reid could not hear him above the noise of the engine, and instead of replying to whatever Jessop had shouted, he held out his arm and pointed to the left, in the direction of the Albert road. Jessop acknowledged this and carried on driving.

Reid waited where he stood and watched the car go. He wiped the sweat from his brow and face and then ran a hand through his hair. The same restless, chattering birds that filled the air above the cemetery also flew back and forth along the narrow lane, gorging themselves on its riches.

18

The following day, Reid went with Alexander Lucas to the barn at Prezière to see for himself the bodies that were to be delivered to him. The two men had spent the previous evening together, when Reid had told Lucas of Jessop's errand, and when Lucas, in turn, had suggested the visit to Prezière. The coffins for the bodies would arrive at Morlancourt station separately, and the purpose of the visit was for Reid to ensure that the condition of the corpses would not present him with further problems upon them finally being delivered into his care.

The two men arrived at the ruined hamlet shortly before dawn.

Reid saw that the bodies had been separated and laid out individually, each with as much of its uniform and kit as had been found, and with all metal buttons and insignia attached.

The barn was smaller than Reid had anticipated. Its roof and the upper half of three of its walls had collapsed, and heavy tiles, rafters and masonry had fallen into the space where the bodies had originally been laid.

Lucas told him that the walls had continued to collapse when they'd started their work and that this had delayed them. But now all the bodies had been lifted clear of the walls, fully identified and laid out prior to their removal.

Reid went first to the corpses, and Lucas followed him. He gave Reid a cloth to fasten around his nose and mouth. Reid knew that many of Lucas's men had worn full masks during the worst of the work, but in the two years since the men had died, the worst of their corruption and putrefaction had long since passed.

Even at that early hour, a small group of Lucas's men was gathered a short distance beyond the ruins in what remained of the farmyard.

'Wheeler's sending lorries tomorrow,' Lucas said. 'In the absence of coffins, he wants the remains bagging up today ready for loading. There's a road from here to Villier, and the railway there connects to Morlancourt. Are you ready to take them?'

'Most of the graves are dug. I'm hoping the rest will be completed today. Bodies from elsewhere are being held back in Saint-Quentin for the time being. We'll cope.'

'Glad to hear it. We've been ordered to leave here ourselves within an hour of the bodies going.'

Looking at the corpses now, Reid guessed that they could be transported, buried, and their graves filled and levelled in a single day's work.

Lucas went to his men and returned with a cardboard folder.

Reid looked at this final documentation and saw that some of the sheets had been marked at the top right-hand corner with a pencilled cross. He remarked on this to Lucas.

'It was how I indicated the suspicious deaths,' Lucas said. 'Whatever Wheeler insists on having delivered to you, I still wanted to do something to . . . I don't know . . . something to signal to anyone who might look at the sheets in the years to come that *something* had happened to those particular men, at least.'

'All they'll see will be the pencil crosses,' Reid said. 'It won't necessarily signify anything to them.'

'I know. But I wanted there to be *something*, however slight or ambiguous or uncertain.'

Reid understood him perfectly and so said nothing.

'It was something we all decided on,' Lucas said, indicating the watching men.

Reid had always envied Lucas this easy rapport with his workers, many of whom had volunteered for the work they now undertook, and who stayed longer with their units. He continued looking through the forms.

'Half of them?' he said.

'Approximately that. Twenty. All with head wounds, and all with the worst of the burning.'

'Do you think the others were retrieved from the battlefield and added to their number to try to hide what had happened to them?'

'It's a possibility.'

'Has Wheeler – anyone – seen the completed documentation yet?'

'You mean has anyone seen the crosses? No.'

'What will you say if he asks you about them?'

'We thought about that. I'll say that they were the corpses we were able to identify immediately, that the others took a little longer.'

'Knowing all the doubts you've already raised, he won't believe you.'

Lucas lit a cigarette and gave one to Reid. 'To tell you the

154

truth, I'm past caring what Wheeler does or doesn't believe. Besides, once the bodies are buried and the final pieces of paperwork are buried even deeper in the Commission Records Office, then who is ever going to know or be able to confirm or even *guess* what the crosses signify?'

'I suppose so,' Reid said.

The two of them walked the full length of the corpses and then back again, looking down at the remains of each man.

Lucas stopped at one body and drew back the tarpaulin which covered it. 'This is the eighteen-year-old,' he said.

There was little left to show what the boy had once looked like. A head, a torso, arms and legs, all still clothed and held together, and all of this looking to Reid exactly like the khaki-clad skeleton it had become.

In earlier days, countless bodies – identified and otherwise – had been delivered to him like this, but more recently, and especially after the second depot at Saint-Quentin had been established, all of the bodies and remains he received were hidden from sight. It surprised him now to realize how long it had been since he'd looked at an actual corpse like this, and he understood immediately and forcefully what it was that separated him and his own workers from Lucas and his team.

Standing close together, neither man spoke for a moment.

And then Lucas cleared his throat and said, 'Anyhow, we've done what we do; now it's your turn.'

Reid closed and resealed the folder he held.

The two men left the bodies and went to sit together on a stack of timber. As the sun appeared more fully on the horizon, birds started calling and then flying around the ruined buildings at the far side of the yard.

'They probably used to nest in the barn,' Lucas said.

'When I was a boy, my farmer grandfather told me that each autumn all the swifts and swallows and martins on his farm used to burrow into the earth and then transform themselves into toads, waiting to hop back out into the daylight the following spring.' Reid smiled at this sudden memory of the old man, who had died when he was eight years old and already away at school. 'He said that the birds spent the winter as toads buried in the ground, and then, come the spring, they transformed themselves back into birds again and shot up into the air. Apparently, it was what one of the Greek philosophers believed happened. No one could account for where all the birds disappeared to each autumn, see?'

Lucas leaned back where he sat. 'It sounds a bit like us,' he said.

'What does?'

'Burrowing ourselves into the ground and transforming ourselves into different creatures completely for the past few years.'

'Toads?'

'Why not? What did most of us do except burrow ourselves into the ground to make ourselves as safe and as inconspicuous as possible, and then sit there trembling and fearful and waiting for the sun to shine again?'

'And transform us back into men?'

'Most of us,' Lucas said. He motioned to the bodies. 'Let's face it,' he went on, 'we *are* changed creatures – there's no getting away from that.'

'No, I suppose not,' Reid said.

'For good or ill, we're none of us the men we once were.

And nor can we now ever be the men we might once have set out to be.'

Reid said nothing.

'I've just had a dozen release forms come through,' Lucas said. 'Twelve of my best workers. Some of them are over there now.' He nodded to the gathered men. 'All twelve of them will be home by this time next week – sooner even. I'm glad for them, but I'll be sorry to lose them.'

'You'll end up with a workforce like mine,' Reid said.

'I know.'

Both men laughed at this.

'Home,' Lucas said. 'Walking in and out of their own front doors, in and out of their own rooms, picking up the morning newspaper and worrying about the weather and the football results as though none of this had ever happened to them.'

Neither man believed this.

It was clear to Reid that Lucas's thoughts remained with his own family, his wife in particular, and that the uncertainty of what might now be happening to her weighed on his mind.

'My grandfather also said that to have the swallows and swifts return to their old nests in your eaves and gutters each year brought good luck to your home,' Reid said.

Lucas watched the birds flitting over their heads. The first of the day's insects had appeared in the warming air. 'Whatever luck they might once have brought here . . .' he said.

The journey to Prezière had been a revelation to Reid. Back at Morlancourt, and even more so to the west of the place, there remained little to see of what the war had left in its wake: a few old supply roads gouged across the growing crops; a few pieces of abandoned transport and artillery in the corner of a field or parked up alongside someone's newly rebuilt home. But beyond Péronne, and especially towards Saint-Quentin, the landscape showed little *except* what had happened there two years previously. Villages and hamlets still lay in ruins; vast swathes of land remained unclaimed and were still pocked with deep holes. Whole woods and copses, though growing again and green in places, lay felled and tumbled and rotting.

At Temple, they had passed a field in which lay seven tanks, all of them tilted and trackless and already half sunk into the soft ground. At Averne, the metal bridge still lay where it had collapsed into the canal. And beyond Calat there remained an unexplored cemetery where dozens of crosses and rifles still lay planted in the earth. Someone, somewhere, Reid supposed, knew that the place existed and was keeping watch over it prior to it being examined and its bodies exhumed.

On every road they had come along as they travelled towards Prezière there were warnings of unexploded ordnance and uncleared mines. At most junctions and crossroads, unexploded ammunition and spent casings stood stacked in mounds as tall as houses.

At Railly they had been forced to wait in a queue of nighttime traffic while a crew of mine-clearers had led their teams of horses across the road. An entire field was filled with coils of rusted wire, and in its corners stood giant smoking pyres of the planking and boarding retrieved from the nearby trenches, their dense, sooty smoke rising into the air as dark and solid as ink spilled in water.

Eventually, Reid rose and told Lucas he ought to return to

Morlancourt. The two men arranged to meet there later in the day.

As he was being driven out of the yard, Reid looked back through the open rear of the lorry and saw Lucas return to the corpses. He watched as he stopped at the skeleton of the boy he had uncovered, and then as he knelt beside it and drew the tarpaulin back up over the remains as carefully and tenderly as a father might draw the bedclothes over his sleeping child.

19

Caroline Mortimer sat alone by the church gate where she and Reid had sat together a week earlier. He approached her along the empty street on his way to the station. The previous day, upon his return from Prezière, he had learned that the nurses' bodies she awaited would now be arriving in Morlancourt later than she had previously been told. They were currently in the mortuary at the hospital in Daours. The curt message Reid had received from Jessop said only that the delay had been caused by 'unforeseen circumstances'. It was another of those phrases with which he was long familiar, and which he had quickly learned never to query. He sensed something of the man's malice following their encounter two days earlier.

Caroline looked up at his approach. She held a letter in her lap and pushed this into her pocket as Reid's shadow finally arrived beside her.

'No Mary?' he said to her. Since the arrival of her fiancé's body, the younger woman – or so it seemed to Reid – had hardly left Caroline's side, causing the pair of them to remain apart.

'She's gone,' Caroline said, surprising him.

'Oh?'

'I went with her to Saint-Quentin yesterday. She was hoping to travel on to Boulogne today.' It was a short and straightforward enough journey to make.

'I didn't realize that was what she intended doing,' Reid said.

'I doubt if she *intends* anything much these days. She said she'll come back when the cemetery is finished and finally has its official opening.'

'I see.' Caroline's remark reminded Reid of the delayed arrival of the nurses. 'Your nurses are coming later than I'd anticipated,' he said.

'I know. I saw Captain Jessop in Saint-Quentin. Quite by chance. He told me you were falling behind in your work here. He called them "our fallen roses". Does it help, do you think – all this mawkish phrase-making?'

'Sometimes. Perhaps. I hear the same few phrases repeated often enough. Popular appeal, I suppose.'

'For people who have no idea of the truth of the matter?'

'I suppose so.'

'Captain Jessop told me that Colonel Wheeler had no intention of sanctioning the delivery of the women until he was certain you were ready for them.'

'There's always *someone* to blame for these delays,' Reid said.

She reached up to him and told him to sit beside her, which he did.

'The graves have been dug and waiting for a few days now. I imagine Wheeler considers us to have other priorities.' The first of the bodies from Prezière were due to arrive at Morlancourt later that same day.

'Don't worry,' Caroline said. 'I'll wait as long as it takes.

Mary tried to persuade me to return home with her. She told me I was wasting my time being here.'

'It might have been for the best,' Reid said. 'I mean, now that we know the women are all gathered together and waiting to come.'

'You make it sound as though they were going on an excursion.' She smiled at the thought.

'I only meant . . . Did Jessop say how long the delay might be?'

She shook her head. 'All Mary wanted was for me to go on telling her what to do. She wants constant reassurance, that's all, like a child, until she finds the strength to stand on her own two feet again.'

'It might take her years,' Reid said.

'I don't doubt it. I was at Netley hospital shortly before coming back out here, so you might say I've seen the men for whom all of this will *never* truly end.'

Reid looked along the lane towards the seemingly deserted station. He guessed from the wisps of smoke rising from its low chimney that Benoît was already at his desk and awaiting the train. He felt reassured by the constancy of the man.

'I suppose you could have gone home and then returned when the nurses' arrival was confirmed,' he said. 'Things are usually a lot more predictable these days.'

'I'd prefer to stay,' Caroline said firmly. 'There are too many frayed edges to all of this. Do you know what I mean? Too many things left unfinished, undone. No, I'll see the women where they belong and *then* I'll go home.'

'Of course,' Reid said.

She held his arm. 'I know none of this is any of your doing,' she said. 'Of course I know that. It's just that . . . I

162

don't know . . . Saint-Quentin was full of women like Mary. Women, whole families, young children even. All of them just as lost, and all of them wandering and searching.'

'For something they may never find?'

'Some of them, yes. Captain Jessop said they were becoming a real nuisance. He said most of them expect the Commission to arrange for them to travel to see the graves. Apparently, they prefer to visit in groups, organized parties. They're holding up the work in some places. He said that the problem was that no one on the Commission had the authority to refuse them permission to visit wherever they wanted, only to warn them of the dangers that remain. He said that sometimes those dangers just added to the thrill of the visits. Apparently, it makes some of the women—'

'Feel closer to their lost loved ones?' Reid's scepticism was clear.

'I suppose it gives them *something*.'

'Four French schoolchildren, six- and seven-year-olds, were killed at Avesne two days ago,' Reid said. 'Their first day back at their rebuilt village school. An unexploded mine sitting in the foundations. Four years, it must have been there.'

'I heard about it,' Caroline said.

After that, neither of them spoke for a moment.

Then Caroline said, 'Captain Jessop also complained that they were being hounded by newspapermen wanting to write stories about what was happening with the cemeteries. There's a great demand from home.'

'To go with all the unrest, I daresay,' Reid said.

News of the protests and near-riots, the continued shortages and labour strikes and the rising number of the unemployed filled all the English newspapers, which reached Morlancourt a week late.

'Captain Jessop seemed to think it would be a good idea for the newspapermen to be somehow organized and presented with their stories, rather than wandering around independently and writing whatever they choose.'

'Meaning what?'

'Meaning, I suppose – and I'm sure this was Captain Jessop's feeling too – that some stories were more worthy of being told, of serving a higher purpose, than others.'

'A higher purpose?'

'Of satisfying the need of people to be told what's happening.'

'More dressing-up and telling people only what they want to hear.'

'It would all be for the—'

'Don't say it,' Reid almost shouted.

'Don't say what?'

'That it would all be for the greater good.'

'I was going to say that it might all be for the benefit of those who *wanted* to see what was happening to their loved ones, who needed to see that their deaths were finally being commemorated in some way.'

Reid signalled his apology to her.

'Besides,' Caroline went on, 'Captain Jessop said Colonel Wheeler was already considering the benefit to the Commission – its appeals for funding and resources, say – of giving the newspapermen what they've come to see.'

Reid began to sense what she might be telling him.

'Is he considering sending them here?' he said. 'To report on your nurses?'

164

He knew by her hesitancy in answering him in her usual open way that his guess had been right.

'Believe me, I did nothing to promote or encourage the idea,' she said. 'It's the last thing I want.'

'Hence the delay in delivering the bodies,' Reid said absently.

'Colonel Wheeler and Captain Jessop had clearly given the matter some consideration before I encountered him,' she said. 'He imagined I'd be pleased at the prospect of letting the newspapers report the burials.'

Reid wondered if Jessop had deliberately kept this from him at their recent encounter, or if his own remarks then had deterred the man from telling him what had already been decided.

The previous day, a note had arrived from Wheeler telling Reid to make the ground at Morlancourt appear 'presentable' in case anyone should turn up there unannounced. Reading this, Reid had imagined that Wheeler was referring to the unwelcome tourists; now he saw that the cryptic instruction might have related to something more specific.

He told Caroline about the note.

'Captain Jessop seemed to believe that you now have a cemetery that might soon reveal its final form to anyone with the vision to see it.'

'The vision?'

'I suppose he meant imagination. He said that at least the disarray and turmoil of the early work is over. And that now you've started setting your stones in place, even though they are as yet in the bare earth, then it wouldn't require too much extra effort to gain some idea what the place might look like when it's finally completed.'

'The man has no idea whatsoever of the "extra effort" required to do that.' He imagined announcing the news to his workers.

'I promise you, I did nothing to encourage the idea.'

Reid resisted telling her that Jessop would have given no consideration whatsoever to anything she might have said on the matter.

'He said that a small piece of prepared ground might be presented to the newspapermen as an oasis amid the wilderness, and that the occasion of the arrival of the nurses at such a place would give the story so much more impact.'

'Wheeler used to refer to the plots as "battlefield gardens",' Reid said. 'I think that was another of Jessop's inventions.'

'I daresay Colonel Wheeler will give you plenty of notice if any of this does come to pass,' Caroline said.

'I daresay,' Reid said. It all now seemed an inevitability to him.

The pair of them stopped talking to exchange greetings with an old farmer who was leading his solitary cow along the lane towards the fields beyond the church. The man brought it into Morlancourt each morning to sell the milk directly from the animal's udder at the doorstep.

Caroline clearly already knew the man, and when he took out a small metal bowl and half filled it with milk and offered it to her, she accepted it and drank it, savouring each mouthful. The man nodded vigorously at her every word of praise. He explained to Reid that these 'last drawings' were considered the finest the cow had to offer and that they were a cure for most minor ailments. He made the gift even more precious by adding that, before her recent death, his wife of almost fifty years had always insisted on the milk being saved for her. He then told Reid that his wife was now in heaven, tending to their two sons, and that since her death a year after the war's end, he had always thought of her when he had drawn and sold this last of the day's milk.

When Caroline gave him back his bowl, he leaned close to her and told her that not so long ago – before the war – the young newlywed women of Morlancourt would pay whatever he asked for the milk because it helped them beget their children.

Caroline laughed at hearing him say this, but the old man insisted it was true. He laughed with her, rinsed out the bowl in the nearby trough and wiped it across the globe of his stomach.

The old farmer then left them, following the cow, which continued untended through the slow routine of its day.

'"Beget"?' Reid said once the man was out of earshot.

'What else would you say?' A line of the cream lay along her lip and she wiped this away with her finger.

He was about to say more when she closed her eyes briefly, and he knew to remain silent. She had told him during their first encounter that she had no children of her own.

'Perhaps the milk would have helped me to beget my own sons and daughters,' she said.

'Is that what you wanted?'

'Of course,' she said. 'But it wasn't to be.'

'Do you regret it?'

She considered her answer. 'It was a loss to both of us,' she said. 'But happily neither of us pointed a finger at the other.'

He struggled for something, anything, to say to her, and she saw this and shook her head.

'I saw Alexander Lucas earlier,' she said. 'He said he was

on his way to investigate some recently found bodies at La Chapelette.'

'His wife's unwell,' Reid said. 'Or she was. He's waiting to hear from her. Or from someone to let him know what's happening.'

'He was with the postman when I saw him. We both received letters.'

'Was it from his wife?'

'I don't know. He'd only just been given the letter when I saw him. He said he had a lorry waiting for him and that he was already late. He seemed distracted.'

Beyond the church, the farmer slapped the flanks of his cow, urging it through the gate of a nearby field. The man closed the gate, leaned on it and lit a pipe.

'Wheeler's been piling on the work,' Reid said. 'On Alexander.' It was all he could bring himself to tell her of the bodies at Prezière.

'Of course. Will he apply for leave, do you think? To see his wife, I mean.'

'I don't know. He hasn't said anything.' Reid had suggested it to Lucas several days ago, and Lucas had said he was undecided about what he might do.

'Surely Colonel Wheeler would look favourably on any such application?'

'Perhaps.' It was true: there was nothing Wheeler would like better than to see the back of the man. And once Lucas was home in England, strings might easily be pulled by Wheeler to keep him there.

'The men in the hospital at Le Havre petitioned the authorities to have their rum ration delivered to them even though they were out of the line,' Caroline said. 'They insisted it would help them in their recovery, that they'd be fit and well and back on Active Service again much sooner if the rum was delivered to them in their beds.'

Reid smiled. 'I knew men in the line who were hardly sober from one day to the next for weeks on end,' he said.

'Perhaps they just—'

'There was no "perhaps" about it,' he said.

In the far distance, beyond the signal box, Reid heard the whistle of the approaching train. In another ten minutes it would arrive, and he would be waiting for it. He imagined Benoît walking out on to the platform and looking along the tracks, his watch already in his hand.

He rose and looked into the churchyard.

'The farmer's wife and sons are buried in there,' Caroline said. 'Mons. It's why he brings his last remaining cow past the place each morning.'

'And why you accepted his milk today?'

'Of course. Did you not see how slowly he moved going past the graveyard?'

A second, closer whistle sounded – the crossing beyond the canal – and Reid started to walk away. He stopped and turned back to Caroline. 'Shall I see you later?' he asked her.

She, too, rose from the seat, looked him slowly up and down, and then straightened her back and saluted him.

Reid laughed and returned the gesture.

'Dismissed,' she said to him, and he turned on his heel and marched stiffly away from her, swinging his arms as he went.

Ahead of him, the smoke of the engine finally appeared above the long curve into the station, turning slowly to steam as the driver finally made the approach to the platform and gently applied his brakes.

20

Later that same morning, an aeroplane appeared in the sky to the north of Morlancourt, circled the village and then flew low over where Reid and his men were working. Most of the diggers stopped what they were doing to watch the machine and to wave to it as the pilot flew even lower over them, crossing the cemetery from one side to the other and then banking along the line of the road to return. The man himself was clearly visible to everyone on the ground as he leaned over the side of his cockpit and waved back to them.

Reid was standing with Drake at the edge of the trees when the machine appeared.

'He wants to watch himself,' Drake said as the plane banked again to make a second circuit of the site.

'The telegraph poles?' Reid said. Though now wireless, the poles still stood along the road, and followed the temporary railway to Bray; nowhere were they either upright or evenly spaced.

'Everything,' Drake said. 'I saw a Bristol Five clip the church spire at Carvin, beyond Arras. Folded up like it had been grabbed by a giant hand. It came down in a hundred pieces.'

'Was the pilot . . . ?'

'Killed. Along with his observer. They sent some of us out to pick up the wreckage. The Red Cross came for the bodies.'

There was still a makeshift airstrip at nearby Quierrieu, and a few aircraft came and went from the place.

At the first distant note of the engine, Reid had imagined it to be the lorries bringing the Prezière corpses.

He had made a careful list of all forty-two names and he had this with him now in readiness. He had already announced to the men that the bodies were coming by their unusual route, but had been unable to give them a time. For all their sakes, he hoped the lorries arrived there soon.

One of Wheeler's aides had contacted him to say that when the burials were completed, the relevant paperwork was to be given to Wheeler personally at their next meeting.

Above them, the aeroplane climbed higher in the sky and then turned away from them in the direction of the river.

The men in the cemetery were slow to return to their work after the diversion. Reid remarked on this to Drake, and the sergeant shouted to those workers standing close to them. The men returned only reluctantly to their labours.

'No one's exerting themselves on account of what they've got coming later,' Drake said. 'If Lucas couldn't bring the bodies first thing, you should have insisted they wait until tomorrow.' It was a rare criticism from the man, but it would have served no purpose for Reid to try to explain to him what little true authority either Alexander Lucas or he possessed in the matter.

The waiting holes and their neat mounds of excavated soil lay in four rows close to the cemetery entrance, where the broad path would shortly be divided into several narrower paths reaching in among the headstones like the fingers of a hand. The chalk base of these lesser walkways had already been laid, and if the spreading paths did resemble a hand, then it remained a skeletal one.

Drake left Reid and walked among the more distant of the men, sending them back to their work. It was another warm day and most of the labourers worked stripped to their waists.

Almost an hour after the plane had gone, Reid finally heard and then saw the first of Lucas's approaching lorries. He called Drake back to him and told him to gather the men together and to instruct them on the work ahead. He showed him the simple plan he had drawn up allocating the holes. The men would work in groups – some carrying the corpses from the lorries to their waiting coffins, others lowering them into the excavated graves, and a third group coming along soon afterwards and filling in the holes.

'Will we get them all done today, do you think?' he asked Drake. It had been another of Wheeler's stipulations.

'Are you asking me or telling me?' Drake said, as astute as ever, and then leaving Reid as the first of the lorries negotiated the narrow entrance.

Reid waited a moment and then followed his sergeant down the slope.

Four lorries had appeared, three of which were covered. Only the fourth remained open, and Reid was surprised to see a dozen men sitting there holding picks and shovels of their own.

Alexander Lucas climbed down from the cab of the leading vehicle. He spoke to the driver and then came to Reid.

'I brought some help,' he said. He called for the men to disembark and then told Reid to. employ the newcomers where they were most needed.

'I was contacted last night by—' Reid began to say.

'Me too. Wheeler wants me to find a telephone and let him know when the burials are underway.' The nearest telephone was back in Morlancourt and both men knew that. 'He can wait,' Lucas said.

They watched as the first of the bodies were unloaded and carried to the waiting coffins. Even from that distance, Reid could clearly see the names and numbers marked on both the hessian sacks and the casket lids.

'This will be the last work most of them do,' Lucas said, meaning his own men. 'When I asked Jessop about my replacement teams, he told me to be patient. I told *him* that I'd already been sent the dockets for the fresh retrievals at La Chapelette. He told me to leave it with him,' – he mimicked Jessop's voice – 'that he'd see what he could do. Why does the bloody man always have to make everything sound as though he's doing you a great favour, and as though it involves twice as much effort from him as it ever does from you?' He took off his cap and ran his hand through his hair.

Waiting a moment, Reid said, 'I saw Caroline earlier.'

'By the church?'

'She said you'd received another letter.'

'I did. From my wife's mother again. Posted four days ago. Elizabeth's been taken into hospital. They're convinced now that it's scarlet fever, though no one seems to be very certain about much else.'

'Unless—'

'Unless she's keeping the worst of it from me, yes.'

It wasn't what Reid had been about to suggest, but he let this pass. He heard Lucas's concern in everything he said.

'Is your daughter still well?' Reid said.

'Susan. Yes. So far, anyway.'

'Caroline was wondering if you'd considered applying for leave.'

'At first. But then all this Prezière business piled up in front of me and I wanted to see it through to the finish.' It was an excuse, and Lucas did nothing to disguise this.

'And now?' Reid said.

'I don't know. What would I achieve by going home? What good would I be? Besides, now that I've done Wheeler's dirty work for him, you know as well as I do that he'd be more than happy for me to be left over there and chained to a desk for the rest of my time.'

'And so you'll go to La Chapelette and retrieve the bodies there?'

'I suppose so. Certainly somebody has to. Besides, I'll be home for good in a few months' time.'

'Of course you will.' Their conversation petered out in these further half-veiled excuses and diversions.

Both men turned to watch as the lorries were unloaded and as the coffins were carried to their graves. Lucas's men seemed to imbue Reid's workforce with something of their own enthusiasm and he saw how much they had achieved since the lorries' arrival.

'I went to La Chapelette yesterday,' Lucas said eventually.

'Is it a new discovery?' Reid said, happy for the subject to have changed.

'Our primary findings suggest between eight and twelve bodies, and not the two we were initially told. In addition

174

to which, they're going to be considerably more difficult to identify than the poor sods at Prezière. We've already got our people going through the records of the place.'

'What do you know?'

'Local witnesses who came back said they'd been told that pits had been dug and bodies and parts buried all together after the retreat there. Pioneer Battalion troops, by all accounts. And some Ulster Division men, though God knows what *they* were doing there. Apparently, most of the deaths were the result of a barrage. I've already told Jessop that we'll need longer than the two days he's suggesting. I also told him I'd looked at the rosters and that, currently, I was the man best qualified to get the job done.'

Reid wondered if Lucas wasn't overstating the case – both for the time required for the retrieval and for his own participation in it.

'I told Caroline that I'd probably taken precedence over her nurses,' Lucas said. 'This morning. The delay. She told me I was forgiven and absolved.'

Reid, in turn, told Lucas about the farmer and his cow, and Lucas laughed.

'When I told Jessop about the extra time I'd need, he spent ten minutes telling me how hard dear old Wheeler is working on all our behalves. Apparently, last week, hard-working Wheeler went back to London to meet the Prime Minister and to address a few of his committees.'

'You think he can see a knighthood shining on the horizon?'

'I wouldn't be surprised.'

They were interrupted by Drake, who came to them and told them that all the coffins had been carried to sit beside their allocated holes and were about to be lowered into them.

Reid told Drake to let the men rest for twenty minutes. He told him to fill the graves furthest from the path and then to work back in the direction of the entrance. He asked if the work would be finished by four, when all the more strenuous labour on the site was usually halted in the heat of the afternoon sun. Drake looked at the coffins and the additional labourers and said he didn't see why not.

Then Drake turned to Alexander Lucas and said, 'I was talking to a man in Albert a few days ago – Provost Crew, served for two years in the Battle Police – said he remembered you from Ginchy. Name of Anderson.'

'It rings no bells,' Lucas said.

'Spoke very highly of you, as it happens. Said he was in the clearing-up brigade the morning after the so-called assault at the place.'

'I was certainly there,' Lucas said. He turned from Reid to face Drake.

'He said you were knocked about a bit, that you were lucky to walk away from things.'

It seemed to Reid that Drake was almost pushing Lucas to say much more.

Lucas said nothing for a moment, concentrating on lighting another cigarette. 'There were a hundred and fifty of us who were a bit more than knocked about a bit,' he said eventually.

'He told me that, too. If I see him again – not very likely, considering – I'll tell him I spoke to you. Tell him you came through, shall I?'

'You do that,' Lucas said, but with no enthusiasm. 'You tell him I came through. Perhaps he'll have some idea of how many of the other hundred and forty-nine did the same.'

'I'm sure Sergeant Drake only meant—' Reid said.

'But, as you say,' Lucas went on, his voice raised, 'it isn't very likely that you'll see him again, this Anderson, so we'll never know, shall we? Not much call these days for the Battle Police squads, I should imagine. Not now that all the battles have been fought and paid for by others.'

Drake said nothing in reply to this.

It had always struck Reid as a ridiculous title, a ridiculous conjunction of both words and responsibilities.

He wondered at the true nature of what had just passed between the two men, guessing only that both knew more than they were letting on. There was nothing suspicious in any of this; neither Drake nor Lucas were given to this kind of fond, embellished reminiscing. Besides, Reid doubted if many men would have anything to say in favour of the disliked police battalions.

He was distracted from these thoughts by the arrival of several of Lucas's men, who came to tell him that two of the lorries and some of his workers were about to leave for their new quarters in Amiens. Lucas agreed to let them go. The remainder of his men would return to their quarters in Saint-Quentin in the remaining vehicles when the work was finished.

The men left, and Drake walked with them back to the waiting holes and coffins.

When they were again alone, and just as Reid was about to suggest that they too return to work, Lucas took a postcard from his tunic pocket and gave it to him.

At first, Reid thought this had something to do with the communication Lucas had received from his wife's mother, but turning the card to read it he saw that it was nothing more than a dirty, unsent Field Service card made out by one of the men who had been retrieved from Prezière, and who now, presumably, lay in one of the nearby coffins.

'According to that,' Lucas said, 'he was in good health, his spirits were high, and he was in a quiet part of the line. He'd been recently wounded, but only lightly, and was hopeful of being moved into a quiet sector as a result. His next letter home was going to be written at the first opportunity, despite having heard nothing from there for some time. He hopes everyone is well and hopes, too, to see them all soon.' He took back the card from Reid. 'As you can see, none of that wonderfully reassuring news ever reached anyone at home.'

'Was he—'

'One of those men with a head wound? He was. He still had the field dressing over his forearm where he'd been hit earlier. Shrapnel, probably.'

'Suggesting he was at Prezière when the Germans overran the place.'

'And wondering, like everyone from Prezière all the way back to Paris, when all that overrunning was finally going to come to an end, yes.' Lucas turned to watch the departing lorries reverse through the gates into the lane beyond. Men ran and jumped on to them. Others stood nearby and watched them go. A cloud of blue smoke formed above the vehicles and then drifted slowly in their wake.

21

As Reid had anticipated, and despite the additional help brought by Lucas, that day's work ended later than usual, and it was almost eight in the evening before he and the last of his exhausted men were able to leave the site.

Several hours earlier, following the departure of Lucas and the remains of his workforce, and when it had become clear to Reid that the work would not be completed by the end of the usual working day, he had gathered everyone together and told them they would need to work longer. He had made one of his small, hopeful speeches to them, explaining something of the history of the bodies from Prezière and offering them time off in lieu in the days ahead. But the mood of the workers had remained sullen and unwilling, and it was only when Drake had intervened and given most of the men the following day off that they had acceded to Reid's demands and returned to their labours.

Later, when the work was finished and as they were all preparing to leave the site for the night, Drake returned to Reid and told him that he had made his offer to the men based on the knowledge that there would be no bodies on the following day's train, only stores.

Reid asked him how he knew this.

'A sergeant pal at the Albert depot,' Drake said. 'It looks as though Wheeler or Jessop imagined we might need at least two days for this little lot.'

'How much do you know?' Reid asked him. 'About the bodies, I mean.'

'What does it matter?' Drake said. 'It's done now.'

'Will there be *anything* on the train?'

'Supplies, I should imagine. Nothing you and me and Benoît's boys can't manage.'

It occurred to Reid, as Drake was telling him all this, that neither Wheeler nor Jessop would be in any position to object to these concessions now that the men from Prezière were buried and all the necessary paperwork would soon be handed over.

Drake left him then, to catch the last of their own departing lorries.

Reid walked the two miles back to Morlancourt alone.

Approaching his *pension*, he saw Caroline Mortimer sitting at a table of a nearby café. A man in uniform sat with her, his back to Reid, and at first he imagined this to be Lucas.

Only when Reid drew closer, and when Caroline saw him and rose to greet him, did the man turn and reveal himself to be Jonathan Guthrie.

It had been Reid's intention, following their encounter and loose arrangement earlier that morning, to return to his room, wash and change his clothes, and then go in search of Caroline.

'Captain Reid,' Guthrie said, standing as Reid reached them.

Caroline pulled out a chair for Reid.

'You look exhausted,' she told him.

Reid told them about his day's work.

'Of course,' Guthrie said. 'Edmund said you were taking them on board today. Well done.'

Taking them on board, Reid thought. *Of course*.

Caroline filled a glass from the bottle on the table and gave it to him.

Reid emptied this in a single swallow and she refilled it.

'It's foul stuff,' Guthrie said. He picked up his own glass and sipped it.

Not what you're used to at your dinners with Edmund.

'Alexander was here earlier,' Caroline said.

'Yes,' Guthrie said. 'He told us you'd be along shortly.'

'We invited him to join us and await your arrival.'

'Apparently, he had a bit to do,' Guthrie said. 'As I'm sure we can all appreciate. These are busy days for all of us. Captain Jessop put it most succinctly last night when he responded to a toast with the observation that we are laying the foundations here for a lifetime of remembering. Quite a phrase, I'm sure you'll agree.'

Caroline signalled to Reid that she regretted the man's overbearing presence as much as he did.

'I'm surprised Colonel Wheeler didn't want you out there with us today to say a few words,' Reid said to him, his voice betraying nothing of his true intent.

'As a matter of fact, he *did* consult me on the subject. However, both he and I came to the conclusion – and especially taking into account your ongoing labours at the place – that anything of that nature might be somewhat premature.'

'Only, you seemed keen earlier to become involved at every opportunity,' Reid said.

'I'm sure the appropriate occasion will present itself soon enough,' Guthrie said. 'Besides . . .'

'Yes?' Reid said.

'Sorry?'

'You said "besides".'

'Oh, I merely meant that those men today will be honoured alongside everyone else you are interring at the place when the time comes to do so. The Commission, as I'm sure you're aware, has great plans for when the time is right.'

'I see,' Reid said, draining his second glass.

The exchange was ended when a waiter came out and put a basket of bread and a pot of pale butter on the small table. The butter immediately attracted several flies, which walked in circles around the rim of the pot until Caroline put her handkerchief over it.

'Did you manage to lay them all to rest?' she asked Reid. 'Alexander told me that they far exceeded your usual day's work.'

'We did,' he said. 'In lieu of which, Drake has promised the men a day's rest tomorrow.'

'Drake?' Guthrie said, a note of forced incredulity in his voice. 'Your sergeant? I'm not sure if Edmund—'

'No, me neither,' Reid said. 'But it's done now. And given the circumstances, I'm sure Colonel Wheeler will understand and agree to the break.'

Guthrie considered this. 'Quite,' he said.

Reid knew that everything he said or suggested would be repeated to Wheeler, but rather than be made wary by this, he felt strangely pleased at the prospect.

Guthrie spun the glass he held. 'Yesterday evening, I tasted my very first Yquem '09. Nothing like one of the great vintages, of course, but still . . .'

'Quite,' Reid said, catching Caroline Mortimer's quick smile as she pulled the bread apart and started to chew on a piece.

'I wish they'd *cut* the stuff,' Guthrie said. 'Instead of forever handling it like they do.'

Caroline called inside for another bottle of wine.

'Jonathan was just telling me that Colonel Wheeler has asked him to conduct the Sunday-morning service in Saint-Quentin,' she said to Reid.

'I volunteered my services and Edmund was only too happy to accept,' Guthrie said. 'So you see, I do have my uses, I do serve *some* purpose in all of this, however limited when compared to the efforts of others.' He lifted his glass, as though about to propose a toast, perhaps even to himself. 'Better still, I have succeeded in persuading Mrs Mortimer to attend the service.' He turned to Reid. 'Perhaps you yourself – and Lieutenant Lucas, of course – perhaps you, too, might see your way to accepting a small measure of spiritual consolation in these unsettled times.'

Consolation?

Guthrie went on. 'I shall, of course, be speaking of your work here – not you, specifically, you understand, but of the Commission's great labours as a whole – and of all that is being achieved on behalf of the living *and* the dead in pointing the way towards a hopeful and more enlightened future.'

'I'm sure,' Reid said.

In Albert, there were two services every Sunday at the

Army church two streets back from the Commission's hotel headquarters, and though all the serving men stationed in the vicinity and employed on the Commission's work were encouraged to attend at least one of these, very few did so. Someone had come up with the idea of distributing mail from a lorry outside the church following the morning service, but even that had failed as a lure.

'Well?' Guthrie said.

'I doubt I shall be in your congregation,' Reid said. It was far from the answer he would have given the man had Caroline not been present.

'I thought perhaps you might accompany Mrs Mortimer now that she finds herself abandoned here.' He smiled at Caroline as he said it.

'Abandoned?'

'He means Mary Ellsworth,' Caroline said.

'I have, of course, also been working on my service for her nurses,' Guthrie said. 'I'll pull out all the stops, so to speak, rest assured.'

They were interrupted again by the same waiter, who came to see what they had called for.

Caroline asked him in French for another bottle of wine, something better than the bottle on the table if he had it. He began to insist that what he had already brought out for them was of good quality, but Guthrie stopped him by holding up his palm to the boy, and then by throwing what remained in his glass to the ground.

Caroline apologized to the waiter for this crude display, and he picked up the empty bottle and left them.

'Well, I certainly think he received our message loud and clear this time,' Guthrie said, pleased with himself.

'Oh, I'm sure he did,' Reid said.

A thought then occurred to him. 'Will you be officiating at the opening of the cemetery?' he asked Guthrie. 'I mean when it's finally completed and opened to visitors?' He had never known when this was likely to be, exactly, and he had certainly never imagined that he himself might still be there to actually attend any such ceremony, or even be invited as a guest of honour. The event, when it did finally come, he guessed, would be attended only by the higher-ranking Commission members still in France, by officers representing the regiments interred there, and by the families of the buried men, their only true mourners. He and his workers, he knew, would be like the gravediggers at any ordinary funeral – standing back and hidden from the grieving family.

He regretted asking, and braced himself for Guthrie's answer.

'Naturally,' Guthrie said. 'Here and elsewhere. Myself and others. In fact, it was another of our points of discussion last night. Edmund was outlining the timetable for the completion of various sites. I won't be here the whole time until then, of course. My calling at home, you understand. But when the call does come, you can rest assured that I shall answer it and return to do my sacred duty.'

Everything Guthrie now said clothed him further in his self-anointed glory. The man looked as self-satisfied as Reid had ever seen him.

Seizing his advantage, Guthrie went on, 'You know as well as I do, surely, Captain Reid, that everything these days is aimed towards some greater goal, that there is *purpose* in everything, however menial-seeming, that we do here. I am a Man of God, and it is where your own charges now rest –

in His Holy Kingdom, and secure in the knowledge of His grace and His comfort and His protection.'

It was a ridiculous and convoluted thing for the man to say, especially considering where they were and the day just past, but, as ever, Guthrie was pleased with himself and these unassailable confections.

The waiter returned with a new bottle, already opened, put it on the table and left before any of them could confront him further. Caroline called out her thanks to him as he disappeared back into the café's dark interior.

Where they sat, the evening sun fell on the wall above them, casting the crumbling brickwork and painted plaster into shadow. The empty building next to them had recently been flattened and the rubble piled in mounds across the empty site. Pieces of shattered furniture and doors and window frames stood waiting to be burned. The children of Morlancourt made this and other similar sites their playgrounds, and several – Reid couldn't tell whether they were boys or girls – ran back and forth across the broken ground. Benoît had told him that the lost building had been Morlancourt's last remaining boulangerie, and watching the running children now and listening to their cries, he found himself wondering what the place might have looked like all those years earlier, before the war had come and pressed its hand upon the place.

Guthrie sipped at the new wine and grimaced. 'It's every bit as bad as before,' he said, drawing Reid from his brief reverie.

'What did you expect?' Reid said to him, and he raised his own glass for Caroline to fill.

Then Guthrie rose from his seat. 'I'm afraid I have to

leave,' he said. 'As you might imagine, I have a great deal to prepare if I am to be ready for Sunday.' It was only Wednesday.

'Of course you do,' Reid said.

'Of course,' Caroline repeated. She lifted her hand to the man, which Guthrie took and kissed.

The chaplain took a step away from them, then paused and turned.

'Oh, I almost forgot to say, Captain Reid.'

'Say what?'

'Something else I discussed with Edmund and Captain Jessop yesterday evening.' Guthrie took an envelope from his pocket and laid it on the table in front of Reid. 'It seems that you are to expect the man from Neuville on tomorrow's train. Chap called Etherington. I hope allowing your sergeant to be so gracious with his favours to the men won't cause you any problems in the matter.'

'Drake was told there would be only supplies.'

'I'm sure he was, but believe me, the man is definitely coming.'

More subterfuge? Reid thought, but knew that to contest anything Guthrie now said would only give him further advantage.

'Then I'm sure we'll be ready for him,' he said.

'Even without your labourers?'

'With them or without them.'

'Then I shall——' Guthrie stopped abruptly.

'What? Tell Wheeler?'

'If you must know, it was Captain Jessop who asked me to let you know.'

'He could have come himself,' Reid said.

'I daresay the man has a hundred other, more pressing things to do.'

'Of course,' Reid said. He rubbed at the earth caked in the hairs of his forearms. He suddenly felt as exhausted as Caroline said he looked.

'I shall leave you,' Guthrie said, having completed the drama of his departure.

Just go, Reid wanted to shout at the man.

When he was finally lost to their view, Reid picked up the envelope and opened it. He read it and laid it back down. Caroline gestured to it and he indicated for her to read its few details.

'He was executed on General French's personal recommendation,' she said. 'It seems a second charge of Dishonouring the King's Regulations was dropped for the sake of expediency. I don't even know what that means.'

'Me neither,' Reid said.

'But you know what they *say* it means?'

He nodded. 'Besides, French was notorious for never considering appeals. Everyone out here knew that he had become a bloodthirsty embarrassment to the War Office. It was one of the reasons he was replaced by Haig.'

'I had no idea,' Caroline said.

'Of course you didn't.'

'He was a volunteer, Etherington,' she said. 'William. He'd been hospitalized on three separate occasions.'

'What, really, does any of that matter?' Reid said.

She waited a moment. 'At least now his family will have somewhere to come and to remember him,' she said.

'And all the time they're grieving – all those years to the end of all those other lives – they'll know every detail of what put the man in his grave. It's likely that the men who were called upon to take part in his execution are now dead and mourned and grieved over themselves. Or, if they're not dead, then they're men living with what they did for every day of the rest of their own lives.' He stopped talking, aware that his voice was raised and that he was being watched by others at the tables.

Caroline folded the sheet of paper containing Etherington's details and put it back into its envelope.

Reid took it from her and slid it into his pocket.

'Sorry,' he said.

'Please, there's no need. I knew Guthrie had come for a reason. Alexander refused even to sit with him. *Will* you manage? With Etherington, I mean. Without your workers.'

'With a solitary coffin?'

They sat in silence for a moment, Caroline continuing to pick at the bread, Reid considering the following day. The noise of the playing children grew briefly louder as they ran from the remains of the lost building out on to the empty street.

'Did Alexander receive bad news?' Caroline said eventually.

'His wife has been admitted to hospital with suspected scarlet fever. He's concerned for his daughter.'

'I see,' she said, avoiding his eyes.

'What is it?' he asked her.

'Scarlet fever. It has a nasty habit of turning into rheumatic fever.'

'Is it . . . ?'

'Sometimes.'

Neither of them spoke for a moment.

Finally, Caroline said, 'Last winter, I worked at Le Havre. There was an outbreak of influenza. A local man stood at the hospital entrance selling canvas pomanders filled with lavender and spices.'

'I imagine they were as effective as anything else,' Reid said. 'Or certainly no worse.' He realized only then how critical this sounded.

'*Better* in some instances,' Caroline said. 'Or at least the outcome was pretty much the same.'

'At Béthune, in the middle of winter, I saw men scoop up wet stable manure to use as poultices to protect against frost-bite.'

She poured the last of the second bottle into their glasses.

'Should it really be this sour?' she asked him.

'Perhaps we should have asked Guthrie to perform another of his miracles for us.'

'Cheers,' she said, pulling a face the instant the glass touched her lips.

22

The next morning Reid arrived at the station to see both Caroline and Lucas sitting together on the sunlit platform. He had gone there earlier than usual in the hope of getting some assistance from Benoît in unloading what little was due to arrive.

Upon seeing Reid, Benoît came out of his office and walked with him to where Caroline and Lucas sat talking.

As the two men passed the open doorway of the goods depot, Reid looked inside and was surprised to see Drake and a dozen of his workers also waiting there.

Drake came out to him.

'We heard,' he said simply. 'The bloke from Neuville.'

'How?'

Drake smiled at the question. 'We live in a barracks,' he said. He motioned to the men starting to congregate around him. 'More of them volunteered, but I said we'd only need the dozen.' He nodded his greeting to Benoît.

'I see.'

'There were one or two who objected, but not *that* many, not considering.'

'Of course,' Reid said. He thanked the gathering men.

'We'll wait on your word,' Drake said.

'They are all soldiers,' Benoît said to Reid as the two of them returned to the platform. 'It's natural.'

'I know that,' Reid said.

'I called on a couple of my neighbours, but then sent them away when your men arrived.'

'You knew, too? About the body, I mean?'

Benoît nodded. 'Our own generals . . .' he said and then fell silent.

They arrived beside Caroline and Lucas.

'It seems the world and his dog already know,' Lucas said.

'So I see. I still wish Wheeler had seen fit to deliver the man as part of a normal consignment instead of all this.'

Caroline rose, put her arm through Benoît's and drew him with her further along the platform in the direction of the coming train. She talked with him of his work and then stood with him beyond the shade of the buildings in the full glare of the rising sun.

'Have you heard any more?' Reid asked Lucas. 'From home, I mean.'

Lucas sat with his feet apart, his hands on his knees. 'Since yesterday? No. How did the work go?'

'All done. I left a few spaces in case any more turn up.'

'Unlikely,' Lucas said. 'Besides, according to Jessop, there's soon to be a change in policy and men are going to be buried wherever there's room, closest to where they're found. I suppose it makes sense.'

'It makes *his* kind of sense, you mean. Jessop's. Ours *still* not to reason why, eh?'

It was clear from Lucas's lack of enthusiasm, and from the lack of his usual resistance to Wheeler and Jessop's ill-considered decisions, that his thoughts remained elsewhere, and so Reid stopped talking.

It was his intention, if the waiting men agreed, to take more of the engraved headstones out to the cemetery. He was keen now, especially knowing what Wheeler planned for the place regarding the arrival of the nurses and the gathering newspapermen, to replace as many of the temporary markers as possible with the stones to suggest a greater degree of completion and permanency. The stones for the men from Prezière would not arrive for some time, but there were sufficient others already stacked and waiting at the station for a considerable difference to be made to the appearance of the cemetery.

Left to his own devices and schedules, he would have preferred to have waited until all the burials were completed before planting the stones, but he understood that other considerations now held sway. Besides, perhaps Lucas was right – perhaps the time had come to stop fighting Wheeler and to finish the work and then simply leave.

It had been Commission policy until now to salvage all the temporary grave markers and then, upon a small payment, to deliver these to the families of the dead.

As far as possible, photographs had been taken of all the known graves, and these too had been sent, also for a small charge, to the next-of-kin. The practice had been stopped only when greater and greater numbers of grieving relatives expressed the desire to visit the actual graves.

In the months immediately after the Armistice there had been a great demand for the replaced grave markers, and they had been retrieved, dismantled, sent, reassembled and then replanted back at home. Sometimes this had taken place in local churchyards with small ceremonies attached, but more often than not the crosses – most little more than two simple pieces of crate-wood with a name and number roughly scraped or scorched into them – had been erected in family gardens and allotments, and on farmland and village greens.

There were still those in the War Office who believed that 'home soil' cemeteries and a national memorial ground would have been the better option from the very start of the retrieval and burial work.

On one occasion, early in their meetings, Wheeler had declared his support for the plan for a separate cemetery for the three hundred executed men. Afterwards, when the plan was vetoed by Parliament, Wheeler had continued to insist that it was how many in the Army Graves Service had felt at the time.

Lucas nodded towards Caroline and Benoît.

'He's been here since before six. He and his wife went to their son's grave before he came to work.'

'Because of what's happening today?'

'Perhaps. They go together three or four times a week, although I imagine his wife goes every day and keeps it to herself. He was telling me that she still cries every time she sees the stone.'

'He was their only child,' Reid said.

'I know. He told me she argues with him. She wants to know why he isn't grieving for the boy as painfully as she is. She accuses him of being unfeeling.'

Reid looked at the man. 'She's wrong,' he said.

Caroline was still holding Benoît's arm, pointing something out to him on the far side of the tracks.

'He thinks that when the cemetery's finished there'll be

no more use for the station and the government will close it,' Lucas said. 'Have *you* heard anything?'

Reid shook his head. 'Only the same rumours. It's just as likely that they'll keep it open and running for the visitors who'll come.'

After that, neither man spoke.

Close to seven, the whistle of the approaching engine sounded, and both men turned to see the plume of smoke rising above the flatness.

Caroline and Benoît came back to them.

'I make it ten seconds late,' Reid said, causing Benoît to smile and shake his head.

'Would you prefer me to leave?' Caroline asked Reid. She motioned to Drake and the others, who were emerging from the depot and forming themselves into a line between the doorway and the platform's edge. She reached beneath the bench and picked up a small bunch of wild flowers from the shade there. 'I thought . . .'

'Please, stay,' Reid told her, aware what her presence would add to the occasion, surrounded by all these men.

The train appeared, slowed and drew to a halt.

Drake came to Reid, saluted and said they were ready.

Reid wondered what to tell him. He took the documents concerning the man from Neuville from his case. 'Business as usual, I suppose,' he said.

'The cart's at the far side,' Drake said. He indicated the cart and its waiting horses at the rear of the station.

'Take him straight through,' Reid said. He realized only then that it was unfair of him to order the men to return to take out the stones, and so he said nothing of his original plan for the day. 'Then you can tell them to go.'

'That was my intention,' Drake said.

A few minutes later, the solitary coffin was manhandled from the floor of the wagon at the rear of the train, and Drake and five others lifted it on to their shoulders and carried it into the depot, pausing only to allow Caroline to reach up and lay her small bunch of flowers on its lid.

Reid, Lucas and Benoît stood to one side as the casket was carried away.

Eventually, Reid saluted the coffin, and Lucas followed him.

Caroline and Benoît both bowed their heads and muttered separate prayers.

The pall bearers and their load were lost for a moment in the deep shadow of the depot before reappearing at the waiting cart a moment later.

Reid heard Drake calling to the man holding the reins, and then telling the men to return to the platform and whatever else waited to be unloaded and carried into the depot.

After this Drake came back.

'Thank you,' Reid said to him.

The other men came through the shed singly and in pairs and started in their usual desultory manner to unload the remainder of the day's sparse cargo.

Caroline returned to Reid. 'I had a note from Colonel Wheeler,' she said. 'My nurses will definitely be here in a fortnight's time.'

Wheeler had never guaranteed specific delivery so far in advance before, and Reid guessed that the promise now had more to do with whatever else he was planning for the ceremony than with any need for expediency on her or the nurses' behalf.

'I see,' he said.

'I imagine he has a great deal else to consider,' she said, letting him know that she too was aware of Wheeler's as yet unformed plans.

'I suppose so.'

'He promised me their stones will arrive between now and then so that they might be put in place at the ceremony itself,' she said.

'Of course.' It was customary to allow the freshly filled graves to settle for at least a month before they were topped up, levelled, and the stones and concrete foundations added. Any stone-laying at the actual arrival of the women's coffins would be done solely for the benefit of the watching crowd. Again, Reid revealed nothing of the contrivance. 'I'm pleased,' he said, 'that you've finally got a date after waiting for so long.'

Something distracted her, and she turned away from him to look along the platform. 'Look,' she said.

Reid turned too and saw Benoît wiping his face with his handkerchief. Ernaux had climbed down from the train and stood beside his friend, his arm clasped across Benoît's shoulders.

'He's remembering his son,' Reid said absently, as though the man's behaviour needed some explanation.

'Of course he is,' Caroline said.

Lucas came to them and said he was leaving. He told them he intended riding on the train back to Amiens, where he hoped to pick up more of the paperwork regarding the retrievals at La Chapelette. He, too, paused to look at Benoît and Ernaux still standing at the platform's edge.

Closer by, the driver of the train climbed down and walked

alongside his engine, tapping the shining wheels with an iron bar, creating a loud clanging sound which echoed all around them in the early-morning quiet.

23

At the start of the following week, Reid travelled again with Lucas to Amiens to attend a Commission meeting there.

According to the agenda Wheeler had sent out in advance of the gathering, it now appeared that the building of the larger cemeteries further afield and the plans for the giant memorials to the missing were now of greater consequence to the Commission than the completion of the numerous smaller burial grounds already underway. It was equally obvious to anyone who knew Wheeler, and of his personal ambitions, that these larger sites and their monuments were of far greater interest to him as he continued to manoeuvre himself for promotion.

Reid and Lucas arrived at the designated hotel, however, to discover that neither Wheeler nor Jessop were present. A note was handed to Reid by the concierge, explaining that the two men had spent the previous evening in Paris and would be at least an hour late. It was hoped that the proceedings would await their arrival.

Others congregating there were given the same sparse information. It angered Reid that Wheeler had not seen fit to let them know of the delay sooner, but Lucas, as usual, was unconcerned by the news, remarking only that it gave them time to go to a nearby bar for a drink. When Reid pointed out that it was not yet mid-morning, Lucas only laughed and told him to please himself, just like Wheeler and Jessop clearly did.

The two men went together to a bar they had visited before, where Reid ordered coffee, and Lucas cognac.

Reid asked about the retrievals at La Chapelette, but nothing Lucas said of the place and its bodies revealed any of his usual concerns or commitment to the work. And when Reid asked him again if he had received any further news of his wife, Lucas simply shook his head, emptied the glass he held and returned to the bar.

When Wheeler and Jessop did finally arrive – closer to two hours late than one – Wheeler drew everyone together and told them of the work proposed for the monument at Ypres, in Belgium, and over which, therefore, he had no control or influence whatsoever. But both Reid and Lucas guessed by the way he spoke of the monument that he was already convinced of his own elevation within the Commission. Morlancourt and all the smaller cemeteries surrounding it had clearly become something of a backwater as far as Wheeler was concerned, and he was determined not to allow himself to be caught there.

He spoke of progress in most of the cemeteries as though the work on them was all but completed, and when Reid attempted to interrupt him and question these assumptions, Wheeler said there was no time for such discussions. He spoke as though Reid and not he had been the cause of their delay.

Lucas, Reid noticed, said nothing during Wheeler's hour-long speech. He sat low in his chair, his arms across his chest, his head bowed, and at times seemed half asleep in the warm and airless room.

Wheeler never once mentioned Lucas or his work, and this, Reid also saw, suited Lucas perfectly.

Prior to Wheeler's arrival, as Reid had watched Lucas rise unsteadily from where he was sitting in the bar – he had laughed and said he was exhausted – Reid had again suggested to him that he should apply for compassionate leave, but Lucas had insisted that he preferred to stay and complete his work. Reid knew not to persist in the matter, and knew too that he should certainly not intercede with Wheeler on Lucas's behalf.

Upon returning to the hotel, another of Wheeler's aides had taken the completed Prezière paperwork from Reid. When Reid had asked the man to sign for the documents, he had been told that this would not be necessary, and the man had walked swiftly away from him.

Now, sitting in the stifling atmosphere of the hotel room, and sensing that both Wheeler and Jessop were already guessing at the extent of Lucas's intoxication, Reid knew not to draw any further attention to him. All he wanted now – all either of them wanted – was for the meeting to come to an end and to leave Amiens.

Wheeler finally drew the gathering to a close at four in the afternoon by asking if anyone else at the table wished to share anything of importance. It was a common ploy of the man, knowing that most of them would be eager to leave and make the unpredictable journeys back to where they were stationed. He also made it equally clear to them all that, having spoken himself, there remained nothing of comparable importance left to be discussed.

A few minutes later, as Reid and Lucas were leaving the hotel, Jessop came to them and said that Wheeler would like to see them both. They could do nothing except accede to this, and Jessop led them back to the same room, in which Wheeler now waited alone. Having delivered the two men to him, Jessop left.

Lucas said bluntly that, having wasted the morning waiting, they now had a train to catch.

'Of course you do, Lieutenant Lucas,' Wheeler said, and then, having considered Lucas's remark and his boldness in making it, added, 'Quite.' He then turned his back on them, studying his reflection in the giant gilt-framed mirror that hung above the marble fireplace. 'I merely wished to ascertain – to confirm, that is – that your work at La Chapelette was underway.'

'And everything at Prezière finished, yes,' Lucas said.

It was telling that Wheeler had waited until the meeting was over and everyone else had departed before asking Lucas this.

'I took delivery of the bodies five days ago,' Reid said.

'And buried them?'

'And buried them.' Both Jessop and Guthrie would already have told Wheeler this.

'Excellent,' Wheeler said to Lucas. 'Then rest assured, I shall include a commendation on your work when I next find myself answerable to my own superiors. You, too, Captain Reid.' In the mirror, he looked from Lucas to Reid and then back again. 'I don't suppose . . .'

'What?' Lucas said. 'You don't suppose what?'

'I was merely wondering,' Wheeler went on hesitantly, 'whether or not Captain Reid had seen fit to bring his latest plans of the cemetery, so that I might better consider the necessity—'

'I didn't,' Reid said. 'If you'd told me beforehand that you needed them . . .' Both he and Lucas took pleasure in the man's discomfort.

'No,' Wheeler said, and then, again, 'Quite.'

'Besides, the men are buried and the graves filled and marked,' Lucas said. 'What difference will seeing the plots and the names on a plan make?'

'Of course,' Wheeler said. 'You're quite right; it will make no difference whatsoever. I suppose all I wanted was to satisfy myself that everyone involved in our task here was continuing to work to the same exemplary standards to which we at the Commission have become accustomed.'

'Quite,' Lucas said, causing Wheeler to turn from the mirror and look directly at him.

'I could send it to you,' Reid suggested, before Lucas could antagonize the man further.

'That would be most appreciated, Captain Reid,' Wheeler said, his eyes still on Lucas, who was now considering a tray of decanters on a nearby table.

'I'll send it to you first thing in the morning,' Reid said.

'Better still, I shall send someone to Morlancourt to collect it from you. Shall we say noon? I'm sure everyone concerned will be only too relieved to see an end to the matter.'

'Of course they will,' Lucas said, his voice low.

Wheeler ignored the remark. 'I'm sure *you*, at least, take my meaning, Captain Reid,' he said, his slight emphasis more than making its point.

'Of course,' Reid said. 'We both understand you perfectly.' He turned to Lucas. 'Don't we?'

'Perfectly,' Lucas said eventually.

'And Caroline Mortimer?' Wheeler said to Reid. 'I suppose she's told you about her nurses finally coming. What is it, ten days now?'

'Of course,' Reid said. He started to tell Wheeler about the problems he was experiencing with the water along the edge of the cemetery.

Wheeler laughed as he started speaking. 'And the Commission men in Mesopotamia complain endlessly about shifting sand. At Lone Pine – Gallipoli, you know – they complain about having only bleached bones – no actual corpses as such – to gather up and bury. Mind, that's the colonials for you – all they ever seem to do is complain about one damn thing after another.'

There was a further silence as neither Reid nor Lucas responded to the remark as Wheeler had hoped.

'In fact,' Wheeler went on, 'I was hearing only yesterday of the need for experienced supervising officers out in that particular neck of the woods.'

'Turkey?' Reid said.

'And beyond. Persia, Mesopotamia, the so-called Holy Land, that sort of thing.' The remark, and the way Wheeler now looked at him, made Reid wary.

'Are we finally building cemeteries out there, then?' Lucas said. It was something the Commission had long deliberated on. The families of the men killed in the Middle East campaigns did not feel the same way about their lost sons and husbands being buried there as those who had lost men in France and Belgium did.

'We shall build them wherever honour and decency demand it of us, Lieutenant Lucas,' Wheeler said firmly, his eyes remaining on Reid as he spoke.

'Of course we shall,' Lucas said.

'We need capable men,' Wheeler said to Reid, confirming everything Reid was starting to consider. 'Men who understand the rigours and extent of the challenge to be undertaken. And men who can now embrace and embody the ideals in which we are clothed.'

Lucas, too, sensed what Wheeler was suggesting, and said, 'And men with time left to serve?' It was said solely to alert Reid, and Reid understood this.

'Of course men with time left to serve,' Wheeler said. 'You can't begin to imagine the headaches I've had concerning the loss of all our conscript and time-served labour.'

'Funnily enough, I probably can,' Lucas said. He went to the decanters and poured himself a drink.

'You want to transfer me elsewhere?' Reid finally said to Wheeler.

'It was merely—'

'Now? Before—'

'Before what?' Wheeler said sharply. 'Your work at Morlancourt is almost finished, surely? Surely the place can now be handed over to others to complete the finishing touches? Tell me – how many more bodies are you actually anticipating?'

'I'm not sure,' Reid said absently. 'A hundred – fewer. There's no definite—'

Complete the finishing touches.

'There you are, then,' Wheeler said, as though his argument were already won.

Reid struggled to remember what remained to be done at the cemetery. The bodies coming to him now – the nurses and those retrieved from Prezière excepted – were mostly 'prior retrievals', gathered in from the surrounding district. The men from Prezière would in all likelihood be the last large consignment of new discoveries. It was the same in all the cemeteries, so long after the war's end. It was why the Commission's work on the giant monuments and the much larger national cemeteries was now of such interest to Wheeler.

'And the remaining graves required are already plotted, at least, if not actually dug?' Wheeler said, drawing Reid back from these thoughts.

It was why Wheeler had wanted to see the plans: so that everything might now be handed over to someone else.

'Yes,' Reid said. 'More or less.' He felt like a man being pushed in his chest, never allowed to regain his balance and to push back.

'I often cite your work at Morlancourt to all our more recent appointees,' Wheeler said. '"Go and see him," I tell them. "Go and see Reid. Any doubts on how to proceed – go and see old Reid over at Morlancourt."' He smiled at the remark, at the rhyme of the words.

It was another of the man's tactics – to confuse and divert with easy flattery.

'And so you'll consider my proposal?'

'For me to leave?' Reid could still not fully grasp what was being asked – demanded? Ordered? – of him.

'For you to continue your excellent work elsewhere, to share your expertise with those in sore need of it, and to give to others what you have selflessly and tirelessly given at Morlancourt, yes.'

'Selflessly *and* tirelessly,' Lucas said, returning to them with a drink in his hand.

'Lieutenant Lucas,' Wheeler shouted at him, his temper finally breaking, 'I would appreciate it if – as very much behoves even a junior officer of your rank and distinction – you could keep at least some of your uncharitable thoughts to yourself. You fool no one, Lieutenant Lucas, no one. Yes, you, too, have worked selflessly and tirelessly on our behalf, I *know* that, we *all* know that. But there is only so much leeway, so much slack, that I am prepared – that I am *able* – to grant, even to you. I am by nature a tolerant man, Lieutenant Lucas, but I should perhaps give you notice here and now that my tolerance has its limits. Your behaviour today . . .' He stopped speaking, letting the remark hang.

'Then I apologize unreservedly,' Lucas said eventually.

'And mean nothing by it,' Wheeler said calmly. 'Captain Reid?'

'I'll consider it,' Reid said.

'That is all I ask,' Wheeler said, finally turning away from Lucas, and afterwards ignoring him completely.

'I still have things to do,' Reid said.

'Of course you do, of course. No one is suggesting that a new position be found for you tomorrow. Of course you have things to do. All I need to know is that you are agreeable to the notion. No one is suggesting that there is any true urgency in the matter. As you can well imagine, the work in these outer realms – Mesopotamia, wherever – proceeds at a considerably slower pace than it does here. No one is asking you to pack your bags tonight.'

Mesopotamia? Had Wheeler even made that much clear before?

For a moment, Reid wondered if that was exactly what Wheeler *was* now suggesting to him – that the transfer *had* already been arranged and confirmed elsewhere, as though his own acceptance of the idea of relocation was just the final stamp on a mound of otherwise completed and waiting papers, and as though this *fait accompli* were considerably more imminent than he could ever imagine.

'I have Caroline Mortimer's nurses to take care of,' he said, the thought and words coming to him simultaneously.

'Of course you do,' Wheeler said. 'And you are precisely the man for the job. Precisely the man. I daresay Mrs Mortimer herself would countenance no other. And I daresay she will be as happy and as relieved as the rest of us when the work here is done and she, too, is finally able to return home, to move on to pastures new.'

He waited for Reid to agree with him, but Reid, still absorbing everything he had just been told, remained silent.

And then, with no indication that he was about to leave, Wheeler walked briskly to where he had been sitting at the head of the table, picked up his cap and cane and case, and left the room.

'I shall no doubt be in touch,' he called back to Reid as he walked away along the corridor. The door to the room swung shut behind him with a solid click.

For a moment, neither Reid nor Lucas spoke.

Lucas fetched them both drinks.

'Did I actually agree to anything?' Reid said, still uncertain of where he now stood within the machinery of his eventual departure. He looked into the glass he held.

'You're off to live in the desert,' Lucas said, emptying his own glass. 'Like Saint Antony the Hermit.' He held up his watch. 'The train.'

The two men left the hotel and walked to the station.

'You have to admire the man,' Lucas said at one point along their short journey. 'He does know how to set his perfect little traps.'

'And all we know,' Reid said, 'is how to go on blindly wandering into them.'

'Quite,' Lucas said, again mimicking Wheeler. 'Quite.'

Part Three

Part Three

24

'They all used to complain about the chloride of lime put in the water,' Caroline said. 'Every single one of them. Some of the nurses used to fetch jugs from local houses to avoid spoiling the taste of the tea.' She sipped the cup of water she held.

'At the front it was usually the butter,' Reid said. 'Tinned butter. Margarine. It used to melt and then solidify over and over. By the time we opened the tins, it was usually rancid. The men used to throw it away, until it attracted vermin.'

They sat together close by the collapsed bridge over the canal, and beside a late-flowering verge which curved back towards Morlancourt.

'The yellow is charlock,' Caroline said, pointing. 'And the white is wild chamomile. Some of the older nurses used to boil it up to make tea.'

'It sounds disgusting,' Reid said.

'It was. Most of the patients took it, sipped it and pretended to like it, and then threw it away when the women had gone. It was more the act of kindness they appreciated than the drink itself.'

'I was once ordered to gather up all the sheepskin fleeces in my company and then to burn them because of the fleas they harboured. They were a big thing in the winters. The Army and Navy store sent out tens of thousands of the things. The men who'd worked on the land back at home pushed them under their tunics, wool-side innermost. They were very effective.'

'Until the fleas.'

'It was something else you learned to live with. A lot of the men hid their fleeces and went on wearing them. I knew a man in a field survey company who stitched several of the things together to make a cumbersome jacket for himself. He ran an observation group, Royal Engineers. He used to look like a polar bear walking around. The jacket was grey within an hour, and seemed to forever steam. He even had a balaclava made of the stuff. When the order came for them to be collected and burned, he wrote to his MP, telling the man to complain to the War Office on his behalf.'

Caroline smiled. 'Was he successful?'

'I'm not sure. He was killed soon afterwards. He was sent out to set off some Bengal Lights to mark a new line of advance. The story that came back to us was that one of them was faulty and that it blew up in his face rather than burning steadily.' He stopped talking. It was always difficult to prevent these seemingly insignificant tales and recollections from moving towards their abrupt and unavoidable endings. Reid drank from the flask he had with him, then offered the spirit to Caroline, which she drank diluted in her water.

'I was watching a Charlie Chaplin film when I heard he'd been killed,' Reid went on. 'We were good friends. I was in Saint-Quentin. With the Sixteenth Battalion, Manchesters. I can't even remember why I was there. Funny how some small details stay with you while others disappear completely.'

'We showed the films in some of the hospitals,' Caroline said. '"A tonic for the troops". At the Tincourt clearing station, we projected them on to the wall of one of the wards. Everyone looked forward to them, staff and patients alike. Some of the nurses were old enough to be the mothers of the boys in their care.'

They sat in silence for a moment.

'You'll miss the work,' Reid said eventually.

'Nursing the wounded? I suppose I will. I mean, I do. Not that there aren't . . . back at home, I mean.'

'Of course.'

'A lot of the women said the same. Out here they knew that they were doing something important, something of real value to the men under their care. A lot of them will have found it hard to settle back to their lives at home, carrying bed pans and making beds. I knew women out here who were little short of surgeons when the need demanded, especially in the field stations. I'm a dab hand at removing bullets and shrapnel from flesh wounds myself.'

'I'll remember that,' Reid said. He resisted the urge to touch his own faint and waxy scars.

The water beneath them was rippled across its dark surface by the evening breeze. Dense reeds along both banks swayed slightly, and Caroline turned her face back and forth in the draught of cooler air, pulling her collar from her throat. A solitary fisherman stood on the far bank and raised and lowered his pole over the unproductive water.

'I used to sit with the dying men,' Caroline said. 'Some of them wanted me to be their mother, some their wives or sweethearts. All they really wanted, of course, was someone to sit and talk to them. We were told – instructed – to keep all our conversations cheerful, hopeful. "Optimistic of a good outcome" – I think that was the phrase.'

'We were all forever hopeful of that, I suppose,' Reid said.

'Some of them were delirious with their infections. Some of them, I imagine, might even have believed I *was* their mother or sweetheart.'

'What did you say to them?'

'Whatever they wanted to hear. I imagine there was deceit on both sides.'

'Not deceit,' Reid said.

'What else would you call it? Consideration? Compassion?'

'Of course it was compassion,' Reid insisted.

'And after you've done it ten times, twenty, thirty?'

There was nothing Reid could say to this, and so he remained silent. He wondered how much longer the need for all this story-telling, this tying-up of loose, unravelled ends, this release of long-twisted tensions would last. Until they were all returned home? Until a decade had passed? Until another war was started somewhere else? Until the last man and woman of this one had died and been buried and then forgotten?

'I imagine we mean the same thing, whatever words we use,' Caroline said.

'I suppose so.'

'We used to find those French instructions in the men's pockets,' she said. '"*Je suis*," and then their names and outfits, followed by . . .'

'"*En cas d'accident m'apportez au . . .*"'

'That's it,' she said. 'We used to joke with them that there seemed to be an awful lot of "accidents" happening out there and that they really ought to be more careful. The funny thing is, most of them used to ask us constantly when they would be well enough to return to their friends back where all these accidents were happening. Their officers used to come to visit them, especially in the forward field stations, and all some of the wounded ever talked about was being back at the Front and doing their "bit". Even the ones who'd already been told they'd be going home when they were well enough to travel.'

'Even the men who knew they were dying?' Reid said. He regretted asking as soon as he'd said it.

Caroline considered her answer. '*Especially* those who knew they were dying. I suppose they needed to believe it more than most. In Le Havre, I sat with a Highland sergeant. Black Watch. He'd been badly wounded at a place called Zonnebeke, in Belgium.'

'"The Storm of Zonnebeke",' Reid said. 'Third Ypres.'

'A severe stomach wound. It was a miracle that he'd lasted long enough to reach us at base. Sorry, not a "miracle" – luck, chance, the skill of the medical staff who first saw him in the field and clearing stations. Whatever saved him, he came to us with his records already marked up.'

'Meaning?'

'Meaning all *we* could do for him was to make him as comfortable as his injuries allowed.'

'And could you do that?'

'To some extent. His wounds meant he couldn't eat or drink. I spent most of my time with him wiping his face with a cold cloth and holding cigarettes to his mouth. His wounds were mostly undressed. The night he died, he told me everything he could remember about his home and his family. He'd worked in the harbour at Portree on Skye. He was also a part-time farmer and gamekeeper. I told him I'd go and visit the place when the opportunity arose.'

'Was he married?'

'With six children – all girls bar a solitary son. He was anxious because the boy was almost seventeen and keen to join up.'

Reid did a quick calculation and guessed that the war had ended before the boy was old enough to enlist.

'It sounded a good life,' Caroline said. 'He loved his work and his family. He was also an itinerant preacher, and that sustained him, too. I remember him telling me that he knew precisely what had happened to him – his injuries – and what was likely to happen to him now, and that there was no need whatsoever for any pretence on my behalf. He just wanted to talk, to tell me everything that was good about the life he'd lived and all the good he believed he himself had done in the world. He wanted me to *understand* something.'

'The life well-lived?'

'Perhaps. But it was more than that. He never said it, but he wanted me to understand that he had no regrets, even after what had happened to him. Some of the others who overheard him telling me all this, and who also heard his groans when his pain became unbearable, shouted for him to shut up, to talk about something else.'

'Because they couldn't accept the fact that he had resigned himself to dying?'

'And that they ought to reconcile themselves to the same thing happening to some of them. Yes. Some of them even wanted me to leave him alone, to make him fall silent.'

'And did you?'

'He died later that same night, approaching dawn. I stayed with him. I remember the rising sun passing across the wall at the end of the ward. He'd told me it was his favourite part of the day. He recited poetry in Gaelic. Even after all this time I can still remember the exact pitch and tone of his voice. When he knew he was close to the end, he thanked me and asked me to let go of his hand. I laid his arms by his side for him. He asked me to pull the sheet up over his stomach and chest. He closed his eyes and died in an instant, in a breath. I said a prayer over him and then sat for a few minutes thinking about his wife and children. He'd lost all his photographs of them back in Belgium. I suppose the truth is, he just wanted someone to *know* about him, about the man he'd once been before he got caught up in everything here.'

'Of course,' Reid said. He held her arm for a moment.

He remembered the occasion when he and a raiding party had entered the empty German trenches at Serre, where they'd come upon an abandoned, wounded man lying on the floor of the trench, calling on them not to shoot him and holding up in front of his face a photograph of his wife and two young children, as though this were his final flimsy protection in the world. Reid had spoken to him, looking at the photograph and then telling the man to put it safe in his pocket. He had finished his work in the trench and then returned to his starting point. He later filed his report and made no mention of the abandoned man.

He had heard nothing afterwards of the outcome of any of this, and the following day he was withdrawn from the line in the general retreat west.

'One of the visiting officers once referred to the nurses

as "God's Comforters",' Caroline said, interrupting his thoughts. 'I wanted to slap him in the face. No, worse – I wanted to shout at him and to push him out of the ward.' She continued angling her face into the breeze as she said all this, finally tilting back her head and closing her eyes.

Reid tried to remember where the Black Watch and other Highland regiments were now buried, but could not recall. It was another of the Commission's aims eventually to create a giant directory of the burial place or memorial listing of every single man.

After they had sat together for a few minutes longer, Caroline stood up and said she was returning to Morlancourt.

Reid's instinct was to rise and walk with her, but instead he told her he would stay. She leaned over him and kissed him lightly on the forehead.

Across the canal, the distant fisherman raised his pole into the air and walked away across the adjoining field.

It was a world of restless ghosts, Reid thought to himself, all of them wandering blindly in unplotted circles around all those other restless, wandering ghosts.

He remained where he sat for almost an hour longer, and then he too rose from the embankment and returned to Morlancourt in the settling dusk.

25

Following their return from Amiens, Reid saw nothing of Alexander Lucas for the next few days.

On the second day, he received word from Jessop confirming that the bodies of the nurses would be arriving at Morlancourt in a week's time. Jessop also told him that Wheeler was now organizing a ceremony both to mark the nurses' arrival and to accommodate the gathering newspapermen. It was no more or less than Reid had expected. Jessop was also at pains to tell him that the ceremony was now deemed necessary by Wheeler on account of all the good it would serve.

The good it would serve.

Jessop asked him if he was in full agreement with the plan, and Reid told him he was. It seemed a small enough concession to make. He would have arranged it himself had the occasion not already been taken over by Wheeler and made to serve his own purpose. He would have organized it with Caroline Mortimer, and he felt certain that the pair of them would have arranged something considerably more fitting than whatever Wheeler was now proposing.

He sought her out soon afterwards and told her everything Jessop had just confirmed to him. She, in turn, showed him the note she had received directly from Wheeler on the subject. Reid read it and saw how much more definite everything was made to seem, and what a prominent role Wheeler himself would play in the affair. Jonathan Guthrie, no doubt, would also take his part.

'More work for you, I imagine,' she said as Reid handed the sheet of paper back to her.

'Not really,' he said. 'The graves are dug; that's always the hardest part. I suppose you know that Wheeler wants to put on something of a show for the press.'

'I guessed as much by the way he avoids any mention whatsoever of the men jabbing their pencils at him.' She raised her hand to a group of passing local women, who called their greetings to her.

'Is it what you want?' Reid said. 'Most of the cemetery still resembles a building site.' He was careful not to say 'battlefield', which would have been a considerably more accurate description.

'I daresay it hardly matters,' she said. 'To them, I mean – the women.'

'No.'

'You're just angry because the day will now better serve the glorification of Wheeler than—'

'Than the women who deserve that glory ten times more?'

She smiled at the remark. 'Listen to yourself, Captain Reid. Glory, indeed.'

'I daresay neither of us is in a position to deny the man anything he wants,' Reid said.

'We never were. When the idea of burying the nurses out here was first suggested, it was dismissed out of hand. We've come a long way since then. Besides, who's to say that letting the journalists and the photographers watch the whole thing and then write their stories and take their photographs won't all be to the good?'

'Perhaps you're right,' he said.

'But you personally will never agree with that?'

'No,' he said. 'I know there's a demand back home for these things to be done, and for everyone who wants it to participate in some way or other. But to my mind that's not what they're doing, not truly.'

'Because no one who wasn't out here themselves will ever truly grasp what's happening now?'

Even Reid could see how worn that particular line of reasoning had become.

'Let's just see, shall we?' she said, folding Wheeler's note and pushing it into her pocket.

Ever since his confrontation with Wheeler in Amiens, Reid had started to prepare himself for his removal to the periphery of the man's concerns. To Reid, the path that once lay before him in France and then, presumably, back at home, which had seemed so straightforward and definite – *preordained*, almost – had now suddenly disappeared, leaving only this unknown and unknowable terrain ahead of him.

'Has anyone said anything to you about Guthrie's involvement in the occasion?' he asked her.

'Nothing. But you know as well as I do that the pair of them ride around on each other's coat-tails. Perhaps I ought to get in touch with him and find out what he intends doing.'

Before Reid could say any more, they were interrupted by the noisy arrival of a lorry, which drew up beside them where they stood on the narrow street.

'My transport to the cemetery,' he said. He'd been waiting

for the lorry when the message from Jessop had arrived, followed shortly afterwards by Caroline. 'Now that we know what's definitely going to happen, I'll get as much ready as possible,' he said. 'Wheeler will want the place looking its best.'

He climbed up beside the driver and sat looking down at her as the man struggled with and swore at his gearstick, which refused to move. He warned the driver about the language he was using.

Eventually, the lever came free and they started their journey. When Reid looked back, he saw that Caroline had already gone from the street.

There had been no new bodies on the train earlier, only supplies and an additional forty stones, and these had been unloaded and then taken to the cemetery under Drake's supervision.

The sergeant was waiting for him when he finally arrived there.

Reid told him everything he could about the arrival of the nurses and the ceremony that was about to take place. As usual, Drake knew most of this already. The two men walked together to the waiting graves.

'It's a good plot,' Drake said. 'Get the grass down and the planting finished and we can then put some seating at the back of the graves. It'll be a good view for anyone sitting there.'

They went to the spot indicated by Drake, and Reid saw what an overview of the place the slightly elevated site afforded them.

'Will we be ready, do you think?' he asked him.

'If we're not, then they'll have to take us as they find us.

What's Wheeler going to do, call the whole thing off?'

Reid shielded his eyes and looked at the work going on around them. The flooded graves had been pumped dry and made secure. Mounds of chippings had been delivered to help with the finished drainage.

'We'll need to prepare some ground close to the graves for the newspapermen to gather,' he said. 'Something to make the place look less . . . less . . .'

'Less like the unfinished graveyard that it is?' Drake said, smiling. 'I wouldn't worry too much about that if I were you. The photographers will be far more interested in getting their pictures of Wheeler and the other bigwigs all turned out in their pomp and glory. You know how these things work.'

'I suppose so,' Reid said, reassured by the sergeant's understanding and acceptance of everything that was about to happen.

'They want their show, that's all,' Drake said. 'It's all some of them *ever* wanted.'

Reid said nothing in reply to this. He continued looking over the site around them. In an enclosure by the entrance, the brilliantly white stones had been stacked in rows, ready to be taken to the waiting graves. Nearby, a cloud of blue exhaust fumes hung above a group of men still engaged in unloading that morning's cargo. Elsewhere, men worked alone and in pairs, smaller parties than usual now that the majority of the graves had been excavated and the paths, lawns and flower beds were being prepared. The rows of completed graves, their stones already in place, ran in broken lines throughout this apparent confusion. A definite order was finally emerging wherever he looked around the site.

At the cemetery's edge, a line of French labourers swung their scythes through the tall grass and undergrowth, the dry stems falling neatly behind the cutters. The smell of wood smoke drifted over the scene from the small fires the men insisted on lighting, whatever the day's heat, to brew their tea.

'It's a rare sight,' Drake said absently. 'All this. I daresay when the place is finished, you'll never even know we were here.'

'I imagine that's the whole point of the exercise as far as some are concerned,' Reid said. He took the cigarette Drake offered him.

He saw where the outermost of the pale, narrow paths had been laid, reaching towards the cemetery's edges like the thinning branches of a tree.

After a moment of silence, Drake said, 'Do you think it will ever happen again?'

Reid wondered what to say to him. 'I don't see how it can,' he said eventually. 'At least, not like this.'

'I wouldn't put anything past us now,' Drake said.

'"Us"?'

'Us. You and me. The men in charge. The men doing their bidding. To my mind, we've done it once, we'll do it again.'

It surprised Reid to hear him talking like this, revealing a part of himself Reid had never seen before.

'We're soldiers,' Drake went on. 'What else are we *for*?'

Reid couldn't agree with this, but neither could he bring himself to counter Drake's honest reckoning. He lifted his eyes and scanned the horizon, already lost in the day's haze. Everywhere he looked, there was nothing to distinguish between the bleached colours of the land and the pale, almost colourless sky above. Birds flew and called above the trees; snatches of noise, of conversation and laughter rose muted and distorted from the men and machinery below.

'Eighty-two degrees,' Drake said. 'Benoît. The thermometer in his office. Warmest day yet, apparently.' He wiped his face on his sleeve.

The two men walked to where the nurses' waiting graves lay. Some of the holes still contained a man with a shovel straightening the sides and rims of the cut earth. Elsewhere in the cemetery, the early graves had been dug unevenly from the ground, but these now were receiving all the care and attention of graves prepared in a small country churchyard.

At the arrival of Reid and Drake, the men climbed out of their holes and congregated at the mound of their discarded tunics and shirts.

Reid left Drake with the diggers and walked towards the entrance alone. As he passed the other labouring men, and despite his earlier reservations about the forthcoming ceremony, he could not help but feel that, however premature or contrived the occasion might prove to be, it did at least mark a vital junction in his own time and work there – another of those hitherto unsuspected boundaries he was about to cross, beyond which nothing could ever remain the same for him.

Some men, he knew, embraced all possible change and uncertainty in their lives ahead, whereas others clung with a kind of desperation to the known and the dependable and the endlessly reassuring to support and guide them. France, Mesopotamia, England – what, really, did it matter where he was, or what work he undertook there, when the world might never again turn soundly on its axis, and when none of its usual checks and balances might ever right themselves?

What if Drake had been right in his speculation and the same thing *were* to happen all over again? And then again after that, and again after that.

He felt the sweat gather and run on his brow and cheeks. He walked to the cemetery's edge, and then beyond, following a narrow path into the abandoned, weed-filled fields, where he was finally alone and unobserved, and where all he could hear was the humming and droning of the insects he disturbed as he continued his wandering at the height of the day's stifling heat.

26

Reid next saw Alexander Lucas two days later, and when he remarked on the man's recent absence from Morlancourt, Lucas said simply that he'd been unable to return each evening because of the work he was now undertaking at La Chapelette. It seemed an uncharacteristically dismissive thing for him to say, but Reid, aware of Lucas's greater concerns, did not pursue the matter.

Their encounter took place shortly after Reid's return from the cemetery to his room, where Lucas sought him out and asked if he wanted to go for a drink. Despite Lucas's abrupt remarks of only a moment earlier, Reid knew immediately that the seemingly casual invitation was much more than that.

The two men walked in silence to the small bar at the end of the street.

Reid's first impulse upon arriving there was to sit as usual at one of the tables which lined the road, but Lucas insisted on them going inside. It was much cooler in the small room, and little of the early-evening sunlight penetrated its half-shuttered windows.

Lucas pointed to a corner table and then went to the bar alone, returning with a bottle and glasses.

'I went to Amiens,' he said eventually, draining his glass and sitting with both his palms pressed to the table.

Reid considered what he was being told. 'In connection with more retrievals?'

'To see Muir and apply to him directly for leave. I received another message from Elizabeth's mother.' Gregory Muir was Lucas's own Graves Registration Officer, now Wheeler's superior in the Commission.

'Is your wife no better?' Reid asked him. He wondered at Lucas's change of heart. He refilled both their glasses. The air in the bar was thick with dust and smoke. A pall of this already hung above the tables containing the room's few other drinkers, a group of local men quietly playing cards.

Lucas shook his head. 'It's not just that. My daughter is now ill.'

'With similar symptoms? I mean—'

'It seems so,' Lucas said.

'I'm sure that—'

'And the War Office, according to Muir, is refusing all requests for compassionate leave for the next two months.'

'On what grounds?'

Lucas shook his head at the question. 'Apparently, if I'd applied when I first heard my wife was unwell . . .'

'What? You would have been successful?'

'Perhaps.'

'But there are *always* exceptions,' Reid said.

'Muir assured me he had every sympathy, but that the War Office is being very insistent. The only men being allowed back are those at the end of their time who have no intention of ever returning here.'

'What are they afraid of?' Reid said.

'The way Muir told it, it all made perfect sense, and he made it perfectly clear to me, given the circumstances, that *I* was the one behaving unreasonably.'

'Did he say when the restriction would be lifted?' It was beyond Reid to suggest to Lucas that he might now change his own mind and accept the office work back at home that Wheeler would be only too happy to arrange for him. He wondered at the man's insistence on staying this long. He wondered, too, at the true nature of the balance that had been tipped now that Lucas's daughter was ill and not just his wife.

'He told me that over three hundred men died of the influenza at Amiens hospital alone during that first winter,' Lucas said.

'Influenza? But this is a different thing entirely, surely? They must know that much, at least.'

'Perhaps,' Lucas said. 'And perhaps they've just finally decided to stop taking chances. Perhaps it really is as simple as that. Or perhaps the Army doesn't want to lose any more of its labour force while the weather's so good and while so much remains to be done. The autumn and then the winter will be here soon enough. You can see their point.'

'Not where men like you and I are concerned,' Reid said. 'You, especially. Surely, Muir could acknowledge that much, at least?'

'Because I deserve special treatment? He waved the War Office order in my face. You know as well as I do how these men pick and choose their responsibilities.'

Neither of them spoke for a moment, and then Reid said, 'Some of them behave as though they wish the war were still running its course.'

'I came to *that* conclusion a long time ago,' Lucas said. 'I was with Muir a month before the end, when everything looked cut and dried, when he announced to the room that it seemed a great pity to him that we seemed to be losing the will to continue fighting with our earlier vigour – they were his words – and that it was an equal pity that the retreating Germans couldn't be "forced to bleed" for a few months longer to secure a proper peace afterwards.' He raised his glass. 'To "proper peace".'

Reid left his own glass on the table. 'What will you do?' he said.

'What *can* I do?' Lucas said loudly, causing the nearby card players to pause in their game and look across at him. He signalled his apology to them and the men returned to their game.

'Perhaps you should have gone to Wheeler first,' Reid said, already knowing how the suggestion would be received.

'If you say so. All the time I was talking to Muir he was fiddling with a pair of white kid gloves, stretching them over his fingers, tamping them tight. He told me he'd only just received them, a gift from his wife on their wedding anniversary, don't you know. When he knew I wasn't going to persist with my request, he relaxed and asked me what the shooting was like hereabouts.'

'The shooting?'

'He led his local hunt back at home. He has a painting on his wall of Saint George slaying the dragon. I imagine it's a great reassurance to him.'

'I daresay he sees himself up on the horse.'

'I'm sure he does,' Lucas said.

After a further brief silence, Reid said, 'What, exactly, have you heard about your daughter?'

'Only that she has a fever and is unable to eat or drink. The same early symptoms as Elizabeth. The letter was four days old again. It wasn't that long ago that we had mail from home within a day.'

'No urgency now, I suppose,' Reid said.

'None whatsoever. I bumped into Jessop in Amiens. When he insisted on me telling him why I was there, he told me I should have gone to him first, that he could have saved me a wasted journey. Perhaps I should change my request and ask to accompany you into the desert instead and search out my bones there.'

'Which you would stand considerably less chance of ever identifying.'

'Perhaps not. But, then again, perhaps identification isn't the great be-all and end-all men like Wheeler and his crew keep insisting it is.' Lucas turned in his chair and called for the barman to bring them another bottle.

When the man had done this, and as Reid paid him, Lucas said, 'You remember your sergeant remarking that he'd spoken to a man called Anderson? Battle Police?'

'Who'd known you? At Ginchy?' Reid struggled to remember what else Drake might have said, but nothing came to him.

'Jessop was also at Ginchy. There was an occasion when he was waiting for me and a reconnaissance party to get back to one of our observation posts before an assault the next day. We'd been out all night, the best part of ten hours. Myself and nine others.'

233

'What happened?'

'We were caught by a lucky German flare and then machine-gunned. Somebody in our trenches had loaded tracers by mistake, and when they returned fire, they aimed them directly over us.'

'Alerting everyone to the gun's position?'

'And ours directly ahead of it. The tracers had probably been intended for anti-aircraft fire.'

'What happened?' Reid said again, already guessing.

'I lost five men, all killed,' Lucas said. 'The rest of us took shelter in a sunken lane, a hundred yards from our line, much the same from theirs. Nothing happened after that. A few more flares – ours, mostly; someone hadn't told the idiot firing them that we were still out there trying to keep our heads down. Two of the men I lost made it to the lane and then died there of their wounds. One man – my sergeant, a man called Howitt – was shot in the neck; the other – Howitt's cousin, as it happened – was hit twice in the stomach. You can imagine the wounds and the men's chances. They were both dead within minutes of me strapping them up. Those of us who were left sat with them for the rest of the night and then came back to our line an hour before dawn. I daresay if we'd waited where we were, then the following day's assault troops would have found us soon enough.'

'Either that, or our barrage,' Reid said.

'I don't think one was ever planned. It was open country-side, still farmed. I doubt the place had ever been even lightly shelled. When I got back, I went to write my report, sat down at a table in the farmhouse where I was billeted, and fell asleep. Jessop found me and woke me two hours later.

I'd missed stand-to. The assault had been and gone, and I'd missed that, too. Not that anyone except Jessop seemed to notice. The assault had found only empty trenches. No one was injured; no one was even fired on. The men who'd taken part walked back singing from the old enemy line. Jessop said he'd seen the same thing happen elsewhere. He said the Germans, expecting to see us first thing, would fall back, and that they'd then creep forward into the line after we'd returned to our own trenches. When we received the order to go back and occupy the same supposedly empty trenches the following day, *then* they'd be waiting for us. To make sure this wasn't what was happening at Ginchy, Jessop said I'd been ordered to go back out on a similar patrol that same night. I told him to find someone else. I'd been out four times in the previous week. Apart from those five men, I'd already lost two others only days earlier. The sector had been quiet for months. I told Jessop that all we were achieving with the patrols was to stir things up. Muir was our CO at the time and Jessop sent for him.'

'What did Muir say to your objections?'

'My refusal? What *could* he say, especially in front of Jessop? He told me I was disobeying an order and that there would be consequences.'

'What happened?'

'Jessop insisted I be written up on a charge of Cowardice in the Face of the Enemy.'

'And did Muir agree with Jessop in laying charges?'

'Not a bit of it. Bloodthirsty he might have been, but Muir was never a man for digging out trouble where it didn't exist. His first instinct was to throw the thing out – to deal with it himself – but Jessop was insistent. The Battle Police came for me less than an hour later. It didn't help matters that I'd fallen asleep where I sat at the table. While they were handcuffing me, Muir said he'd get in touch with General Headquarters, and that in the unlikely event of a Field Court ever being convened, then he'd speak in my favour, along with the few remaining men who were with me that night at Ginchy.'

'I take it the court was never called,' Reid said.

'Muir finally managed to get the whole thing thrown out. It seems Jessop had done the same thing twice before. Two men are still in military prisons because of him. The matter was further helped by the fact that when we did finally get back to the German line, and contrary to what Jessop had suggested, they'd withdrawn even further than on that first night.'

'And now you think Jessop is still whispering into Wheeler's ear?'

'He can't help himself,' Lucas said. 'So you see where I stand.'

'In no real position to push Muir into doing *anything* for you.'

'Something like that.'

'And Jessop will presumably have repeated to Wheeler everything he already knows about you.'

'I daresay it's a card Wheeler is happy to keep up his sleeve until the need to play it arises. After the Armistice, Muir waited until a few days before he was due to return to England and then sought Jessop out to tell him exactly what he thought of him. He did it in front of a crowd of others, and when he'd finished they applauded him.'

'And you? At Ginchy, I mean.'

'Muir sent me out of the line for a month. I went to Boulogne to take charge of a new depot there. When I got back, I found that Jessop had also been transferred. Our paths never crossed again until he turned up all spick and span, sitting alongside Wheeler in Amiens.'

Reid wondered why Lucas had told him none of this before, but knew that these were the stories some men – those men like Lucas – quickly left behind them as they prepared to return to the paths of their other lives. It also occurred to him that this might have been why Lucas had turned up at the station on the day the executed man was delivered there. It was beyond him to ask.

Several new customers came into the bar and sat at the tables closer to them. Reid and Lucas exchanged greetings with the men, who then began their own sparse, subdued conversations.

In the short time they had been there, the smoke in the small room had thickened considerably, and was drawn in elaborate, shifting patterns around every movement. The cloud across the dirty ceiling had sunk lower, and was now pierced at the front of the bar by the thin rays of the falling sun.

Reid told Lucas about the confirmed delivery of the nurses' bodies and how Wheeler proposed to mark their arrival.

'I heard,' Lucas said, but showed little interest in the matter.

The two men parted an hour later, and rather than return to his room, Reid walked in the last of the day's warmth to where the railway crossed the Sailly canal. He stood on the metal bridge and looked down into the barely flowing water. The sides of the bridge were still warm to his touch, and he waited where he stood, his hands on the parapet, until the sun finally dropped to the distant horizon and then sank into the land, drawing down the darkness all around it.

27

Reid walked what he imagined to be the final mile from the Bray road to the cemetery at Fricourt; now that there was a brief lull in his own work, he had been asked by Wheeler to report on the early excavations there. It was a plot of around two hundred graves currently in its laying-out phase, and was expected to contain a mass grave of men of the Tenth West Yorkshires. The surrounding land was open and sparse.

At the junction of the Maricourt road, a field of irretrievable vehicles lay abandoned, overgrown and rusting in the heat – lorries, mostly, but with gun limbers and a few dismantled artillery pieces among them.

As he approached the field, Reid saw men moving amid all this waste – metal dealers, he guessed, from either Bray or Etinhem. A sudden fountain of sparks and the loud banging of heavy hammers revealed where they were already at work salvaging whatever remained of value to them. He paused at the gateway, where others stood with their horses and carts, waiting to take the metal away.

He asked the men if much remained to be retrieved, and they told him, in their usual guarded manner, that they would make scarcely any profit on what little they were able to take. It occurred to him only then, listening to the men decry their labours, that they were there illegally, stealing the metal rather than collecting it under contract from the Army.

'Have you been sent?' one of the men asked him suspiciously, confirming this guess.

He reassured them that he had no connection whatsoever with the field of abandoned scrap, and told them of his visit to the nearby cemetery. The men relaxed at hearing this, and offered him water from their clay pots. Reid accepted and gave them cigarettes in return.

'Where's your car?' one of them asked him.

Reid explained that he didn't have one, and that he'd been given a lift only as far as the lane's end. They offered to lend him one of their horses, saying that the animal would make its own way back to them if he released it at the cemetery gate.

'It's not *that* far, surely?' Reid said. He had only visited the place once before – a week after his arrival in Morlancourt – and he guessed it now to be close by the next long bend in the road.

The wreckers shared smiles at this, but did not persist.

'They tell us these places are full of dangerous ammunition, corroded shells and gas canisters,' one man said.

'But only to keep you away?' Reid said, causing them all to laugh.

Several of their companions arrived, leading horses which dragged large pieces of metal behind them, just as foresters used the animals to clear away felled trunks.

Another of the men told him of the tales they heard of those being killed and maimed by the unexploded shells still being ploughed up as the surrounding land was returned to its original use.

'Are you not afraid of disturbing something?' Reid asked them.

'The whole country has been disturbed,' one of them said simply. 'What is this compared to that?'

Reid guessed by the way those standing beside this speaker fell silent and then briefly bowed their heads that they knew something of the man's own losses during that greater disturbance.

'Of course,' he said.

A man arrived dragging an engine behind his horse. The others shouted at him that the engine was worthless, that there were hundreds already salvaged and repaired in every garage and workshop within fifty miles of the place. The remark prompted further loud and prolonged laughter and protestations.

Reid thanked the men for the water and resumed his journey towards Fricourt.

Turning the bend in the road, he was disappointed to see that the village was still not in sight ahead of him, and then surprised to see a car coming along the road towards him.

He stood to one side to let the car pass, but as it came close it slowed and then drew to a stop beside him. Reid was surprised again to see Jonathan Guthrie sitting beside the driver.

'I was on my way to the plot at Fricourt,' Reid explained. He hadn't seen the chaplain since their encounter a week earlier in the company of Caroline Mortimer at the small bar.

'Walking?' Guthrie said. He took off the goggles he wore, revealing the circles of paler flesh around his eyes and making himself look both startled and ridiculous.

'Only from the Bray road.'

'But still . . .' Guthrie looked back and forth along the empty lane.

'You?' Reid said.

'I've just been to the same spot,' Guthrie said, pointing in the direction of the place.

'The West Yorkshires?'

'Colonel Abrahams. He's a friend of my father. Seventh Green Howards. Knowing I was close by, he asked me to pop over and take a look. Infantry, not many, ten or twenty or so. He wanted me to see that they were all safely delivered and then to say a few words. Apparently there'll be no official opening ceremony as such.'

'And you were given a car?' Reid asked him. And a driver.

'Seek and ye shall find, ask and ye shall receive. Captain Jessop gave me a chit for the transport depot. When I told them I didn't drive, they threw in the driver.'

The man beside Guthrie leaned forward and raised his hand to Reid.

Reid wondered how much Guthrie already knew of his recent visit to Amiens. He wondered, too, what the man was preparing for the arrival of the nurses at Morlancourt.

'If I'd known you were coming this way, I could have diverted and given you a lift,' Guthrie said.

A distant loud bang – metal on metal – distracted them both and Reid told Guthrie about the men scavenging amid the abandoned lorries.

'Stealing, you mean?' Guthrie said.

'I'm not sure. I suppose they see it as a way of getting back on their feet.'

Guthrie shook his head at the remark. 'More excuses,' he

said. 'These people take advantage at every possible opportunity. We make every conceivable effort on their behalf, and all they do in return is complain and then do the opposite of what we ask of them. The diggers at Fricourt, and beyond at the Highland cemetery, are mostly locals. You should give thanks that you employ soldiers. Apparently the Germans are also looking to build a cemetery at Fricourt.' He smiled. 'I'd like to see them get that one past the Commission.'

'Of course,' Reid said, unwilling to rise to the man's remarks.

More noises distracted them and Guthrie said that perhaps he ought to go and speak to the men. He asked Reid how many he had counted there.

'I didn't,' Reid said. 'Count them.'

'Still . . .'

'Besides, I doubt you'd be telling them anything they didn't already know,' Reid said.

'And perhaps that's precisely why I *should* say something,' Guthrie said.

'Do whatever you see fit,' Reid said. 'Though I doubt they'd appreciate—' He stopped abruptly.

'Appreciate what? Appreciate being told of their wrongdoing by a man like me?' Guthrie touched the collar he wore.

Reid stayed silent for a moment, and then said, 'They consider it their *right*, their due. Something from which they might benefit rather than lose, for once.'

Guthrie shook his head at this, as though Reid were an ignorant child and he a wise teacher.

Only then did it occur to Reid that if Guthrie *did* confront the men, they might consider him to have been sent to admonish them by Reid. 'It's not really any of our business,' he said, but with little conviction.

Guthrie remained silent. He looked at his watch and then at the driver beside him, who now sat with his head back and his eyes closed as though he were asleep. Guthrie finally rubbed at the fine dust which covered most of his face. 'I ought to be getting back,' he said eventually. 'Let Abrahams know that his happy warriors are all safely settled. He wants me to go and dine with him in Paris. Perhaps a few days back in civilization will help to raise my flagging spirits.'

'I daresay,' Reid said.

Guthrie looked around them. 'I sometimes wonder if our continued wandering in this particular wilderness doesn't begin to have an adverse effect on us all. A change of air, of scenery, perhaps that's what's required to encourage us all in our endeavours.' He paused. 'Edmund told me of the proposition he'd put to you, about your own imminent change of scenery.'

'Imminent?' Reid said, wishing he'd contained the word and everything it revealed to Guthrie.

'I told him you were a fortunate man indeed. It was always my own ambition to visit the Holy Land, and is something I shall no doubt undertake when my labours in this neck of the woods are less in demand.'

'Wherever I go, I'll still be burying the dead,' Reid said, again wishing he'd remained silent.

'And a noble and much—' Guthrie began to say, when he was silenced by a further loud bang – an actual explosion this time; a small one, perhaps, but definitely an explosion – from the direction of the field around the curve in the road.

Both Reid and Guthrie turned to look. The driver woke with a start and stood up to scan the nearby land. In the distance, a thin plume of pale smoke rose into the air above where the wreckers worked.

Other than the driver dropping back to his seat, none of the three men spoke or moved for a moment.

Then Guthrie said, 'As you say, I imagine they well understood the risks they were taking.'

'Perhaps we should go to them and see if anyone's injured,' Reid said.

'We'll know soon enough,' Guthrie said.

Several minutes later, a slow-moving horse and cart appeared on the road ahead of them, four men sitting abreast on its plank seat.

They came without any apparent urgency to where Guthrie and Reid awaited them. Arriving alongside the car, one of the men Reid had spoken to earlier showed them his loosely bandaged, bleeding hand.

'Was no one else injured?' Reid asked the men.

All four of them shook their heads.

'Where are you taking him?'

'To the doctor at Fricourt,' one said.

'And after that to Mametz to make a claim for compensation,' another added, at which all four men burst into laughter.

The man with the bandaged hand unwound the cloth to show his injury to Reid. Blood pooled in the man's palm and was smeared along his forearm.

'Can you move all your fingers?' Reid asked him. He had asked fifty other men the same question.

The man clenched and opened his fist several times, causing fresh blood to flow. He refastened his bandage. Reid guessed the blood would be even more in evidence by the time the men arrived in Mametz.

After that, the driver of the cart shook his reins and the horse continued on its slow journey.

When the men were beyond hearing, Guthrie said, 'See?' He then told his driver to start the engine and continue their own journey back to Amiens. 'I daresay I shall see you in Morlancourt very soon,' he said to Reid as he slid the goggles back over his eyes.

'Of course,' Reid said.

The car left him, making a faltering, chugging sound as it gathered speed along the road. Reid stood and watched it go. He looked in the direction of the smoke, but it had already thinned and drifted and was now barely visible where it rose off the land.

28

The following morning, the whole of Morlancourt knew about the imminent arrival of Caroline Mortimer's nurses.

Reid learned this from Benoît, who came out of his office the instant Reid arrived on the platform. Again, as during the previous few days, there were no bodies to be unloaded, only further supplies and materials sent by Wheeler in advance of the forthcoming ceremony.

It seemed to Reid as though the demands and diversions of only a week earlier had all now either ceased to exist or were being held in abeyance by Wheeler until the women were delivered and then buried. Everything, he realized, was reaching its natural conclusion in the place, his own authority and tenure there included.

He saw from the docket Jessop had sent him the previous evening that the load being delivered to them that particular morning included several hundred folding chairs, plank walkways, scaffolding and a marquee complete with all its poles and ropes, and he saw immediately how much extra work was involved in the unloading and then setting-up of all of this.

Having emerged from his office, Benoît waited while

Reid told Drake and the waiting men what to expect. There were fewer men than usual, and Drake explained to Reid that those who were absent had finally received their discharge papers and were refusing to continue working at the cemetery. There had been no reasoning with the frustrated, impatient men, and no orders had come from Commission Headquarters insisting that they continue.

'The men in charge don't want any more riots,' Drake said softly. 'They've pushed people too far and now they're paying the price.'

'They could at least send us some new arrivals,' Reid said, already calculating how to complete the work now being demanded of him with this reduced workforce.

'There's no stopping some of them once they've got their travel warrants in their hands,' Drake said. 'They'll all be waking up drunk in either Boulogne or Calais some time later this morning. And this time tomorrow, they'll be doing the same in Birmingham, Manchester and Liverpool. I doubt if any of them will ever pick up a spade again.'

Reid smiled at the remark. As usual, Drake seemed considerably less concerned by the loss than he was.

'How many are still here?'

'Sixty-two,' Drake said.

At the height of the work, Reid had commanded almost two hundred men. Recently, since the bulk of the actual graves had been dug and the work had turned to preparing the appearance of the cemetery, this number had been halved. Now he had lost almost forty of those men overnight.

'Spilt milk,' Drake said. 'We'll manage.'

'Of course we will. We always do.' Reid left the men and went to where Benoît awaited him.

Benoît beckoned him into his office, and Reid saw by the way the man avoided his eyes until the two of them were finally sitting facing each other that something was wrong.

'Your nurses will finally come,' Benoît said. 'I have been instructed by my own superiors to assist you in any way possible. They have offered to send more men if necessary.'

'Thank them for me,' Reid said. 'I doubt it will involve much – not here at the station, at least. The Commission will want to put on its main show at the cemetery itself.'

'Of course.'

'Apparently, we're kowtowing to the newspapers and to public demand back in England.'

Benoît did not understand the phrase and so Reid explained himself.

'But surely that's a good thing,' Benoît said. 'For the people back in England to see.'

'It's what Wheeler and his superiors clearly believe.'

It had also been rumoured that other Commission members and an array of invited guests would now attend the ceremony. None of this information had been delivered to Reid directly, and this angered him as much as the lack of forewarning concerning his depleted labour force.

'They're sending two hundred chairs today,' he said.

'Two hundred,' Benoît repeated, considerably more impressed by this than Reid.

It had even been rumoured that representatives from both the War Office and the Medical Council were also coming over from London to participate in the event, so great was the demand from the newspapers. And with every one of these tales and rumours, Reid saw yet again how far beyond his own control the ceremony had now moved.

'They were brave women,' Benoît said. 'To come here and do what they did.'

'They were indeed,' Reid said.

'And Mrs Mortimer has worked hard to achieve all this on their behalf.'

'She has.'

Benoît busied himself preparing them coffee.

When this was ready, Benoît surprised Reid by taking a bottle of cognac from the drawer in his desk and pouring them both a glass. It was not yet seven in the morning. Soon the whistle would sound at the canal halt and a few minutes later the train would appear.

Finally, waiting until they had both sipped the spirit, Benoît said, 'They're closing the railway. The branch line and the station. It seems we are soon no longer to serve any true purpose.'

'Following the completion of the cemetery?'

'And the others by the river, yes. Temporary narrow-gauge lines can be more easily laid and operated where necessary.'

Reid could think of nothing to say to the man.

Benoît must have long since realized that the line would soon close, but this knowledge had clearly done little to cushion the blow now that it had finally been confirmed.

Reid knew that Benoît had been born only three miles from Morlancourt, and that he had lived and worked there all of his life – almost sixty years.

'There's a great new plan for the whole country,' Benoît said, sipping his cognac again. 'Hereabouts, especially. From Paris to the coast, and east into Belgium.'

'I daresay a great deal was destroyed and damaged,' Reid said.

'Of course. And now, we are told, each and every one of us must grasp this unique and precious opportunity to build anew for the glory of France in the future. Mile upon mile of lesser lines will become redundant, replaced by new and direct connections and by new and better roads.'

'Including here?' Reid said. He put down his glass and sipped the bitter coffee instead.

'The main line will now run directly from Amiens to Saint-Quentin. I am told that I will be offered an opportunity to apply for work in the stations there.'

Every word Benoît spoke pushed him further away from the likelihood of this ever happening. Besides, it was unlikely that he had any intention of leaving his own small kingdom of Morlancourt or of applying for any kind of work in either of these much larger places.

'Is that a possibility?' Reid said.

'It would mean going to live elsewhere,' Benoît said. 'Otherwise how would I get there and back every day once the railway has gone?'

'You might consider—'

'Besides, my wife would never leave.'

Reid was glad the brief pretence was over.

'Twenty years ago, perhaps, ten even,' Benoît went on. 'But not now. She would never abandon Pierre.'

And neither would you.

'Of course,' Reid said. It was the beginning and the end of all Benoît's reasoning and argument. 'Will you retire, then?' he said.

'I'm fifty-eight. All my wife ever really wanted was to become the grandmother to a brood of noisy, demanding grandchildren. It was once all the consolation she sought for her hard life.' He sipped his coffee and brandy in succession.

'When will it happen?' Reid asked him.

'They say within the year. The two others here have already made up their minds to go to Saint-Quentin. They're young men. They have no true commitments here beyond their parents. Besides, both served in the war and both were wounded. We may not provide such grand burial grounds for our own dead, but France has always been a good mother at pushing certain of her children to the front of certain queues. I don't blame them – it's a great opportunity for them. If they stayed in this backwater they would only turn slowly and unhappily into me.' He smiled at the suggestion.

'It sometimes seems as though the whole world is about to become a completely different place,' Reid said.

'Oh, I don't doubt it. And nor should you, Captain Reid. We shall all wander amid the ruins and the rubble for a few years more, and then a whole new country filled with prosperous towns and factories and farms will slowly rise up around us. All this suffering must surely one day be repaid. Surely, one day, we shall all see the *purpose* of everything we have just endured.'

Reid said nothing to contradict the man's forced and desperate belief. He wanted to ask Benoît why he insisted on accepting the empty promises made by his own politicians. He wanted to tell him that England hadn't been reduced to ruins and rubble, but that even there things were no better for the ordinary man.

Eventually, Benoît seemed to sag where he sat. He drank the last of his cognac and let out a sigh. 'Do you think *anything* will ever go back to the way it was before?' he said.

'Some things,' Reid said, but did not elaborate.

'Important things – things that matter?'

'I hope so.'

'And for people like me and my wife – all those people for whom things can *never* be the same again?' Benoît looked at the empty glass he held, and for a moment Reid thought he was going to throw it to the ground, or against one of the walls, but instead he set it carefully down on his desk.

'Will there be other changes here in Morlancourt, do you think?' Reid asked him.

Benoît shrugged. 'What can change with the railway gone? We shall just go back to being what we have always been. Perhaps it would have been better for us all if the war *had* come more violently to the place. At least then there would be some *need* for all this grasping of the future.'

It then occurred to Reid that at some of the more recent Commission meetings there had been discussions concerning the employment of local labour to maintain the finished cemeteries. Gardeners would certainly be needed, and occasionally stonemasons and builders. The gates and paths, monuments, memorials and boundaries would have to be tended. The register of burials at each site would have to be kept up to date for visitors to consult. And those same visitors, presumably, would also need knowledgeable guides and somewhere to stay, somewhere to eat and drink, perhaps even someone to drive them back and forth between the new stations and the cemeteries.

He told Benoît all this, but to his surprise and disappointment, the station master showed little real enthusiasm for what he was suggesting.

'It's worth a try, surely?' Reid said.

Eventually, unable to listen to Reid's speculation on all

he was proposing, Benoît said, 'And your Colonel Wheeler
– you truly believe that he would act on *your* recommendation?' He reached out and held Reid's arm for a moment.
'Please, my dear friend, do not prostrate yourself before the
man on my account. These men – our so-called superiors –
they see only themselves in all they do. The rest of us – you
and I, my son, your soldiers – we are all only profit and loss
to them, borrowed honour and other men's glory, that's all.
All that truly matters to these men is their own standing in
the world, their own reputations, bought with the lives and
suffering of others.' He released his hold on Reid's arm, put
both hands in his lap and bowed his head.

After this, neither man spoke for several minutes, both of
them content to sit in silence and listen to the voices of the
men along the platform waiting for the train.

Eventually, a distant whistle sounded. Benoît took out his
watch, looked at it, held it to his ear for a moment, and then
put it back in his pocket.

'Six minutes late,' he said. 'There have been delays at the
canal junction all week. The seven-twenty from Calais to
Charleville will also be running late, and because of that,
the signal at Douai will sit against the drivers for longer
than usual to let the mainline trains through. The two mid-
morning coal trains in from Liège will run late, but no one
will care about them. The drivers won't even bother to try and
make up their time.' He smiled at his simple understanding
of all this, and at the small, inconsequential problems being
encountered by all these other men.

Watching him, Reid saw again how perfectly suited Benoît
had grown to the world he inhabited; how that world and all
its inter-connected and tightly fitting parts had become an

integral part of the man himself; and how, in turn, Benoît had shaped the world around him by the varying measures and degrees of influence and authority he exercised over it.

'So, you see,' the old station master said eventually, breaking the silence between them.

'I do,' Reid said.

Benoît rose and opened his door and walked outside.

Reid waited where he sat for a moment, listening to the gentle rattling of the coffee pot where it sat on the iron stove. Powdery ash fell from the stove to the worn floorboards, adding its own sudden smell of scorching to the room's other odours.

29

Later that day, as Reid arrived back in Morlancourt from his work, he saw Alexander Lucas and Caroline Mortimer sitting together beside the trough at the entrance to the churchyard. As he came closer he saw that Caroline was holding Lucas by his shoulders, and that Lucas was hunched forward, his head down, his hands clasped to his chest. Closer still, and Reid heard that Lucas was crying, the noise muffled by his posture and by Caroline's embrace.

Reid went to them and sat beside Lucas, putting his own arm across the man's back and trying with his other hand to raise Lucas's head from his chest. Lucas tensed at the gesture, and for a moment he remained as he was. But then he re-laxed and slowly raised his head, lowering his hands from his chest to his knees. He wiped his face with his sleeve.

Caroline gave him her handkerchief, and when he refused to take it, she wiped his face herself.

'Elizabeth died,' Lucas said eventually, telling Reid what he had already guessed. Either that, or his daughter.

Lucas dropped the ball of paper he held into Reid's lap. It was a telegram, and Reid flattened it and read it.

Lucas's wife had died two days previously. His daughter, though still suffering, was no worse and was now expected to recover. The message was from Lucas's mother-in-law and said nothing else. No cause of death was mentioned, and no definite diagnosis of what she'd been suffering from. The few stark details seemed devoid of all compassion and understanding, a final cruelty almost. Reading the telegram, Reid was reminded of those he himself had sent during the previous years, all of them containing at least some measure of vague or distant consolation. He folded the paper and put it back into Lucas's waiting hand.

'I'm sorry,' he said.

Lucas turned to face him, but said nothing. Then he turned to Caroline and thanked her for having sat with him.

'Telephone someone,' she said. 'Find out more. Find out about your daughter. Talk to her doctor.'

'I don't even know where she is,' Lucas said absently.

'Then let me do it for you. It surely can't be—'

Lucas rose abruptly at the suggestion. 'No. I mean . . .' He looked around them, at the churchyard and the empty lane.

'At least telephone either Wheeler or Muir,' Reid said. 'Let *someone* know what's happened.'

'*Them?*' Lucas said. He took several paces away from the bench, stopped and turned. He seemed about to say something more, but then he turned again and walked quickly away from them.

'I'll find you later,' Reid called after him, feeling Caroline's hand tighten on his arm to stop him from going after the man.

Lucas raised his hand in reply.

Reid and Caroline then sat without speaking until Lucas was lost to sight.

'I found him here,' Caroline said eventually. 'Almost an hour ago.'

'He applied to Muir for compassionate leave,' Reid said.

'And was refused?'

Reid looked away from her. 'They behave as though the whole thing were still happening,' he said. 'This regulation, that regulation.' He told her what Lucas had told him following his unsuccessful visit to Muir.

'His wife might already have been dead by then,' she said.

'I suppose so.'

'I'm sure everything possible is being done for his daughter,' she said.

'She's five,' Reid said. He lit a cigarette and leaned back on the bench, closing his eyes and feeling suddenly exhausted after his day's work.

'Are you preparing for Monday?' Caroline asked him. She leaned back on the seat and sat close beside him.

He told her what had been delivered earlier.

'A marquee?' she said.

'Just like a garden party. Sorry – I didn't mean . . .'

'I appreciate all you're being asked to do on my behalf . . . theirs. I've had a succession of messages from Colonel Wheeler and Captain Jessop informing me of some new detail or other. I think I'm supposed to be even more grateful for everything that's now happening.'

'It wasn't what you expected,' Reid said simply. She too, he guessed, was hiding the disappointment she felt now that her own involvement with the dead women was being turned into such a public spectacle, and now that all these others – all these men who had never known the nurses, who had never known what they had been there to do and what they had endured and then suffered in doing it – now that all these others were being invited – encouraged, even – to share in and comment on that grief and loss and sacrifice, far in advance of the women's families and fellow nurses being afforded that same opportunity.

'I'm sure the whole thing will proceed according to plan,' Caroline said, confirming his guess.

Reid resisted laughing at the phrase. 'I'm sure it will,' he said.

'After all,' she went on, 'what are plans and preparations for, if not to ensure success?'

'Exactly,' Reid said.

'Jonathan Guthrie has sent me his order of service,' she said.

'Of course he has.'

'He said he'd be only too happy for me to say something on the nurses' behalf.'

'That's generous of him. And will you?' Reid opened his eyes.

'Of course I will. I heard from Mary Ellsworth yesterday. She's gone to stay at a rest home in the Cotswolds.'

'A rest home?'

'That's what she said.'

'Do you think she'll come back here when she finally feels up to it?'

'I daresay the passing of time might help matters,' she said.

'Time being the great healer, and all that?'

'I meant she might finally be able to better understand her own reasons for wanting somewhere to mourn and to remember.'

Reid had supervised the burial of Mary Ellsworth's fiancé less than an hour after his body had arrived in Morlancourt. At the time, he had been relieved that the woman had not insisted on leaving the station and accompanying the coffin to its final resting place. The dignity of the small ceremony arranged by Drake in the goods depot had far outweighed the perfunctory burial at the cemetery itself.

'I can let you have the details of his grave,' he said. 'If you intend writing back to her.'

'I'm not sure,' she said, surprising him.

'It's all talk of memorials and monuments at the Commission these days,' he said. 'The popular politicians are promising the families back at home that no one will go unremembered.'

'Even if they remain unfound and unburied?'

'Half of all the actual burials consist of unidentified men. It's still more common than people think.'

'Or than the Commission lets on?' She took the cigarette from Reid's mouth to light one of her own, blowing on its glowing tip and scattering sparks into the air around them.

Behind them, the church bell pealed its cracked note for a minute and then stopped.

'The end of the day,' Caroline said.

A man came out of the church and walked past the gravestones to the far wall, climbing over it and dropping into the field beyond.

'I see they've decided on a name at last,' Caroline said. The dying note of the bell sounded for almost as long as its ringing.

'A name? For what?' He thought at first that she was talking about the cemetery.

'For the war. The Naming Committee. The No-men-cla-ture Committee.'

'And?'

259

'"The Great War".'

'More window dressing,' Reid said. 'They do like everything to be neat and tidy and festooned with flags and bunting, these people. Festooned with flags and then with a gilding of grandiosity – something noble and fitting – thrown in for good measure.'

'I daresay most people will think it a good thing,' Caroline said.

'I daresay they will.'

'And would you honestly deny them that small consolation?' she said.

Reid considered his answer. 'No, I suppose not,' he said.

'Because, after all—'

'Because, after all, I'm just as much a part of all that tidying-up, of that gilding, as any of them?'

'I was going to say it seems to me that what most people want now – the families of the dead, I mean – is simply a way of getting on with their lives, and that all this pomp and ceremony and tidying-up – yes, *your* tidying-up included – is a means of helping that to happen.'

'I suppose so,' Reid said again, not wanting to argue with her.

'Of bringing – I don't know – some certainty and purpose to so many unsettled lives. And, yes, you *are* a part of all that.'

'Two sides of the same coin,' he said.

She smiled at him and held his arm again. 'If you say so.'

'Wheeler likes to talk of a "common bond", of the cemeteries and memorials connecting those who were here with those who stayed at home and did their bit there.'

'It's what all the newspapers are saying – it's what people want to hear. Perhaps you should give the man more credit.'

'Never,' Reid said, causing them both to laugh.

They were interrupted by the reappearance of the man who had come out of the church and then climbed over the church wall. He came back through the graveyard and stopped in front of them. It was the bell-ringer, who came to the church at least six times every day to carry out his duty there. The man took off his cap and commented on the weather. He told them there was talk of coming rain, of a thunderstorm, even.

'Tonight?' Reid asked him, aware of what a change in the weather would mean for the work still to be done at the cemetery.

The bell-ringer shrugged. 'Sunday,' he said. Two days away.

It seemed unlikely to Reid that the timing of something so dramatic, of so sudden a break in the prolonged heat, could be predicted with any real certainty.

The man looked up into the pale, clear sky above them.

When he had gone, Caroline asked Reid if the rain would affect his preparations.

'Unlikely,' he said. 'Besides . . .'

'It will happen whatever the weather?' She turned to watch the bell-ringer talking to others further along the village street.

'Or it will have been and gone by Monday.'

After that, neither of them spoke for several minutes, and then Caroline said, 'Will you go and find Alexander?'

'Of course.'

'What do you think he'll do?'

Reid shrugged, unwilling to speculate.

'Surely, Muir can't refuse him now?'

Still Reid refused to be drawn.

She rose beside him. 'If there's anything whatsoever *I* can do . . .'

'Of course.' He felt suddenly unsure of what else he might say to her.

She walked away from him – not, as Reid had anticipated, towards the few scattered buildings of the place, but away from the village and its church and into the open countryside beyond. He resisted the urge to call after her, or to catch her up and walk beside her, to make it clearer to her, perhaps, that he was as powerless as any of them to alter to even the slightest degree the course of events ahead.

Instead, he watched her closely as she followed the line of a grubbed-out hedge, and then as she turned and was lost to him amid the wild grass and weeds which rose first to her waist and then to her shoulders, then swallowed her up completely, as though she were a swimmer walking into a calm sea, who wanted to be covered by the water before bursting shouting and gasping at its surface and reaching up into the air above.

30

Reid found Lucas later that evening. He'd gone first to Lucas's room and had found it empty and in disarray. His clothes and equipment lay scattered over the floor and narrow bed, as though everything had been recently and hurriedly unpacked and searched.

Eventually, he found Lucas sitting alone in the open cobbled yard at the rear of one of the bars, overlooking the distant canal.

Only as Reid approached close behind him did Alexander Lucas finally turn and acknowledge him.

'I can leave you if you'd prefer,' Reid said.

'No, please.' A half-empty bottle stood in the shade of Lucas's chair.

Reid pulled a chair to the table and took an empty glass from another.

'It's not my first bottle,' Lucas said.

The line of distant water shone in the setting sun, looking like molten metal in its foundry bed.

'Nine months ago we dug up forty temporary graves at a place called Ayette,' Lucas said as Reid poured himself a drink. 'Irish. Connaughts, Munster and Leinster regiments. Every man had a bottle with his name and all his details

263

tucked into his tunic. On the second day, one of my men pulled out the bottle to take down the details and it blew up in his face. Booby-trapped. We used to find it a lot in the early days, mostly in those marked temporary graves. Someone would dig the hole and bury the men and then the Germans would overrun the place and put the grenades in. I used to give a little speech at least once a week about looking out for the things.' Lucas sat with his eyes closed as he said all this. 'I used to tell them – the slightest doubt, anything you can't see, anything out of the ordinary, then leave it alone.'

'What happened? At Ayette.'

'The man was killed outright. Two others were badly injured. One of them was blinded and lost his jaw.' He shook his head at the memory. 'As replacements, they sent me a full squad of boys from the British Empire Service League. I sent them straight back.'

'Because they—'

'Because they were boys. And because they didn't have the first idea about what they were doing, what they were likely to come across.' He opened his eyes and smiled. 'I once retrieved some of the Third Warwickshires for the cemetery at Serre, and they sent me a party of conscientious objectors to do the digging. Two of the men were professors of archaeology from Cambridge. I tried to send *them* back, too, but that definitely wasn't on. They were a good crowd. Some of them applied to work with me on a regular basis, but you can imagine how that went down with the powers-that-be.'

Reid nodded. Six months earlier he had worked with a similar group of men in one of the Commission's nurseries at Arras, propagating and multiplying the plants required for the cemeteries. He told Lucas this, but Lucas remained lost in his own thoughts and said nothing in reply.

A waiter appeared in the open doorway at the rear of the bar and called to them. Without turning, Lucas raised a hand to the boy and a few minutes later another bottle was brought out to them.

'I've no money,' Lucas said. 'I told him when I arrived that I was waiting for you.'

Reid paid the boy and waved away his change.

'I don't know what I'm expected to do,' Lucas said when they were alone again. 'I don't know what's expected of me.'

It was impossible for Reid to answer him.

Beyond the canal a line of men walked across a field carrying forks and hoes. They sang and shouted to each other as they walked, lacing the evening air with their distant voices.

'I once saw some brigadier or other tell the choir of a Welsh regiment to stop singing, one Sunday morning in the trenches up the road here at Morval,' Lucas said.

'Because they were attracting attention to themselves?'

Lucas shook his head. 'Because he said they sounded too sad, too morose. He said they were having a bad effect on the morale of the others.'

'And did they? Stop, I mean.'

'What do you think? The choir master just went on conducting them and they went on singing for the best part of another hour. One of them asked me afterwards what kind of bad effect the brigadier thought the German machine guns, artillery and mines were having on *them*. They said the same man had told them to lower their parapets by six inches because they were over the regulation height.'

Reid wondered why Lucas was repeating all these small, common tales, and guessed it was to keep himself at a distance from the news he had just received and everything he now had to consider. Keeping himself at that distance and also keeping Reid at that same vital distance from him. Whatever his reasons for this, and for the reminiscing itself, Reid knew it would be unwise to confront him any more directly about what he might do next.

'The Leinstermen – rifle brigade, I think – had been heavily sprayed with creosote to keep flies off the corpses.'

'Successfully?'

'Not really.' Lucas took something from his pocket and gave it to Reid.

At first Reid thought it was the telegram Lucas had received earlier, but unfolding the piece of paper he saw that it was a map. Looking more closely, he saw that it was a simple map of the French coast and then of England and Wales as far north as the Midlands. He remembered what Lucas had already told him about the maps being used to help reassure new arrivals of their eventual return home.

'It was on one of the bodies at La Chapelette. There were one or two others. Men on Active Service were eventually ordered not to carry them,' Lucas said. 'Ridiculous. Look at it – two inches from Boulogne to Paris, half an inch across the Channel. How much information was *that* ever going to give away?'

Reid studied the map and held a fingertip over his own home. 'It doesn't reach as far as Nottingham,' he said.

'I know,' Lucas said. 'I looked.' He held Reid's gaze for a moment and then laughed.

'I was in Amiens, General Headquarters,' Reid said,

'when the Ploughman Order came in.' It was a story of his own, something to maintain their failing momentum.

Lucas shook his head.

'At harvest time. Back at home. They suddenly found themselves short of ploughmen. They wanted two thousand of the men finding within days and shipping back home.'

'Don't tell me – ten times that number suddenly appeared.'

'Something like that. Someone at the War Office came up with a great idea for finding out who was telling the truth. A draught horse was found, and everyone who claimed to know how to plough a field or to work a harvester was told to harness it up. I think they found forty men, fifty at the most.'

'I saw perfectly sound horses being slaughtered at Boulogne, and again at Étaples,' Lucas said. 'They'd served their purpose. There was some talk of giving them to the French farmers to help them get themselves up and running again, but I doubt it came to much.'

After that, neither man spoke for a while, both settling close to the dangerous silence which surrounded them.

Other men came out into the rear of the bar and sat in the yard.

Eventually, Lucas said, 'Are you still bound for the howling wastes of Araby?'

'I imagine so,' Reid said.

'I heard from an old Graves Service man that we are obliterating graves in Persia to prevent them from being desecrated by religious zealots there.'

Reid had heard the same at one of Wheeler's meetings. 'It sounds a different place completely,' he said.

'Just make sure you know what you're getting yourself into

before Wheeler pushes the last of his scattered little pieces into place and then gets himself crowned. The same man who told me about Persia said the Forestry Commission had already approached Wheeler to play a major part in their own set-up, and that he had turned them down. Not much glory in planting and chopping down trees, I don't suppose.'

'No.' Reid refolded the map and gave it back to Lucas.

Lucas waved it away. 'No use to me. Will you go home, do you think? Before being posted.'

'I don't know. I haven't even heard anything definite yet.'

'Jessop wants me to go to Chaulnes,' Lucas said. 'Apparently, a lot of temporary grave sites were overrun there before the Germans ran out of steam down the road. All the records were lost, and whatever's still there will have to be done from scratch.'

'Perhaps they're just trying to keep you busy.'

'Perhaps they are. To keep my mind off things, presumably.'

Unable to hold back any longer, Reid drained his glass and said, 'Your daughter.'

Lucas closed his eyes for a moment and then opened them and looked back to the canal.

'I know,' he said.

And again, both men fell silent.

'I might try the Forestry Commission myself,' Lucas said, but with little conviction in his voice.

'I thought you planned to resume—'

'Perhaps that's just it – plans. What good are most of *them* now? I daresay I'm not the only one being forced to reconsider what lies ahead, how things *might* once have turned out.'

'No, I suppose not.'

'Besides, all those trees, forests – and how long does it take for a tree to grow? – it sounds more . . . more restful. They're talking about planting up hundreds of thousands of acres of the things. It sounds medieval – the twentieth century, and we still need all that wood. It almost sounds as though we're denying the future.'

'Or as though we're planning for it,' Reid said, the thought and words arriving simultaneously.

'I suppose so,' Lucas said.

'Drake reckons it will all be down to aeroplanes the next time around,' Reid said. 'Aerial bombardment.'

'What, no battlefields? I wouldn't try selling that one to the desk-top generals back at the War Office just yet.'

Both men laughed.

'You needn't worry about me,' Lucas said afterwards, un-expectedly, and as Reid considered what to say next.

'No, I know.'

'This war's a long time finished.'

'So everyone keeps telling us,' Reid said.

In the bar behind them, someone put on a gramophone, and a woman's singing voice drifted out to them, occasionally muted and intermittent in volume, as though blown out to where they sat on a changing wind. And then the noise of the bar fell silent for a few seconds and the woman's singing came to them as clearly and as warmly as though she were sitting beside them at the table and they were her only audience.

31

Two days later, Sunday, the day before the ceremony, Reid was woken by someone banging on his door and calling his name. Opening the door, he was confronted by one of his own labourers, who said breathlessly that he'd been sent by Drake to fetch him and to tell him that all the other workers had also been unexpectedly woken and taken to the cemetery several hours earlier. It was not yet nine in the morning, and Reid and his men had worked until late the previous evening.

At the end of that day's work, Reid had told Drake that, with most of the preparations finished, they might rest for a day and then resume an hour or so earlier on Monday morning. The arrival of the nurses was scheduled for later than usual, at ten, to give Wheeler and all the others time to get to Morlancourt.

The man told Reid that he'd come in one of their lorries and that the vehicle was waiting for them in the street below.

Reid dressed and went down with him.

Arriving at the cemetery twenty minutes later, he saw that work had already started on the erection of the marquee alongside the path leading from the entrance towards the site of the eventual memorial. Men were setting out chairs and others were hammering stakes into the ground all around the structure. The marquee stood on a raised platform, and yet more men laid and hammered the plank floor.

Reid saw by the number of workers that, in addition to his own depleted labour force, others had also been brought to the site. A line of lorries blocked the narrow lane and others were scattered across the open ground. It was the busiest Reid had ever seen the cemetery, and it seemed to him then, surveying the activity all around him, that it was a different place entirely from the quiet fields and slope and copse he had been working on almost daily for the past four months.

Going to the marquee, Reid sought out Drake, whom he found amid a group of thirty or so labourers, only a few of whom Reid recognized.

At his appearance, those same few men came to him with their complaints before Drake shouted them to silence.

'They're mostly from Saint-Quentin,' Drake told Reid, indicating the unfamiliar men all around them. 'Wheeler laid on a special train. One of them gave me this.' He took out a folded sheet and handed it to Reid.

It was a list of instructions outlining the work still needing to be completed in advance of the arrival of the nurses. It was signed by both Wheeler and Muir, and informed the reader that someone from the Commission would be arriving at the site later in the day to check that everything had been satisfactorily carried out.

'You weren't aware of *any*thing?' Drake asked Reid, his voice low.

Reid could only shake his head. He wondered who had compiled the list for Wheeler, and Guthrie came to mind.

'It would have been better coming from you,' Drake said. 'You know all the extra hours our own lot have been putting in this past week. This was the last thing they needed. I told one of the sergeants from Saint-Quentin to get on with everything using just his own blokes, but he said Wheeler had insisted on us all being brought out here for the day. No one's saying that things don't need to be ready and waiting for tomorrow, but the overall feeling is that it's all a bit much and that we would have managed everything in the morning. It's *Sunday*, for Christ's sake.'

'It would be pointless trying to contact Wheeler now,' Reid said, knowing precisely how the man would respond.

The canvas sections of the marquee were already rising into place and being bound together.

'I've told the other sergeants to keep their men away from the graves and paths,' Drake said. 'They were everywhere when I got here, walking over the ground we'd already prepared. In fairness, most of them didn't have the first idea why they were here, and some of them didn't even know it was a cemetery until they started wandering round. I got some of our lads to put up ropes to keep the nurses' plot off limits.' He motioned to the men driving stakes into the ground around the waiting graves.

'Will everything get done?' Reid asked him.

'The marquee's the biggest job. It's all starting to look a bit too much like a summer fête for my liking.'

Reid smiled at the remark. 'With Wheeler as Lady Bountiful, cutting the ribbon and declaring the whole thing open and then handing out the prizes?'

'He'd certainly fit the part,' Drake said.

'He wants to send me to supervise work in Mesopotamia,' Reid said.

Drake considered this for a moment. 'I see. Well, I suppose

we'll all be moving on somewhere or other when the time comes. I wouldn't mind a spell in that neck of the woods myself.'

'Perhaps you could come with me,' Reid said, remembering what Drake had told him about his own original posting.

'Perhaps I could. But until then we've got this lot to sort out.'

Reid saw again how the man had laid his calming hand over everything, how his presence and simple reasoning had created a kind of order and acceptance amid the confusion of the day.

'I think our biggest problem now is that,' Drake said, pointing to the horizon.

'The rain?' Reid said, seeing the darkening of the sky.

'You can feel it coming,' Drake said. He tipped his head back and breathed deeply. 'There's already a chill. And look . . .' He pointed to where the roof of the half-erected marquee was already rippling in the rising breeze.

'Do you think it'll get here sooner rather than later?'

Drake shrugged. 'It already looks thicker and darker than it did an hour ago.'

The cloud across the horizon was sunlit along its upper edge, but lower down it completely obscured the land in that direction. Reid guessed the horizon to be twenty miles distant.

He finally turned back to the men still gathered nearby and made a short speech explaining the necessity for what they were doing. He reminded them that they were all – himself included – serving men, and as such were expected to obey the orders of their superiors. It was an unpopular remark to make and served only to unsettle the crowd further. He finished by saying that it would be unfortunate if, after all their earlier work, the following day's ceremony were to be ruined for the want of this one final effort. And again it was something he regretted saying, guessing that to his unhappy audience he was starting to sound like Wheeler.

Before any of them could respond to the words, Drake ordered them all back to their work and the men turned and dispersed.

'Will you stay?' Drake asked him when they were alone.

'Of course.'

'They'd appreciate that. It's why I sent for you.'

'Perhaps Wheeler intended me to spend the day in Saint-Quentin with him and all the others, making the final preparations there.'

'You'd be more use here,' Drake said, at once exposing and dismissing Reid's lack of conviction. 'Besides, it looks like either Wheeler or Jessop will be turning up here later to make sure everything's done.'

'Jessop, most likely,' Reid said. 'Wheeler will save his own appearance for the big day itself, to the sound of trumpets, and no doubt behaving as though he built the whole place himself.'

'He certainly likes his entrances,' Drake said, and then saluted Reid and walked back to the labouring men.

Reid watched him go and was considering what to do next when he saw a car coming along the lane, navigating its way past the lorries there. Imagining this to be Jessop coming to make his inspection, he went to meet the vehicle. Arriving at the gateway, he was disappointed to see Jonathan Guthrie climb down from the passenger seat.

Guthrie looked around him for a moment, clearly pleased

with what he saw, and then he noticed Reid and hesitated for a moment before raising a hand to him.

Reid went to him. 'I imagine Wheeler told you I wouldn't be here,' he said.

Guthrie shrugged at the remark. 'Edmund said you might consider yourself badly treated. Without cause, I might add.'

'And the men?' Reid said. 'How did he think *they* might consider themselves treated? All this could have been arranged and undertaken days ago.'

'I imagine he didn't want to interrupt your own daily routine. What does it matter?'

'Have you seen him? Today, I mean.'

'I held the early service in the military chapel,' Guthrie said, smiling. 'Edmund was in attendance along with a great many others.'

'And now?'

'I believe a luncheon has been planned for the members of the Commission and their invited guests.'

'I meant you,' Reid said. 'Why are you here?'

Guthrie smiled again at the question. 'I daresay you have already made your mind up on that account, Captain Reid. And, yes, I would far rather be at that luncheon than here. I imagine you already know there is bad weather in prospect.'

'Naturally,' Reid said.

'If you must know, I am here because Edmund has asked me to officiate at the ceremony tomorrow, and I came – yes, to ensure that the work was nearing completion, but also so that I might best prepare myself for my own duties. I wanted to see where the graves lie in relation to the marquee, where my congregation – my audience, if you will – will be seated. I take my duties concerning these poor women very seriously,

Captain Reid. Others might be content to leave things to chance, but not I.'

'And by "others", presumably you mean me.'

'Not at all, not at all. I have the greatest respect and admiration for all that you and your workers have achieved here. As does Edmund. As, I'm sure, does everyone else already gathered and waiting. There's an official reception. The War Office is insisting. It may not yet have occurred to you personally, Captain Reid, but there are a great many things to be considered here other than the burial of the unfortunate nurses. There are a great many other straws blowing in this particular wind.'

'Politics,' Reid said.

'If you like. We are none of us immune from these things. Not you, not I, and certainly not Edmund. All talk now is of doing the right thing by both the deceased *and* the bereaved.'

'Because they're the ones still voting?'

Guthrie shook his head. 'I sometimes wonder if we haven't asked too much of you and all the others like you. I wonder if our demands on you shouldn't have ended with the war itself. Please, forgive me. All I'm trying to say in my own clumsy way is that the world now needs men with vision – men who see more clearly than you and I the shape and the needs of the future.'

Everything the man said betrayed his sense of superiority and his own rising ambition.

Reid wanted him to do what he needed to do and then to leave. He wanted to return to Drake and his own men and to talk to them and instruct them on their work as he had always done.

'I honestly believe,' said Guthrie, 'that it is men like Edmund who—'

'Who see that future more clearly? And certainly more clearly than anyone here, say?'

Guthrie looked around him. 'They are honest, working men,' he said. 'Just as they were once honest, dutiful soldiers. Nothing more and nothing less.'

Reid could not bring himself to respond to this.

Guthrie clearly felt something of Reid's rising anger, for he too fell silent, again looking at the men around him, before eventually saying, 'Surely we are all working towards a common goal here – I mean the nurses, and all those others already interred and embarked upon their own Eternal Sleep.'

Everything the man said seemed at once dismissive and provocative to Reid.

He, too, looked around, and he saw in that moment how much more *finished* the cemetery now looked – how the paths and lawns and flower beds and stones had all finally started to take on a satisfying shape of their own. He found it hard to remember the bare, unworked ground of only a few months earlier. What he was finally looking at, it occurred to him, was what all those others would see for the first time upon their arrival the following day.

'Have you heard anything certain about the coming of the rain?' Guthrie said, distracting him from his thoughts.

The coming of the rain.

'No, nothing. Except that it's definitely on its way.'

Reid watched as the roof of the marquee was finally completed and as the whole structure was pulled taut by the gangs of men hauling on its ropes and hammering its stakes deeper. He saw the red cross at the centre of its white circle on one of the gently billowing panels.

'I see,' Guthrie said. The man hesitated for a moment and then added, 'I don't suppose you've seen Alexander Lucas this morning, by any chance?' He continued looking around him as he spoke.

'His wife died,' Reid said. 'He only heard on Friday. I saw him that evening, not since.'

'I was sorry to hear about his wife. We all were. I only ask because it seems *no one* has seen him since the day he received his terrible news. Edmund heard of the death and tried to contact him directly. You do know, I suppose, that before this sad event, Lucas had applied to Muir for compassionate leave.'

'Which he was denied,' Reid said.

'Quite,' Guthrie said. 'Though I daresay with reason. I can't begin—'

'And now Wheeler's convinced that – what? – that Lucas has taken matters into his own hands?'

'Nothing of the sort. Nothing of the sort. Edmund was merely concerned for the man's well-being, that's all.'

It occurred to Reid to ask Guthrie if he knew of Lucas's sick daughter, but he said nothing.

'Or perhaps Caroline Mortimer might know,' Guthrie went on. 'Perhaps Alexander Lucas confided in her. A woman's touch, and all that.'

'Or perhaps he's just gone somewhere to grieve for his dead wife,' Reid said.

'Quite,' Guthrie said again. 'Quite. Though it was Edmund's belief that the pair of them – Lucas and his wife – had been estranged of late. Still, who are we to speculate?

Presumably Caroline Mortimer has said nothing to you concerning the man's whereabouts?'

Reid remained silent.

'No, right, I thought not.'

And before Reid could say anything in response to all this obvious prodding, Guthrie turned and walked back to the waiting car.

Reid remained where he stood, glad to see the back of the man, and pleased that whatever Guthrie now reported of the work at the cemetery, Wheeler would be satisfied, and neither he nor Jessop would appear until the following day. Only the uncertainty of Alexander Lucas's whereabouts might now concern Wheeler, but even that would not distract him from the all-consuming business of the day ahead.

Waiting until Guthrie's car was lost to sight, Reid walked up the slope, shielded his eyes and looked back out to the distant horizon, where the gathering cloud seemed piled to twice its former height, and where there was now no clear divide between this thickening mass and the land over which it slowly flowed and which it darkened in its wake.

32

The rain finally started falling in the late afternoon as work at the cemetery drew to a close. The marquee was fully erected and secured by then, the seating laid out, the completed paths cleared, and all the superfluous building materials and tools moved out of sight of where the burial of the nurses would take place.

The route of the short procession from the cemetery gate to the waiting graves was roped off, and the graves themselves had been made tidy. Cut turf was laid neatly along their edges and the infill soil was carefully mounded and covered. Crosses were laid at the head of each grave, and buckets of flowers and wreaths were stacked in the marquee.

Ensuring that the site was fully prepared, that all of Wheeler's instructions had been followed, and that the drains close to the previously flooded graves were flowing freely in the first of the rain, Reid returned to Morlancourt.

A contingent of the men from Saint-Quentin would stay overnight at the site, using the marquee as a shelter. Canvas beds and provisions had already been delivered to them. Before leaving, Reid warned them about the earlier flooding, but it was clear to him by the way these strangers listened to him that they were unlikely to leave their shelter if the flooding resumed.

Wheeler had instructed that these men, and not a party of Reid's own, should undertake this night watch, and Reid regretted this. Everything Wheeler now said and did made ever clearer to Reid his own loosening bonds and evaporating authority over the place.

He arrived back in Morlancourt at seven, heralded by the dull tolling of the church bell, and was surrounded briefly by the evening's gathering worshippers walking through the rain with umbrellas and avoiding the edges of the road which were already running with water.

He went first in search of Alexander Lucas, and, unable to find him, then went instead to Caroline Mortimer's room.

She let him in and gave him a towel for his face and arms. His jacket was saturated and she took it from him and hung it over a chair, where it dripped on to the thin carpet.

He told her about the work at the cemetery and what he had heard from Guthrie concerning Lucas.

'Do you think he's trying to get back to his daughter?' she said.

'What else?'

'He wouldn't be so stupid. Surely? Besides . . .' Her voice tailed off.

'Besides, Wheeler wouldn't be so inhuman as to deny the man – not after everything Lucas has just been through, everything he's done on Wheeler's behalf?'

She nodded.

'Sorry,' Reid said, knowing even as he'd spoken that her thoughts now were on the arrival of her nurses and the events of the following day.

He watched the water dripping from his jacket to the floor. A loud murmur of conversation and laughter rose up from the room below.

'Newspapermen,' Caroline said. 'Dozens of them.'

'I understood they'd be coming from Amiens with Wheeler and his party in the morning.'

'So did he, I imagine. They're a law unto themselves, those men. They've been talking to people all day. I gave a so-called interview to one of them myself, but he didn't appear particularly interested in what I had to say. He kept asking me if I had some words of consolation for the people back at home. He thought at first that I was here because of my dead husband.' She closed her eyes briefly at the memory of the man.

She went on talking, but like those journalists earlier, Reid only heard half of what she was telling him. His own thoughts were still with Alexander Lucas and the likelihood of him being caught and the consequences of that.

Caroline poured them both brandies and they sat together at her open window looking out at the street below. A small balcony extended a few feet from the window and the rain collected on this and ran over its edge. An occasional gust of wind blew the water in on them, staining the cloth on the table.

The day had lost little of its earlier heat, and the rain grew heavier still. The previously sunlit sky seemed to darken in an instant and the thunder and lightning of the long-approaching storm finally arrived. Almost eight hours had passed since Drake had first pointed out the distant cloud to Reid, and he was grateful that the worst of the weather had held off this long.

Caroline counted the seconds between the flashes of lightning and the rolls of thunder. The rain fell even more heavily, and it poured off the roofs of the buildings opposite them in unbroken streams. The street below became a shallow, fast-flowing river.

Reid flinched at a louder than usual peal of thunder, and beneath his palms he felt the small table shake.

'Are you concerned for the waiting graves?' Caroline asked him.

Reid looked down at his hands. 'They'll drain if the rain stops for long enough,' he said.

A group of men ran shouting across the street and he recognized several of his own labourers among them.

'Guthrie clearly thought I knew more than I was telling him,' he said.

'About Alexander?'

'He's probably already told Wheeler that he believes I'm involved in some way.'

Caroline went to the cabinet beside her bed and took a small album from its drawer. She came back to the table and put it in front of him, drawing the table further into the room beyond the reach of the splashing rain.

Reid opened the album and looked at the photographs it contained. They were mostly of women, individually posed and in groups, all in their nursing and auxiliary uniforms, and often standing with small groups of the men under their care, some also in uniform, some in pyjamas, and some wearing items of both.

'Are they the women coming tomorrow?' he said.

'Not all of them. But some of them are in there.'

She put her finger on the face of a solitary woman standing

amid a group of twenty grinning men, most of whom wore clean white bandages, and some of whom stood with crutches. All of those men able to hold a thumb up to the photographer did so, but the men standing closest to the young woman looked at her rather than at the camera.

'She's coming,' Caroline said fondly. 'Margaret. She was twenty. An auxiliary volunteer. That was taken at Le Havre. Every one of those men loved her in his own way. She was killed at a place called Pernois. The clearing station there was shelled. She lost a foot and a hand and died of her injuries three days later.'

She took her finger from the page, folded it into her fist and held this to her cheek.

'You'll say something for them all at the ceremony?' Reid said.

'Jonathan Guthrie has already told me where I'm to be fitted in. Apparently he'll be saying a few words first. He feels certain our two eulogies will complement each other perfectly. He wanted to know if I could let him have a copy of what I'd be saying. He seemed disappointed that I didn't have something prepared.'

'He'll have been working on his own speech for days.'

'Weeks.'

'He'll no doubt do his usual God and King and Country stuff,' Reid said.

'To which I'll add my simple woman's touch afterwards.'

'You *knew* them,' Reid said. 'All *he* ever knew was how to spread his worthless blessed balm over everything. As though that ever—' He stopped abruptly.

Caroline laid a hand on his arm. 'I've written again to all their parents,' she said. 'Some of them contacted me wanting

284

to know why no one had invited or even *told* them of the ceremony.'

'What did you say to them?'

'I told them that when this cemetery was completed, there would be another ceremony. They were all simply relieved to know that their daughters were safe and finally being laid to rest.'

'Safe?'

'Accounted for, then. That they'd never be completely lost to them, that they'd be cared for in death and that they were now being afforded everything they deserved. Most of them wrote back to tell me what a great comfort it was to them to know all that.'

She spun the album to face her and then turned a few pages, stopping at a photograph of two women standing together with their arms linked at the elbow. She pushed the picture back to face Reid.

'It's you,' he said, recognizing the taller of the two women.

'And my closest friend. Charlotte. That was taken at the field station at Puisieux. We'd been there together for almost a year. I was there when I received the news of my husband's death.'

'Is she among . . . I mean . . .'

'Sadly, no. She left Puisieux on a routine run delivering the more seriously wounded to Calais. We sent them once a week when they were considered well enough to travel. We usually set off in the late evening and returned the next day, mid-morning. Except she never did.' She looked hard at the woman's face as she said all this.

'What happened?'

'We heard nothing for a few days and then were told that

the ambulances had been caught in a barrage on their way back to us. I spent all those days praying that Charlotte had been ordered to stay on the hospital boat with her charges – it happened sometimes, especially if the journey had made things worse for any of the men.'

'But she'd been killed?'

'Four nurses and two drivers. She's already buried, at Étaples. I go occasionally to watch everything that's taking place around her. I wrote to Colonel Wheeler six months ago to ask if she and the others couldn't be brought here. I thought the notion of all the women being buried together might appeal, especially to a man like him. But he insisted that it was hard enough for him to allocate space to the bodies he didn't yet know about, without special provision being made for those already buried elsewhere.'

'Perhaps in the years to come,' Reid said. 'When *everyone* has finally been gathered in. The whole of this country for fifty miles in any direction is little more than one giant burial ground.'

Outside, the torrential rain slackened briefly, but then, after almost ten minutes of silence, the thunder and lightning resumed, and a second storm gathered and flowed across Morlancourt.

'I think the worst has passed,' Caroline said absently. She took back the album and looked at the photograph of herself and the dead nurse.

'Were you very close?' Reid asked her.

'I loved her,' she said. 'I have no sisters or brothers, and Charlotte was like a sister to me.' She paused. 'The pity of it is, I was the one who allocated the nurses and auxiliaries to the Calais convoys. It was always looked on as something of a break for the girls. The ambulances sometimes waited at the coast for a night or two longer than was absolutely necessary – there were always medical supplies to be brought back to us – and knowing this, I always used to allocate the work to those women most in need of some time away from the hospitals. I'd known for weeks that Charlotte was becoming exhausted. She was from Nuneaton, and I remembered her telling me that before coming to France, she'd only ever seen the sea on two previous occasions, both family holidays. There was a nursing depot in Calais so there was always somewhere for the girls to stay and to eat.'

'Did you go on the trips yourself?'

'Rarely. I was always more useful at Puisieux, or wherever else I happened to be. Besides, I was hardly in a position to go myself and leave someone else behind. Even Charlotte took herself off several rotas until I finally insisted on her going. When we heard what had happened to the four girls—' She turned away from Reid to look over the street below.

'I know,' Reid said.

Neither of them spoke for several minutes. Instead, they sat together and watched the distant storm move slowly away from them. In the west, the already clearing sky revealed the light of the day's setting sun and the promise of better weather tomorrow.

'Will you imagine her among them?' Reid said eventually.

Caroline closed her eyes and nodded. 'Of course.'

'It's an easy thing to do,' he said.

'I know.' She finally closed the album.

When Reid next looked at her he saw that she was crying. The tears ran in lines over her cheeks and dripped from her chin on to the backs of her outspread hands.

33

Only later, alone in his room, did Reid finally understand how impossible it was for him to do anything to help Alexander Lucas. There were a few people he might telephone – men he and Lucas had known in either Albert or Amiens – but it was unlikely that any of them would know any more than he did about Lucas's disappearance or his whereabouts now.

In all the months he had known Alexander Lucas, Reid realized, Lucas had spoken of none of these other men except in connection with his work in the Retrieval unit. Besides, any enquiries would have to be put through the Army Exchange in Saint-Quentin, and in all likelihood the operator there would have already been instructed to report any call made by Lucas or his friends. A call in the middle of the day might have gone unnoticed, but certainly not one at almost midnight. Whatever he attempted, Reid would only make things worse for Lucas.

He tried to remember the names of the men he had met in Lucas's company – his labourers at Prezière, for instance – but could not. Besides, Lucas's team there had already moved on or been disbanded.

His best hope, he realized, was if Lucas contacted him.

But that, too, was unlikely. Perhaps detaching himself this completely had been Lucas's intention all along, at least since either making his application to Muir or receiving word of his wife's death. And perhaps it had already occurred to both Wheeler and Muir to keep a close eye on Reid himself in the hope that he might lead them to Lucas.

An hour later, the storm had moved beyond the barely perceptible horizon, and though the far distant clouds were lit occasionally by a sudden flicker of lightning, there was no longer any thunder to be heard. The rain had long since lessened and then slowly ceased, but water still ran in the street outside and dripped from the roof of every building.

Unable to sleep, Reid sat at his window and looked out into the darkness. There was a vague brightness in the sky to the east, which never fully darkened through those summer nights, but closer to Morlancourt it was difficult to distinguish where the buildings and ruins of the place now stood. It was as though the world all around him had no true form or structure in the night, and as though, despite the dim light across the horizon, there was now no end to this shapeless world and the darkness in which it lay.

A solitary lantern shone in the window of a building further along the street, and Reid recognized this as the bar he had visited in the company of both Caroline and Lucas. He watched the light for a few minutes, but there was no movement around it – no shadows of late drinkers coming and going from the place, no sudden silhouette cast fleetingly on a wall – and so Reid came away from the window and sat at his small table.

Despite the storm, the night was humid, and where the heavy rain had fallen against his window and the wall around it, dark patches had appeared on the plasterwork. He touched his palms to these stains and felt the dampness against his fingers. He understood then, in that instant, that living through a long and deteriorating autumn and then an even longer winter in Morlancourt would be a different thing entirely to the summer he had just spent there, and he felt a sudden and unexpected sense of relief at the realization that he would know nothing of the place during these other, harsher seasons.

Eventually, exhausted after his long and unexpected day's work, Reid fell asleep where he sat at his table.

He slept fitfully for several hours and then woke when some movement almost tipped him from his chair.

The room around him lay in complete darkness.

He pulled off his jacket and his shirt, kicked off his boots and lay on the bed. He fell back to sleep, and this time he lay undisturbed until the early dawn, when he woke again and heard the usual muted cacophony of the town all around him. He opened his eyes and then lay without moving, gathering his thoughts and considering everything that had just happened and everything that was about to take place in the day ahead.

34

An hour later, the sky was again blue and cloudless, and at nine in the morning, as Reid made his way to the station, the air was already warm. Gutters still dripped with the night's rain, and the dykes along the roadside were filled with debris and flowing water. A light mist floated above the distant canal, and deep puddles lay along the lower reaches of the lane where it approached the railway. Following the storm, the verges seemed much greener than usual, and the exposed soil of the fields beyond much darker.

Arriving at the station, Reid saw Caroline Mortimer already waiting there, sitting on a bench beside Benoît.

Benoît rose at Reid's approach. 'She was here when I arrived,' he said. 'We've been talking, but mostly just sitting.' He turned back to Caroline, bowed, took her hand and kissed it.

'I'm keeping you from your work,' she said to him.

Benoît shrugged and said he would return to her soon.

Reid sat beside her.

'I couldn't sleep,' she said. She cupped an ear to listen to the birdsong in the trees beyond the depot. 'Look,' she said. She indicated the pots of flowers that Benoît had set out along the platform. Small sprays were fastened to the depot door. 'I think I surprised him,' she said. 'I must have looked like a ghost sitting here in the half-light.'

She wore a pale tan coat, white gloves and a hat with voile folded over its rim.

Reid himself had put on his smartest uniform, and had polished its buttons and belt and straps.

'Have you heard if the cemetery suffered at all in the storm?' she asked him.

'Not so far.'

Drake and his men would inspect the site before coming to the station, and any work which needed doing would be completed before the arrival there of the cortège.

'The place is still full of newspapermen,' she said. 'Some were already up and about as I made my way here.'

Reid had passed several of the men on his own short journey to the station.

He took out a cigarette and offered her one, which she accepted.

'I daresay Guthrie will be coming with Wheeler and the others on the train,' he said. Unusually, he felt awkward, constrained, in her company. The day ahead weighed on them both.

He looked along the track. A faint vapour rose from the warming gravel and the sleepers.

'What will happen afterwards, I wonder?' Caroline said.

'Afterwards?' For a moment, he was uncertain what she was asking him.

'After the ceremony,' she said. 'Will Colonel Wheeler come back here, to Morlancourt, do you think, or return immediately to Amiens?'

But Reid, too, had little clear idea of the day's proceedings beyond what was about to happen at the station. 'I daresay everything will become apparent,' he said. 'The day will run its course and we'll all play our own small parts within it.'

'Of course,' she said.

Several minutes later, a convoy of lorries and cars drew up on the lane beyond Benoît's office, and a group of Reid's men climbed down and congregated there.

'I ought to go to them,' Reid said, rising.

'Of course.'

It seemed to him she was relieved to be left alone.

He met Drake coming through the empty depot and saw that he too had cleaned up his uniform. The men beyond him were also in full dress.

'They made the effort,' Drake said.

'Meaning you gave the order. I appreciate it.'

'I went to the cemetery,' Drake said.

'And?'

'The stream overflowed and the holes along the perimeter have filled up again.'

'And the nurses' graves?'

'They're fine. The boys from Saint-Quentin have been brushing everything dry. The marquee and seating are fine.'

It was a relief to Reid to hear this. He told Drake to go back to the men and to turn the lorries in readiness for the journey to the cemetery.

'We've got three new cars from Amiens,' Drake said. 'Arrived a couple of hours ago. For the dignitaries and Commission members.'

It was something Reid had not considered. 'Tell the drivers to go slowly,' he said. 'I'll go on ahead in the first lorry, set the pace.'

Drake went back to the waiting men and Reid returned to the platform and Caroline.

Shortly before the train was due, Benoît came back out to them and said that there had been a delay, but the engine would be there in fifteen minutes. He stood beside them for a while before being called away.

'I appreciate the flowers,' Caroline said to him as he went.

Benoît looked at the pots and the door. 'It's little enough,' he said. 'Considering.' He walked briskly back to his office.

'They're closing the station in a few months,' Reid told her.

'I heard. I daresay a great deal will change.'

Reid had not yet approached Wheeler with the suggestion that Benoît be put in charge of the upkeep of the finished cemetery.

'I don't suppose . . .' Caroline said hesitantly.

'Alexander Lucas? No, nothing.'

'Perhaps Colonel Wheeler will have some news.'

'If he does, it won't be good.'

'No.' After a pause, she said, 'One of the newspapermen I spoke to referred to the cost of all this gravedigging and memorial-building as a "butcher's bill to the nation".'

Reid had heard the remark before. He listened to the sound of the lorries being turned in the narrow lane.

'And you?' Caroline asked him.

'Me, what?' He knew exactly what she was asking him.

'After today. After Morlancourt.'

'Wherever I'm sent, I suppose.' He'd already told her about Wheeler's proposal concerning his future posting. 'You?'

'Home, I imagine,' she said. 'A few more days here while arrangements are made. I shall want to come back and say a proper farewell to my women. Alone. After that . . .'

Reid was about to say more when they finally heard the whistle of the delayed train, signifying that it had arrived at the canal halt. They both rose at the sound and went to the platform's edge. Benoît reappeared from his office, followed by his two employees. The three men all wore flowers in their lapels.

Drake came back to Reid and said everything was ready. Reid told him to form the men into lines and to await further instructions.

A group of local people, including Benoît's wife, gathered at the station gates to pay their respects.

After them came the journalists and the photographers, most of the men gathering at the waiting vehicles. Others, Reid guessed, would already be making their way to the cemetery to follow the proceedings there.

The train appeared a moment later, attracting everyone's attention and causing them all to fall silent.

Back in Morlancourt, the church bell started its slow and measured tolling, suggesting to Reid that someone there had also been waiting for the signal of the whistle.

The train came slowly forward and stopped at its usual place.

The driver and Ernaux climbed down from the cab and went to stand beside Benoît. They, too, wore flowers in their lapels.

Further along the train, several doors opened and other men climbed out. Among the first of these were Wheeler, Jessop and Guthrie. They stood together for a moment, and then Wheeler, seeing Reid and Caroline further along the platform, said something to Jessop, who came towards them.

Jonathan Guthrie started to come with him, but Jessop

said something to the man and Guthrie turned back and made his way to the solitary goods carriage at the rear of the train.

Jessop took off his cap and held out his hand to Caroline.

'Perhaps you might like to go to your nurses,' he said. He motioned to where Guthrie now stood. 'Don't worry, nothing will commence until Colonel Wheeler gives the word.' He looked through the depot to Drake and the waiting men. 'Perhaps I might have a word with Captain Reid?'

'Of course.'

Caroline left them and walked slowly along the platform. The men and women who now filled it fell silent at her approach and then stood aside as she continued towards the waiting carriage.

'The cemetery?' Jessop said, hardly looking at Reid.

'Everything's fine and waiting.'

'Good.' And then, without warning, Jessop clasped Reid's arm and turned him away from the train. 'You'll be relieved to hear that Lieutenant Lucas has finally revealed himself. In Boulogne. He's being detained at the provost's office there.'

'Detained?'

Jessop smiled at the word. 'I'm afraid so. He was travelling without authority. As well you knew. I'm surprised you hadn't already heard. The deputy provost called Wheeler last night.'

'How would I have heard?' Reid said.

'Of course. How would you?' Jessop looked back along the platform to where Wheeler stood in conversation with men Reid had never seen before, several of whom wore dress coats and top hats. After a moment, Wheeler looked towards them and Jessop quickly raised his hand.

'Your signal,' Reid said, pulling himself free of the man.

'What are you talking about?' Jessop said.

'He sent you to ascertain that everything was ready and that I, at least, was still here and doing his bidding.'

'He's your superior officer, for God's sake, man. What bidding?'

'What will happen to him? Lucas.'

Jessop shrugged. 'Out of my hands, I'm afraid. Out of all our hands.'

'Meaning Wheeler's already washed *his* hands of him.'

'Meaning the best thing for all concerned would be to let others – the men responsible for these things – deal with the whole affair. The Commission itself certainly doesn't want any—' He stopped abruptly. 'Besides, I imagine Lieutenant Lucas might consider himself to have somewhat more pressing concerns at present.'

'Meaning?' Reid said, suspicious of what Jessop was suggesting. 'His daughter, you mean?' He braced himself for Jessop's answer, but Jessop seemed confused by the remark.

'Meaning,' Jessop said, 'that upon being challenged by the port authorities, Lieutenant Lucas suffered some kind of seizure, a kind of fit. The provost's office sent for a doctor. Don't worry, Lucas is fine. The doctor said it was probably caused by nervous excitement, agitation. You know the thing.'

'And now?'

'Lucas? In the hospital there, being well taken care of.'

'Sedated, you mean?'

Jessop held up his hands and smiled. 'I'm not a medical man, God forbid. Besides,' – he looked back to Wheeler and the gathering crowd – 'this is neither the time nor the place. Sharpen up and do your duty, Reid. Just do your damn duty.'

Then Jessop took several paces away from Reid and looked all around him. 'It looks a good show,' he said. 'For the women, I mean, the nurses.'

'People appreciate being able to do it,' Reid said.

'I'm sure they do,' Jessop said, looking back to Wheeler and his invited dignitaries. 'And all to great advantage, of course.' He looked at the journalists and photographers gathered beside the waiting soldiers, making his meaning clear. 'Necessary evils, I suppose.'

Reid gave no answer because none was expected of him. In Jessop's eyes – as in Wheeler's – he too had already ceased to exist.

Wheeler finally detached himself from the growing crowd and came to them.

'Right, good, well, shall we begin?' he said, holding out his hand to Reid. 'Shall we get the proceedings underway?' He put on his cap, tugged at the knot in his tie, clapped his gloved hands together once and then walked quickly back along the platform towards Caroline, Guthrie and all the others.

Jessop walked even more quickly to catch up with him.

Reid remained where he stood for a moment and then followed them towards the waiting carriage, exchanging nods and words with the few people he knew.

Seeing that the first of the day's ceremonies was about to begin, all those on the platform again fell silent.

Wheeler called for everyone's attention and delivered a short speech outlining the day's running order. He then beckoned to Jonathan Guthrie, who came to stand beside him.

Guthrie paused for a few seconds and then bowed his head and said a prayer. Most on the platform copied him.

Only the voices of the nearby newspapermen broke the quiet of the occasion.

When Guthrie had finished, he nodded to Wheeler, who indicated for the door of the waiting carriage to be unlocked.

Reid moved closer to the train and signalled for Drake and his own men to come forward.

Caroline Mortimer, Reid saw, kept her head down and her eyes closed as the carriage door was fully opened and its contents revealed to her.

The coffins had been set out in a single layer, and laid upon most of them was a simple bunch of tied white flowers. Other blooms lay scattered on the carriage floor, where they had fallen during the journey.

Reid continued walking until he stood beside Caroline, who finally raised her head and opened her eyes, letting out an involuntary gasp at finding herself suddenly so close to the coffins. She seemed to sag slightly before steadying and composing herself. Reid held a palm to her back and then briefly took her hand into his own.

The Monster's Lament
Robert Edric

APRIL 1945. WHILE THE ALLIED FORCES administer the killing blow to Nazi Germany, at home London's teeming underworld of black marketeers, pimps, prostitutes, conmen and thieves prepare for the coming peace. But the man the newspapers call the English Monster, the self-proclaimed Antichrist, Aleister Crowley, is making preparations for the future too: for his immortality.

For Crowley's plan to work, he has to depend upon ambitious gangland boss Tommy Fowler who can still get you anything you need – for a price.

And what Crowley needs is a young man, Peter Tait, in Pentonville Prison under sentence of death for murder, whose only chance of survival lies in the hands of a detective struggling to win a desperate appeal that has little chance of success . . .

'A wonderfully edgy piece of wartime noir'
INDEPENDENT

The Devil's Beat
Robert Edric

'We must prise opinion from fact, belief from supposition and guesswork from whatever evidence must exist . . .'

1910. THE EYES OF THE country turn to a Nottinghamshire town where four young women allegedly witness a terrifying apparition. Has the devil really revealed himself to them? Are they genuine victims of demonic possession? Or, as most suspect, does their real purpose lie elsewhere?

A panel of four men must examine the substance of the girls' story and decide their fate: a minister, a doctor, a magistrate, and Merritt, an investigator. But even with a perfect mix of the rational, sacred and judicial, their judgement will be called into question as the feverish excitement around the case grows ever more infectious and hysterical . . .

'A connoisseur of shadows. Edric is excellent on what is truly "devilish" in human beings'
SUNDAY TIMES

The London Satyr
Robert Edric

1891. LONDON IS SIMMERING under an oppressive summer heatwave, the air thick with sexual repression. But a wave of morality is about to rock the capital as the puritans of the London Vigilance Committee seek out perversion and aberrant behaviour in all its forms.

Charles Webster, an impoverished photographer working for famed actor-manager Henry Irving at the Lyceum Theatre, has been sucked into a shadowy demi-monde which exists beneath the surface of civilized society. It is a world of pornographers and prostitutes, corralled under the sinister leadership of master manipulator Marlow, to whom Webster illicitly provides theatrical costumes for pornographic shoots.

But knowledge of this enterprise has somehow reached the Lyceum's upright theatre manager, Bram Stoker, who suspects Webster's involvement. As the net tightens around Marlow and his cohorts and public outrage sweeps the city, a member of the aristocracy is accused of killing a child prostitute . . .

> 'Sharply written, wholly engrossing . . . not just an Edric novel, but the Edric novel'
> GUARDIAN

Sanctuary
Robert Edric

Haworth, West Yorkshire, 1848.

Branwell Brontë – unexhibited artist, unacknowledged writer, sacked railwayman, disgraced tutor and spurned lover – finds himself unhappily back in Haworth Parsonage, to face the disappointment of his father and his three sisters, the scale of whose own pseudonymous successes is only just becoming apparent.

With his health failing rapidly, his aspirations abandoned and his once loyal circle of friends shrinking fast, Branwell resorts to a world of secrets, conspiracies and endlessly imagined betrayals. But his spiral of self-destruction only accelerates his sense of destiny as a bystander looking across at greatness and the madness which that realisation will bring . . .

'A work of art . . . Edric is one of the most remarkable novelists writing today'
ALLAN MASSIE, *THE SCOTSMAN*

'Stunning and ambitious . . . Branwell's close relationship with Emily, the love he feels for consumptive Anne and the disintegration of his bond with Charlotte who looks on him with resentment and hostility are vividly explored . . . Moving and imaginatively reconstructed'
PAULA BYRNE, *THE TIMES*

'The book succeeds in poetically entering into the destructive world of a young man of modest talent who finds himself born into a household of genius'
JANE JAKEMAN, *INDEPENDENT ON SUNDAY*

'Robert Edric has written some of the most interesting and diverse historical fiction of the past thirty years . . . An extraordinary portrait of a man lurching towards self-destruction'
NICK RENNISON, *SUNDAY TIMES*